IMPERFECT MR. RIGHT

SHAKTI SALGAOKAR

Popular Prakashan
www.popularprakashan.com

First Published 2012

(4410)

ISBN 978-81-7991-662-9

Cover Design: Vikas Gaitonde
Typesetting: Satyawan Rane

Printed in India
by Nutech Photolithographers
B-240, Okhla Area, Phase I
New Delhi - 110020

Published by
Harsha Bhatkal for
Popular Prakashan Pvt. Ltd.
301, Mahalaxmi Chambers
22, Bhulabhai Desai Road
Mumbai – 400 026
www.popularprakashan.com

ACKNOWLEDGEMENTS

As a child, I lied a lot. They weren't lies, they were my stories. Instead of reprimanding me, my parents encouraged me to turn the lies into story-telling. Thank you for supporting me.

Papa, your keen observation of people, their circumstances and impact on society, have always intrigued and inspired me. Someday I want to write your story but until then, I remain grateful to you for making me look beyond faces and conversations to find people's stories. And yes, you're hands down the best grandpa in the world.

Manuaai, thank you for being so proud of the smallest of things your granddaughter achieved. On the days I got rejection letters from publishers, all I had to do to cheer up was hear her tell someone, "My granddaughter has written a book," with much pride. The rejection did not matter.

Nani, it is a rare younger sister who functions as an elder sister, a friend and a sounding board for all your ideas. Thank you for patiently listening to the story near that *filmi* fountain in Manchester.

Pranali Raut, thank you for understanding my schizophrenia as I wrote the book. Wasn't it fun to just talk about Rahul and Tanya like they were real people?

Ruchi Kaushal, your 'post-it' markers on the first draft telling me exactly what I needed to change are a prized possession even today. Thank you for falling in love with Rahul and Tanya.

Aparna Andhare, I can't thank you enough for reading through my book at multiple stages and reprimanding me for holding on to every redundant word.

Mariam Zia, my friend from across the border who lived opposite me at Falmer, thank you for *pakodas* and advice that nourished me through the MA course.

Shefali Rajguru, thank you for being curious about Rahul and Tanya's future to the point of threatening me. If it wasn't for you, I wouldn't have gotten my act together and completed the book.

I am grateful to Celia Hunt, Sarah Salway, Sue Roe and Julia Widdows for being supportive, inspiring and encouraging professors at University of Sussex where I started writing the book as a part of the course. I am grateful to my classmates Steve Laycock, Virginia Monson and Kevin McGeary for all those fun times working on each other's work. Mary Valiakas, the Bollywood dance number in there is just for you (wink wink).

At age 10, inspired by Enid Blyton, I wrote a sort of long story. It was embarrassingly horrible. But Avinash Paranjape read it and had detailed feedback for me. Avya Kaka if you hadn't taken me seriously then, I'd never have had the ability to take myself seriously as a writer either. For that, and the many other times when you patted my back but never without constructive criticism, I will remain indebted to you.

Bharat Kaka, you always told me that a journalist should know a little bit of everything and everything about something. This helped me immensely while writing this book. Neena Maushi, thank you for being a friend, a philosopher and a warm guide who taught me the importance of being sensitive to others — a trait every writer needs to cultivate. I am very grateful to you, the Raut family, for the love, the values and the encouragement that you have always showered on me.

Kumar Kaka and Sharda Maushi, thank you for the books, the questions, the rhetoric. Thank you for never once making a teenager feel like a teenager and thank you for taking me to my first-ever rock show.

Pratima Maushi, thank you for taking the time to read the first draft of the book and giving me the much needed positive feedback along with some very interesting notes from a cinematic perspective. And yes, one day I will write a profound book...

Even though everybody says that it shouldn't be so, the truth is that every book is judged by its cover. Vikas Gaitonde, thank you for your ideas and thoughts and thank you for putting a beautiful face to my story. And being judged by the measure of this stunning cover is only an honour.

My deepest gratitude to Harsha Bhatkal, Jayanthi Mahalingam, Preeti Singh and the team at Popular Prakashan for giving my novel this opportunity. Thank you for patiently working with me. We – Rahul, Tanya and I – thank you for believing in our story.

Shakti Salgaokar

DEDICATION

The idea for this book was discussed at Barvi Dam guest house on New Year's Eve 2003. Vivek Basrur told me to get everyone present to sign a pact of secrecy because he believed that it was a great story that deserved more than a tranquil evening away from the city to be told.

Nirmala Wadekar or Nimmai, my maternal grandmother was married at 16 and family responsibility took precedence over education. She lived vicariously through her children and grandchildren. As her eldest grandchild, I was lucky to be nourished with not only her cooking but also her dreams for me.

Vivek Kaka and Nimmai, if you were around, I know this book would be your prized possession. I dedicate it to you in hope that it makes you proud, wherever you are.

Chapter 1

Commotion, conversations, shop talk, footsteps, children shrieking — the glass walls of the perfume section at OneStop Mall filtered all of those noises out successfully. He stood in the middle of the most fragrant room in the mall, enjoying the sound of a glass bottle being pulled off a glass shelf, the sound of the bottle being uncapped and the light hiss of the perfume being sprayed into the air. He loved the sound people made as they inhaled the fragrance and the appreciation that followed. He liked the sound of people talking about the perfumes that they had smelt, and he loved these words the most —'I'll take it!'

Rahul Rajgopal didn't just sell perfumes. He was a matchmaker and his job was to match the right fragrance to the right person. He must have been good at this, because although the mall was always swarming with people wanting to buy or just browse through the goods, it was the perfume section that drew everyone in with its mesmerizing haze of mixed fragrances. People might have been drawn into this fragrant world, but it was Rahul they kept coming back for. Rahul's charm and warmth engulfed every person who had ever come into the section, and it was almost impossible for most of his customers to walk by without saying 'hello' to their favourite salesman. They came in to talk a little, to share a little and they all felt loved under Rahul's tender gaze and comforted by the fragrances he picked for them. Rahul and his fragrances were an addiction and his customers were completely and hopelessly hooked.

But not her… she had never ever come into his section. She just never succumbed to the charm of his fragrances, even though she was a regular at the mall. She came often, to buy odd things at odd times, but she had never ever needed a perfume. Today, however, she was walking directly towards him. He felt like she was staring into him as she took long strides toward the glass walls of his fragrant world. The thought of reading her fragrance, talking to her and hearing her voice was a heady one. But he was convinced she wasn't coming in. She could easily be wandering in the mall, looking for some other section. Rahul went back to rearranging the tester bottles on his spotless glass counter.

"I am looking for a perfume for a 35-year-old man," a soft feminine voice said to him in a rather rude manner.

He looked up and there it was — the face that had been intriguing him for the last couple of months. He was taken aback by the hostility in her voice.

"Show me something quickly," she ordered as she fiddled with the contents in her humungous bag.

"What sort of a perfume would you want, Ma'am?"

She looked up with a smirk. "I just told you, anything for a 35-year-old for his birthday."

It had been a while since a customer was rude to Rahul. All his customers thought of Rahul as a friend. Nobody ordered Rahul Rajgopal around, definitely not in his own section.

"Well, these perfumes suit most 35-year-old men. This one," he said spraying from a bottle straight into her face, "is for calm, collected people, while this one is for those who are sort of young at heart. Yes and this one here is for the sporty sort of people and…."

"Just give me something for someone extroverted, funny and romantic," she interrupted before Rahul could spray another strong fragrance on her face. She twitched her reddened nose and glared at him.

"How about this one? It might be perfect. It has a sharp fragrance, but its sharpness doesn't overpower strangers; the base note has a calming effect. This perfume is perfect for outgoing men."

He held out a strip for her. He watched her as she closed her eyes and took in the fragrance. There was a hint of a smile, but when she opened her eyes the smile was gone, as if it had never been there.

"Good, wrap it up. Fast!" she ordered.

He took a box off the shelf and began wrapping it, still staring at her. Her choice of perfume had left an odd sinking feeling in his stomach.

As he wrapped the box, he thought about the person she was shopping for. She really cared for this man. He knew enough from his experience that women bought this perfume for the most important men in their lives. Was this man her husband? Not possible; there was no *mangalsutra* or *sindoor*, but then most Indian girls did not wear it. No ring either. Probably just a boyfriend.... His chain of thought was broken by her cold request.

"Write the card out for me, 'Happy Birthday, Ravi Bhaiyya'."

With a smile on his face he wrote out the card and as he handed her the box, he looked at her face, searching for a reciprocating smile, but her face remained expressionless. She grabbed the gift and handed him her credit card before turning away to start a conversation on her cell phone. He couldn't understand why he felt relieved to know that the most important man in her life was her brother and he couldn't understand why he felt angry with her. Who the hell did she think she was anyway?

He glanced at the name on the card — Tanya Kher.

"Nice name," he thought as he swiped the card and handed her the receipt. She signed it in one swift motion, grabbed the gift and walked off.

This was the most impersonal sale Rahul Rajgopal had ever made and he couldn't believe it. His latest customer hadn't even thanked him! No goodbye either! Rahul wasn't used to this, but now was not the time to brood over Tanya's lack of good manners. He went back to packing perfumes; after all he had had a busy day and there was a busier day coming up tomorrow.

* * * * * *

As she stepped out of the busy mall, Tanya heaved a sigh of relief. Crowds always made her a bit dizzy. Her eyes frantically searched for a cab, but there wasn't a single one to be seen. She started to walk angrily across the pavement towards a taxi stand. Nobody could have guessed looking at her, that her high heels were killing her toes. She walked as if she owned the world, taking long strides, looking straight ahead as if she would trample upon anyone getting in her way and not give a damn. Her business suit added to the no-nonsense attitude which made people turn around and look at her in awe as she tick-tocked down the road. Her eyes finally spotted a cab and Tanya made a run for it.

"Cadell Road, drive fast."

Mumbai cab drivers are used to being asked whether they would do you the favour of driving you to your destination. The cab driver turned around and gave her a weird look.

"Move it, I am getting late," she ordered in her broken anglicised Hindi.

He turned the meter down, muttering, "These modern, pant-wearing girls!"

Tanya ignored him. She had better things to do than to pick an argument with a male chauvinistic cab driver. She looked at her watch and then looked outside at the shimmering river of cars ahead of the cab. Tanya could picture her sister-in-law, cursing her for being late. And that picture made her anxious.

Anita had called Tanya eight times at work to remind her to leave on time. Once Tanya was out of the office her cell phone beeped with reminder SMS-es. However, as she went past the mall, she had remembered that she had forgotten to buy a gift for her brother. After 20 minutes of clueless browsing, she had seen the shiny perfume section. If it hadn't been for the 'friendly' meddling salesman, she thought with annoyance, she'd have made the purchase in half the time. Of course, a gift voucher would have taken her less than a minute to buy, but then, it would have made her the butt of Ravi's jokes till his next birthday.

Tanya hated going to the friendly neighbourhood grocer or the friendly neighbourhood boutique. She chose to make a trip to the mall for the smallest things because the sales staff didn't overwhelm her with the extra dollops of friendliness that always made Tanya a little edgy. After her latest trip to OneStop she now realised that she was stuck with a 'friendly' neighbourhood mall as well!

Her cell phone buzzed in her hand and she knew who was calling without even looking at the screen.

"Anita, I am on my way!! Can't help it — the traffic is terrible! I'm coming!" Tanya fixed her gaze on the red light as she heard her sister-in-law complain.

She clicked off the phone and looked at her watch. She was running late by half an hour and it looked like she was going to take another half hour to reach her brother's birthday party. She was right. The cab screeched to a halt outside her brother's building at exactly half past nine. She threw the money at the cab driver and without waiting for change ran into the lift, almost slipping on the marble floor in the lobby. She had to hit the button a hundred times before the elevator closed, increasing her impatience and irritation.

The doors shut, revealing a reflection on the shiny steel that Tanya did not like. Her hair was completely out of place thanks to the jerky, windy cab ride. Tanya was very particular about how she wore her hair. She never experimented with the length, colour or style. She liked keeping it long, straight and brushed clear, falling over her shoulders. At times she wore it in a ponytail or a bun, but only if it was a hot or a windy day.

Her grey-green eyes always had a stern look in them behind the rather expensive rimless glasses she had been wearing for the past five years, much to Anita's dislike. No experiments. She wore no make-up except for a little bit of kohl and one of the two lipsticks she alternated according to her clothes, most of which were rather formal and business-like. Rarely could anyone catch Tanya Kher in Indian attire and almost never in casuals. In fact, her brother joked about how Tanya was dressed to hit the boardroom at any time of the day.

Today, however, she had managed to pull out a fancy woollen off-shoulder top that Anita had gifted her. She checked her reflection, and smoothed it down over her hips. She didn't want to give Anita another reason to bicker. She had just enough time to straighten her hair with her fingers when the elevator opened on the ninth floor. She got out of the lift and before she could ring the bell, Anita opened the door with a 'where-the-hell-were-you' expression on her face. Tanya gave her a 'you-know-me' smile and shrugged. Anita nodded and pointed to the living room.

The living room looked beautiful with dim lighting and candles. Tanya could hear glasses clinking and people laughing above the lounge music playing in the background. She saw many faces but the one she wanted to see was lost somewhere. She could hear his high-pitched voice from a corner of the huge living room. She glided through the room trying to be as invisible as possible but people stopped for a minute and took notice of Tanya. She looked attractive and something about her was different. Tanya walked past smiling reluctantly at faces, some drunk, some pretentious, some judging her, others appreciative.

"He has to work hard. I mean, the team is in good form but he has got to keep it going. I'm going to miss Gary Kirsten, you know? Tanya! We thought you would definitely make it by my next birthday," he yelled across the hall.

Tanya looked down, embarrassed. She hated being in the spotlight and her brother always managed to put her right into it.

"She's a busy woman, my sister, so I am going to leave you guys for a moment to make the best of the time I get from her," Ravi told the group he had been talking to and put his arm around Tanya.

"Why do you always have to make a joke about me?" she muttered as she handed him the box. "You are getting older but not any wiser."

He took the box and plucked the card off. Holding it in Tanya's face, Ravi frowned. "It says Ravi Bhaiyya! How many times do I have to tell you to stop calling me Bhaiyya? We aren't ten and sixteen anymore, okay? I don't like it."

He frowned as he tore open the wrapping paper, but the frown on his face disappeared as soon as he saw the box.

"Aqua Di Gio! Impressive. It's a pleasant change from the gift vouchers you've been giving me." He nudged Tanya in a playful way. "Met Anita yet? She was hopping mad because you got late!"

"Oh, she met me at the door. She's sort of okay now. I am going to go see if she needs any help around the kitchen."

Tanya was about to make a dash for the kitchen, but Ravi stopped her. "Oi, we have a caterer this time, so there's no excuse for you to hide. These people are decent, you know; they don't bite,"

"I was just being nice," she said walking off towards Gia, Anita's friend, who was one of the few people Tanya looked forward to seeing at her brother's parties. Gia always had exclusive stories and gossip from the television channel she worked for. Gia's constant chatter took all the socialising pressure off Tanya, allowing her to be an intangible ghost.

"Tano! Long time.... Howdy!" she screamed with delight as she hugged Tanya, who knew instantly that Gia had had quite a bit to drink.

"You won't believe this. I am shooting one of our shows in your Delhi offices. It's about these two models. You know sex, high heels, expensive clothes and the works. I was just thinking of you when we finalised things with your guys. I am so glad to see you babe!" She hugged Tanya once again.

"Oh really? That's amazing. Which show is this?" Tanya asked sipping from a glass of wine that Gia planted in her hands. It was white and Tanya preferred red, but she didn't like making a fuss at parties. The bold and confident Tanya became a timid little kitten when it came to socialising, but one could never tell looking at her standing tall with an air of confidence about her. Gia gulped a huge sip of what looked like vodka tonic before answering.

"New one! The boss thinks the glamour will get us the much needed TRP boost. Star is screwing our advertising revenues. Obviously you know that. Silly me," she laughed aloud throwing her head back.

Tanya admired Gia's vibrant personality. You couldn't walk into a party and not notice Gia. She was always dressed in shocking colours and her loud voice and giggles added sparkle to any conversation. Sometimes, Tanya wished she had some of Gia's exuberance....

"Star is hot property as far as prime time slots are concerned, but this guy at your office is offering us great deals if we plan to advertise across all the channels. We are, as a matter of fact, recommending Cee; it is cost effective," Tanya explained with boardroom confidence.

"At least someone's recommending Cee! Oh there's Aneesh; he just broke up with his girlfriend and you know what, she was cheating on him! Let's go say hi!" Gia chuckled.

Tanya nodded her way along as Gia pulled her through the crowd, making conversation, cracking a joke here and there. Tanya enjoyed the fact that she could just nod or smile or say a few words and kill time as she stuck to Gia's side through the party. It was better than standing in one corner and being introduced to random people.

Every now and then, Tanya used the little knowledge she had about the television business thanks to her job, to add bits and pieces to Gia's stories, but even this little socialising was a great effort for her and it tired her out. She hated crowds and she hated parties. She wouldn't have attended a single non-work related party if it hadn't been for Anita and Ravi's enthusiasm.

They hosted a lot of parties and Tanya made it a point to be there, not as a social obligation but because it made them happy to see there. That was the least she could do for the two people she loved most; but in her heart of hearts, Tanya knew they were hoping she would meet someone at one of their parties and settle down. Tanya also knew that though she was single, she wasn't yet ready to mingle. No, not by a long shot....

Chapter 2

"Hello! Good morning!" The chirpy voice came wafting through the glass doors into the perfume section. Rahul looked up from below the counter where he was arranging the bottles and smiled at Rosie D'Mello, the cheerful part-time assistant at the mall. She came by to help Rahul with his counter over the busy weekends.

"Hello darling! Aren't you late? We are opening in 10 minutes," he said pulling her heavily powdered cheeks with affection as she came up behind the counter.

"I am sorry, man. I had to cook for Savio and...."

"No time for excuses, baby. Give me a hand here. We have ten minutes. We'll talk about your morning catastrophe over lunch. Okay?" Rahul handed her an empty crate.

Getting to work by 9.15 every morning was a task for Rosie. Every day she'd make up stories blaming her husband for the delay in her arrival, but everyone knew the real reason was Rosie's make-up and hair regime.

"Yes sir!" she said as she pouted into her compact with deep red lips that she had just touched up with the cheap lipstick in her purse. She took the empty crate to the storeroom and danced back in with a new crate full of fragrances waiting to be displayed on the shiny glass shelves.

Rahul beamed at her and started to line up boxes of Ralph Lauren's Polo Blue on the shelves, giving them pride of place. He suddenly stopped and picked up the tester bottle in the crate. He played around with the tester, drawing patterns in the air with the fragrance. He then closed his eyes and went into a trance, like he was visualising the fragrance perform some kind of a dance in the deep corners of his mind.

"New consignment.... This has been in vogue forever," he said shaking the tester bottle in his hand to the continuing music in his head.

"It's a classic. Hint of spice, a bit cool, a bit strong, a bit mild. Magic. Sophistication. Mmm... here," Rahul playfully pushed the tester bottle towards Rosie, eyes still closed. He knew that opening them would just dissolve the beautiful picture.

"I thought we had ten minutes only. Get to work, men!" She turned to arrange the remaining contents of the crate on another sparsely populated shelf.

"I saw Phoolan Devi come into your section yesterday," she said casually as she placed the bottles on the shelf one by one before examining her perfectly manicured nails to make sure no damage was done to the carefully applied red nail polish. She knew Rahul wouldn't let her apply a new coat now and even if he miraculously did, there wasn't enough time for it to dry.

"Yeah, she bought Aqua di Gio," Rahul said as he filled in the inventory form, "You put ten bottles of Burberry up there, right?"

"Did she talk to you? Even the snootiest of customers are best friends with you. She must have said something, na?"

Ever since he found out she was called Tanya, Rahul had started to dislike the nicknames she had been given by the staff. He liked the ring of the name in his head — 'Tanya'. He repeated the name and smiled to himself.

Rosie obviously hadn't noticed Rahul's attempt to change the topic, but the warning bell came to his rescue. Rosie turned around and checked her chubby self in the mirrored wall behind the counter. She checked every angle to make sure she looked all right. She smoothed down the sweater to make sure her hips wouldn't look too big, but she didn't look very happy. Noticing the frown on her face, Rahul put away his inventory form and held Rosie by her shoulders. "Rosie! You look gorgeous."

Rosie muttered under her breath, "They should change our uniforms. This one makes me look fat."

"Rosie! Two minutes to open and if you looked any better than you already do, I am afraid my customers will be distracted," he said pointing at the perfume laden rack behind the counter, "You wouldn't want to do that to my babies, now, would you?" He smiled at her.

Rosie blushed, making her cheeks go way redder than the no.34 shade of blusher she'd applied earlier that morning. "Shut up, men!" she exclaimed in her Goan accent.

Rosie was the first person to speak to Rahul when he had taken over the perfume counter four years ago. It didn't take Rahul very long to make friends with the entire staff at the mall. To her, he was the best friend she'd never had. Although she told Rahul everything about her life, she barely knew anything about him. He had no close friends and Rosie took pride in the fact that she was the closest to a friend Rahul had at the mall or in the city for that matter.

The opening bell went off and they could hear the shoppers rush in. They both looked at each other and mouthed 'Good luck' at the same time. It was the beginning of a long day.

Customers old and new kept coming in. Some walked away, satisfied with their latest purchase, and some walked away mighty pleased with the attention they got. The teenage girls were Saturday regulars. They'd made friends with Rosie, but they blushed when Rahul tried to ask them if he could help. His regular customers came by expecting a chat in spite of the busy hour and Rahul didn't let them down. He asked after their friends, their fragrances and laughed at the jokes they cracked even though he barely managed to hear them.

"Mr. Sharma, how was your boss's party, I hope you floored him with that fragrance we selected"; "Teenaji, how are you?

Forgotten me and my little bottles have you? Come try this new fragrance. I think you two are made for each other"; "Hey Raj, how are you liking the Azzaro your girlfriend gifted you? I have the perfect fragrance for her. She'll be touched, I promise you"; "Yes sir, I see you're checking the Chanel No. 5. For someone special is it? Good choice, but you might just want to try this one here. You might like it better."

A well-dressed man in his early 40s was observing Rahul from a corner of the section. He was amused at the ease with which Rahul remembered everyone's name and gave them his sales spiel. Within the last half hour, the young man had acknowledged every person who had come in, with a dazzling smile on his face.

"May I help you sir?" Rahul asked the silent observer.

"Just looking around," the man replied.

"You should just smell around here," Rahul insisted with a smile, as he sprayed some perfume onto a strip and handed it to the gentleman. "A brand new fragrance from Armani; it's subtle enough to let you blend with the crowd and strong enough to make sure no one forgets you are around. Just try it out."

"How do you know I'll like it?"

"You wouldn't like a perfume like this," Rahul said handing another sprayed strip, "which would draw attention to you. You like to be a silent observer."

"So you've been watching me?"

"Oh no, just suggesting. Guesswork, you know."

"Look, I appreciate the enthusiasm," the man said smelling the strip in his hand. "But I'm looking around to kill time before a meeting. You're very interesting. Here's my card. Come to me when you want something more from life than just selling perfumes," and he walked off.

Rahul stared after him, ignoring the chaos around him. For the first time in years, Rahul realised that selling perfumes at a mall and being awesome at it wasn't good enough. And all it took was one line from a stranger.... 'When you want something more than just selling perfumes...'.

For the rest of the day, Rahul wasn't himself. He just kept smiling and nodding at customers. The regular ones noticed and asked him if everything was okay. He smiled and said he was okay and went about his business. Rosie knew he wasn't okay, but she also knew that he wasn't going to tell her. He didn't.

Rahul went through the day like a plane on autopilot. Later at night, he wrapped up his work and walked home in a daze. The city seemed awfully noisy and chaotic to him. He shut his eyes tight in the bus. He felt like someone had put him on a super fast roller-coaster. He felt a weird emptiness in the stomach, the kind you feel when the rollercoaster takes a steep plunge after a steady climb. All he wanted was to get home, away from this chaos. He jumped out of the bus onto the street. He climbed the narrow, creaky stairs to his flat and rushed in, shutting out the world.

But the claustrophobia just wouldn't leave him alone. His sparsely furnished flat started to feel cramped. The old walls, almost naked with the peeling plaster, seemed to cave in on him. He slid down the door, eyes shut tight.

He could hear his mother. "You are a special boy, and you are going to make a name for yourself one day. You are destined for higher things. I know it. A mother's heart never lies."

He could hear Ayesha's parting words and he could still feel the words slice his heart to tiny pieces. "I love you but love isn't everything, I need something more than that. I have to take this chance because I don't know if you can ever give me what he has to offer. I can't take this gamble. It's my life, I am sorry,"

Had his mother's heart lied to her? Why had his love not been enough for Ayesha? Was he really destined for something huge? Then, what had he been doing for four years, selling perfumes? Was this his destiny? Selling perfumes in a snazzy mall in the suburbs of a big city that they called the city of dreams?

A tear trickled down his cheek. Rubbing it off with his sleeve, he dug out his wallet. Rahul held up the visiting card of the man who had shattered the glass walls of his life with a casual statement. It said: Avinash Menon, CEO, Cee Television.

Chapter 3

Tanya stirred as the early morning sunshine trickled in through the window of the guest bedroom. A tinkling alarm from the cell phone chased off the last dregs of sleep. Tanya woke up, still tired from the party. She massaged her feet a little, stretched and pushed aside the sheets. She sprung out of bed and headed straight to the bathroom.

Half an hour later, she emerged dressed in the spare shirt and jeans that she'd kept in the wardrobe. Her hair was pulled back into a ponytail, and her well-defined eyes looked fresher than they felt. She could have slept in a little more, but she had a lot of work to do. She grabbed her bag and cell phone from the bed, gave the mirror one last look and rushed out of the door.

The house was messy and the kitchen messier, piled with dirty dishes and wine-stained glasses. Anita's usually spotless kitchen was hard to recognise. Tanya tried to be quiet as she grabbed an apple from the kitchen counter. She didn't want to awaken Ravi or Anita, not on a Saturday morning. She could hear her brother snore. She smiled and noiselessly let herself out of the apartment.

Within twenty minutes, she was walking down the long and empty corridors of Blue, the biggest advertising agency in Mumbai. Most of the lights were out, which made the usually bustling corridor look eerie. The watchman at the reception was sleeping;

Tanya shook her head in disapproval and clicked her card on the electronic reader. She pushed open the heavy glass door and tiptoed past the empty desks. She hated the sound of her heels ringing through the empty office. On weekdays, she felt confident and empowered making her presence felt with her heels, but on Saturdays the office was deserted. She stopped before a large wooden door, and took in the sight of her name written on it in bold steel: Tanya Kher, Media Planning. She felt a rush of adrenaline as she went in. A smile lit up her face as she pulled up the blinds.

She sat down and looked at the two files she had readied before leaving last evening. She opened her laptop, rearranged the pad and a pencil at a certain angle, threw open the files and started hitting the buttons. As seconds became hours, Tanya finished a presentation, answered all her emails, put together a to-do list for the coming week and rechecked a media plan for a major client. She was just finalising some figures when the office phone rang.

"Tanya Kher," she said into the phone, surprised to receive a call on her office line on a Saturday.

"Don't be so surprised, it's me. Why would you run off to office at 9 a.m. on a Saturday?" Even though it was almost two in the afternoon, Anita still had a husky early morning voice.

"Anita, I told you I am working on some very important presentations and…."

"That's been your excuse forever… Tanya, this has got to stop. Anyway, I am not having this conversation over the phone. I am coming over at four and I don't care if you have presentations or meetings or whatever. I will see you at your place at four, sharp!" And Anita did something she almost never did. She hung up on Tanya.

Tanya stared at the receiver, confused and scared. She knew Anita was really angry. She just replaced the receiver and tried to get back to punching numbers into her laptop. She couldn't imagine why Anita was mad at her.

Tanya reached her apartment at 3.30 p.m. She didn't want to take chances with Anita. She couldn't concentrate on work, dreading the endless lecture she was about to receive. She had picked up Anita's favourite double chocolate muffins and cheese-onion puffs from Candies. She had even brought out some beautiful plates to serve them in and matching coffee mugs. Very unlike her, but something she knew Anita appreciated. Tanya went around the white counter that acted like a partition between the kitchen and the living room and sat down restlessly on the spotless white couch.

Exactly at 4 p.m., her cell phone alarm rang, making her jump. She walked across the living room to the French windows. She slid them open for some fresh air. She took in the view of Joggers' Park and the sea beyond it.

She could see little children in the park calling out to their mothers as they played on the swings. Lovers strolled hand-in-hand, old couples sat comfortably together, friends walked their dogs chatting animatedly. Everyone was with someone, someone they belonged with, someone they cared for. And here she was, standing alone, looking at all those people from her perfect apartment. She was beginning to feel sorry for herself, and that, she could not handle.

Just as she shut the windows, the doorbell shrilled. Although she was dreading the conversation, Tanya was glad for the company. She walked toward the door and opened it. There stood Anita, empty-handed.

Tanya remembered her brother telling her once, "Anita showing up empty handed at your place is bad news."

"So? Done with the presentation?" Anita asked as she sat down on the couch, crossing her legs and crossing her hands across her chest, as if she were there to interrogate Tanya.

"Yeah, sort of," Tanya said as she brought her a glass of chilled water.

"Thank you." Anita sipped on the water, and looked up at Tanya who was pacing the room like a child who had done something wrong but didn't know what.

"I got some double chocolate muffins and some onion...."

"Don't even think about it. That's Ravi's trick. It doesn't work for him and it won't work for you."

"Anita, come on. It's not a big deal. I have to work some Saturdays,"

"Some? Did you say some? By some, don't you mean every Saturday?"

"But there's so much work pressure. And I...."

"Tani, we have talked about this before. You can always hire an assistant. And if there's so much work, how come no other employee turns up on Saturday?"

"They have their priorities; besides I left work early on Friday for the party."

"Leaving work at 7 does not qualify as leaving early! They pay you to be in till five, and that too, on weekdays. I hope you are aware of that."

"Anita please... I don't want to discuss this. I enjoy being at work, I like working. You keep telling me get a hobby. Well, work is my hobby."

"You mean punching numbers into your stupid laptop, that's your hobby?" Anita got up from the couch.

Tanya rushed to the kitchen and nervously began to pour the coffee. Anita followed her. "Tanya, there's more to life than work. You needed time, we gave it to you, but you've become a workaholic. It's not healthy to...."

Tanya slammed the mugs down. "What do you want me to do? Come along to parties? Air kiss? Get drunk? Wake up with a hangover, so I can't go to work? Or worse still, do you want me to hook up with one of those guys you introduce me to?"

Tanya's body language was aggressive, but she was almost in tears. She turned to face the window. "Then eventually get married and quit my job to be a wife. Is that what you want?"

"Don't jump to conclusions. You are just getting defensive. All I am saying is that you can't let work eat into your life, bit by bit."

"I am not jumping to conclusions. I know you and Ravi want me to have a conventional life, and I know I am not going to. Just because you quit your job, it's not fair for you to think work isn't important for me. I have been the employee of the year three years in a row. What did you get out of two years of being the best wife you could be?"

Tanya was furious but as soon as she uttered those harsh words, she regretted it. She rushed into her bedroom and slammed the door shut. She didn't hear the front door open or realise that Anita had gone, slamming the door in anger. Tanya flung herself on the bed and sobbed into her pillow.

It hurt that the people she loved the most didn't understand her need to work. She wondered why they couldn't understand that just as everyone belonged with someone, she belonged to her job. Why couldn't they understand her relationship with work? She cringed in shame as she thought of how she had hurt her sister-in-law.

Anita had been a successful journalist before she gave up her career to be a homemaker. Tanya was one of the few who knew that what Anita really wanted was to be a hands-on mother, but she lost a baby and had been unable to conceive since. If there was one sorrow in Ravi and Anita's life, it was their inability to have a child. It was a sorrow well-hidden behind Ravi's jokes and Anita's everlasting smile. Ravi and Anita had begun to parent Tanya, trying to heal her life and in turn heal their own.

Tanya wept. Why couldn't she ever accept their loving concern and try to understand their wretchedly lonely life?

Chapter 4

Rahul stepped out of his dingy apartment with conviction. He stood in the middle of the crowded street, an unknown hunger raging in his soul. He wanted something, something a lot more than fake smiles and shoptalk. He didn't want to feel pleased with himself for selling hundreds of bottles of perfume. For the first time since he arrived in Mumbai, he had serious thoughts about the path ahead. He had to prove that his mother had been right and Avinash Menon was going to help him do that.

He walked in through the revolving doors of Cee TV headquarters in Mumbai. It was a crowded lobby. The receptionist was busy hitting buttons and saying, 'Cee TV reception, how may I help?' The pungent fragrance she wore screamed for attention; so did her voice. Rahul had to stand at the counter for about fifteen minutes before he could get her attention.

"How may I help you?"

"Oh! Actually I am here to meet...." He handed the impatient receptionist Avinash Menon's card. She took one look at it and looked at Rahul again. She signalled him to wait and went on another phone answering spree.

Rahul looked around uneasily. He was the only person who had been still for more than a minute. The silver, electric blue and pink décor made him feel like he was on a spaceship and the hyperactive people around him seemed like robots.

"Excuse me!" The receptionist yelled tapping her pen on the silver counter.

"Oh! Sorry," Rahul looked at her, embarrassed and feeling out of place.

"So you want to see Mr. Menon?" She raised an eyebrow.

"Yes. Actually, I met him…."

"You need to have an appointment and this is the number you have to call."

Before he could explain, she handed back the card with a number scribbled on it and went back to the ever-ringing phone. Rahul kept standing there waiting for her attention, again. She gave him an irritated look and answered a few more calls. When she took a break to sip water, Rahul seized the opportunity.

"Madam, I don't think you understand. I met him yesterday and he asked me to come see him anytime."

Rahul Rajgopal, the charming salesman, stood helplessly on the other side of the counter, stripped naked as his art of persuasion was rendered useless.

"Mr. Menon is the CEO of our network. He doesn't have the time to entertain people who turn up at any time. Speak to his secretary. If you don't mind, I've got work to do," she pointed at the ringing phone and answered it.

Rahul felt like he had vanished into thin air. People walked past him as if he was invisible. At the revolving doors, he turned around and looked at the receptionist and the busy robots. He wanted to matter to these people. He wanted them to give up whatever they were doing and ask him what he wanted. And with that conviction, he pushed through the doors.

Rahul went straight to a public telephone booth opposite the building, picked up the phone and dialled the number written out on the card. He waited for someone to answer, his jaw clenched.

"Mr. Menon's office, how may I help?" a polite voice answered.

"Hi, could I speak to Mr. Menon please?"

"May I know who is calling and what this is regarding?"

"I actually met him yesterday at the mall and he asked...."

"I am sorry Mr. Menon is in a meeting."

"Of course," Rahul said shutting his eyes in anger.

He hung up and came out of the booth. He squinted at the building shining in the scorching afternoon sun. A mischievous smile appeared out of nowhere on his lips and he went back to the booth and dialled again. The voice answered in the same boring tone.

"Mr. Menon's office."

"This is Rajgopal, head of operations, OneStop Shopping Centre. I'd like to speak with Mr. Menon please," Rahul said with a serious expression before breaking into a smile and winking at his reflection in the scratched out panel of the booth.

"Yes of course, what may I say this is regarding?"

Rahul's grim expression was back and in his husky voice he said, "This is regarding… it's a confidential matter we discussed yesterday when he came to the mall."

"Ah! Please hold the line."

Avinash Menon was reading through a pile of concept notes. He wanted to create a storm and he needed new shows to kill the competition. Crappy dramas and 'me-too' talent hunts weren't going to help him. He shook his head uneasily at yet another disappointing concept. The phone rang as he leaned back in his chair.

"Yes, Nina?"

"Sir, I have Mr. Rajgopal on the line for you,"

"Mr. Rajgopal?"

"He is the head of operations, OneStop mall."

Avinash wondered who this fellow was and why he was calling him.

"He says it's about something you discussed yesterday. He said it was confidential."

Avinash broke into a smile as he realised who this person from the mall was.

"Put him through."

"Sorry about the wait, Mr. Rajgopal, Mr. Menon will speak to you now," the lady announced before Rahul heard the voice of the man who was about to change his life.

"Avinash here." This voice had shaken up Rahul's world yesterday, but today Rahul felt a warmth envelop his body. It was a good feeling, a feeling of being worth something.

"Good afternoon, sir."

"Come and see me at 6 p.m. tomorrow. Come to the twelfth floor, and ask for my office. I'll be expecting you," and the phone went dead.

Rahul looked at the receiver and frowned. He looked at his watch. He had 28 hours to kill.

* * * * * *

The Monday morning traffic inched forward slowly on the Queen's Necklace. Tanya looked away from her office window, at her messy desk. Her 'leave at 7 a.m., skip the traffic, be in at 7.45 a.m.' strategy was the reason she had been nominated for the fourth consecutive time for the 'Employee of the Year' award.

She went back to the presentation she had put together for an important meeting. This would reinforce her right to a higher post at the agency and she was determined to nail it. She knew the President had her name on his mind but whatever doubts he had, were about to disappear as she brought in a brand new client with her killer presentation. A ping alerted her to the email circular announcing the employee of the year. It was no surprise to her that she had won it.

She reached out to the phone to call Anita, but she held back and bit her lip in regret. "Time for coffee!" she thought.

Tanya wanted to stop thinking about the weekend fireworks with Anita. The coffee room was filled with murmuring voices and the sound of muffled laughter. Everyone fell silent as soon as Tanya entered.

"Look, here's the employee of the year!" a male voice announced and was lost instantly in the applause and cheering.

Tanya beamed with pride and made her way to the machine. She grabbed a cup and waited for the machine to dispense her coffee as she acknowledged every person looking at her. The congratulations continued as she made her way back to the office. The admiring glances thrown at her convinced her that Anita was wrong. With a triumphant smile, she took a sip of the coffee. Her mouth burnt with a bitter sting. Tanya had forgotten to add milk and sugar to her steaming hot coffee. She walked back to the coffee room, but she entered via the service door. She didn't want to return to the party in a minute and look like a fool. Behind the machine she heard her colleagues' voices.

"Yeah! Employee of the Year. The award is a sham I tell you," she heard someone say.

"Why do they make a big show of nominating people and then hold an elaborate ceremony? Just hand it to her! I mean, if you work round the clock, over the weekend and everything obviously you would...."

"Yeah, I'd say the other nominees won. They do things other than work and still manage to get nominated. But I guess the boring idiot has to win!"

"Don't be mean now. She deserved the award. The ceremony is the highlight of her social calendar."

Tanya's bloated self-esteem shrunk with each word she heard. She felt the need to get away. She walked back to her office but this time, the name on the door made her wince. She turned around and ran for the elevator. She needed some fresh air. Her eyes were red and her lungs were screaming by the time she reached the promenade by the sea.

She had always ignored this promenade. It was right in front of her office. Today she was thankful it existed. She sat down and with each wave that lashed at the rocks, she realised how true the comments were. They were bitching about her, but they weren't lying. It was the truth. She didn't leave the jury any choice and none of the other colleagues stood a chance simply because of her crazy dedication to work. The comments came not out of jealousy, but out of pity and Tanya Kher did not like pity. She wanted to cry but she wasn't going to cry in public. There was only one person she wanted to talk to. Tanya fished out her cell-phone and dialled Anita.

"Anita, I want to talk to you, can you pick me up from my office. It's a bit urgent." She realised that for the first time in ages, she was trying hard not to cry and to sound normal.

"Of course, I'll be there in twenty minutes. Should I pick you up at the main entrance?"

"Hmmm...," Tanya nodded as she pressed her lips hard.

"I'll be there, Tani."

Tanya just wanted to hear Ravi's and Anita's voices, even if it meant listening to them crib about her lifestyle. She gathered herself and walked back into the office and collected her things.

"Meeting?" a woman from client servicing asked her as she stepped out of the lift.

"No. Taking the day off," Tanya spat and walked into the lift, leaving a surprised face behind the closing doors. There was a weird pleasure Tanya felt seeing her colleague's shocked face. She walked to the office entrance and switched off her Blackberry.

* * * * * *

Anita drove silently glancing at Tanya every now and then. She held Tanya's hand reassuringly at every red light. She wanted to know what was happening, but that had to wait until they got home. In the comfort of Anita's living room, Tanya broke down.

"I... I want to quit," she managed, between her sobs.

"Shhh...," she said, handing Tanya a bottle of water from her bag, "Do you want to tell me what happened?"

Tanya flung her arms around Anita's neck. "You... you were so right...," she gulped. "You and Ravi always... I was going nowhere... sorry...."

Tanya couldn't stop crying. The things she wanted to say came out between muffled sobs. "I was stupid… nobody cares… don't want it… want to quit…."

Anita let Tanya have a good cry. It was a while before she fell asleep in Anita's arms. Anita covered her with a rug and dialled a number. "It's Tani. She's broken down… yes. She was saying something about quitting… something went wrong at work. Don't worry," she spoke into the phone as she looked at Tanya sleeping peacefully on the couch. A mother's hand reached out to Tanya's tear-stained face and caressed it with love.

* * * * * *

Tanya felt like she had slept for ages. She glanced at her watch. It was four in the morning. She walked to the window and looked out at the sleeping city.

"Slept well? Must be hungry, na? Let me get you something to eat." Anita's voice startled Tanya.

"I thought you were sleeping," Tanya muttered as she followed Anita into the kitchen.

"You were in bad shape this afternoon, Tani. I can't sleep until I know what happened."

Tanya turned away.

"Whenever you want to tell me…," she said, handing Tanya a glass of water and a plate.

"Anita… I won the employee of…"

"For the fourth time in a row, I know…."

"People at work, they…." The story rolled out with tears as Tanya held Anita's hand tight.

Anita got up at the end of it and wiped Tanya's tears and took her into her arms. "I am sorry, Tani. I really am sorry. I wish we were celebrating your award, but it has become a routine, and that's all the colleagues were saying. Don't take it to heart."

"I don't want to kid myself anymore. I am a loser. Not

because I have lost something, but because in spite of winning all the time, I have nothing. They were right... they were absolutely right."

"You are not a loser. Admitting they were right takes courage. You need to fix what is wrong. Calling yourself a loser is not the way out. And quitting, that's just running away."

"I'm not quitting out of embarrassment. I want to free myself from that office, from that life. I want to.... Anita, when I told that woman near the lift I was taking the day off, there was shock on her face.... And I felt a sense of satisfaction. I just want to give it all up. Shock them. Let them know I am alive."

"Don't rush into it. It'll leave you hollow once again. Just look at you. All this while, you struggled for their admiration, now you want to struggle to shock them. Who are they? You need a break. Just call in sick. Think. That's the answer. Don't rush.

"And don't worry. It will all turn out okay. I called Ravi. He'll be on the first flight out of Singapore. We'll talk about it some more. Fancy a walk?"

Anita extended her hand. A daughter reached out and held her mother's hand.

Chapter 5

With every glance at the watch, Rahul felt his frustration grow. He hated the idea of waiting, the idea of holding his energy still until he could meet Menon and spin the wheel of fortune. It had been barely an hour since Menon had hung up and he couldn't figure out why time had been passing so slowly. The last twenty-eight years of his life had been a breeze. Right now, every minute was excruciatingly long.

He walked back into the apartment he called home, unsure of what he needed to do next. He crashed on the couch which served as a bed when he wanted to sleep, a work desk when he wanted to write out something and a dining table when he needed to eat. He looked at the watch again. Twenty-seven hours to go.

He took out a box that held his treasure — the only thing he carried in his backpack when he stepped into the city of Mumbai. He turned the pages that contained his life; a life he had long stowed away into a dark corner of his mind.

There he was — Rahul, the adorable baby boy, Rahul the mischievous student, a loving son, a loyal friend. The last page held a picture, slightly puffed on the surface where teardrops had fallen a long time ago. It was a picture of two people who were smiling with all their heart as if they were staring at the happiness that lay in front of them. Who could have ever imagined anything could go wrong for these happy teenagers?

Rahul turned back to the first page, wiping away the dust that had blurred the image of a sleeping baby held by his Ma. She was looking at him with all the love in the world. He turned the page to his first birthday. Page three, Rahul's first day at school. He held Ma's hand tight, looking at her with anguish, not wanting to let go, not wanting her to let go. Page four, Rahul was handing a flower to a beaming Ma. Page five, Rahul's tenth birthday; all his friends were around him, and there was Ayesha. Ma missing. Page six, Rahul and Ayesha next to a sand-castle they built on the beach. Ma missing. Page seven, a shaky photograph of Rahul and his mum on her birthday, Ayesha's first attempt at photography. Page eight, Rahul and Ayesha together after their standard ten results, excited about college, about the future, about sharing that future together. This was all that Rahul had. His treasure chest was a bunch of photographs and the memories hidden in those photographs. Why were there no pictures after Ayesha's? The bitter truth was that he had no memories worth clinging to, save the ones with Ayesha. She was all that he had wanted, to make her happy had been his ambition, but that hadn't been enough.

They had almost become a happy family. Rahul, Ma and Ayesha. When their friendship bloomed into love, Ma was hardly surprised. "I knew all along," she had smiled.

It was one of the happiest days of his life, but there was nobody to take a picture at that time.

One night, lying awake on the mats in their little house, Rahul told Ma about his dream. "I want to marry her, Ma. But I don't know how I am ever going to prove myself...."

"If you really want to, you can," Ma interrupted him.

"But Ma, I can't find a decent job. Time is running out. She is twenty-two, and her father is already looking for a match."

"We'll ask for her hand. I'll talk to her parents."

"Ma! I don't even have a job. I have a simple Bachelor's degree. I still sleep on *chatais*. I want to make a name for myself and stand on my own two feet."

"You are a special boy; you are going to make a name for yourself one day. You are destined for higher things. I know it; a mother's heart never lies." Ma never let Rahul underestimate himself. But Ayesha was beginning to lose faith.

"Laugh, laugh. You always laugh. Do you ever think about the future seriously, Rahul?" she had asked him one day.

"Of course, that's why I am saying better things will come along. Even God knows my princess can't be happy with just five thousand rupees a month," he had said justifying his decision to turn down a job.

"Rahul, stop it!" she chided him.

"I have to go. Have to take Ma to the city hospital." He got up.

"Run away from it again. If you can't even discuss our problems, how will you deal with them?"

She didn't ask why Ma had to go to the hospital; she rarely even came to meet Ma these days. Rahul pretended not to hear her. Of course he was worried; he was not a fool. Ma's illness, which he never talked about, rejection letters which he never discussed, had demoralised him. And the one person who was his strength, whose moral support he could seek was busy pointing out his failures. He was crumbling.

Ma was crumbling, too. Her soft soothing voice now cracked and trembled. The hands that always comforted him with their warmth were shaky and cold. Ma was slipping, but he wanted to share only his joys with Ayesha. He could deal with his problems alone, if he had to. It wasn't long before he realised that he needed to tell Ayesha. He couldn't go through it all alone.

When they had sat down on their favourite park bench that evening, Ayesha didn't rest her head on his shoulder like she used to. She sat at an awkward distance and turned to face him. Rahul opened his mouth to speak but she cut him off.

"I have to tell you something. Something very important," she said. Her voice was bleak, without a trace of any emotion.

"Ayesha, I have...."

"An acquaintance in the US has sent a marriage proposal and my family has decided to accept."

"They are not going to force you, you know that."

He wanted to talk about something else.

"He's a doctor, in California. Well-settled, owns a house. Parents are in Mumbai. Looks good."

"Hmm.... A typical good-on-paper guy... I have something to...."

"He's got a great sense of humour, respects the elders. Just the perfect guy," she said.

She was getting on Rahul's nerves now. He hated her silly games and this was not the time.

"Can we talk like two adults? I don't want to play these silly games, where I'm supposed to act all jealous," he said angrily.

"This isn't a silly game. I am just talking about...."

"You're talking about some random guy you will meet twice and then reject." Rahul sprang up from the bench.

"No. You have it all wrong," she said looking away from his piercing gaze.

"Do I?"

"He's my fiancé."

Ayesha's words hit Rahul hard. "What?"

"I have decided to accept his proposal. I couldn't get a better guy than this. Let's face it." She looked away.

"But, you... you and I... what about us?"

"I came here to tell you." She took in a deep breath. "There's no 'us' anymore. I am sorry. I am getting married in two weeks. He has to go back soon. My parents are very happy. He is very happy and...."

"What about you?"

"I am very happy too. I hate to admit it but I am." She looked down.

"Wow! Nice surprise!" Rahul looked at her and laughed.

"So, this is a joke too? Good, I wanted to part with a smile."

She got up and placed her hand on his shoulder. There was awkwardness. He tried to hug her but she pulled away. He tried to hold her hand, but she let go of his fingers. She was disconnected. He laughed and turned away. He wanted to stop her, but he was angry that she didn't want to be stopped. "That's it. You love someone forever. You think you both are a part of each other. And then... Wham!"

Rahul couldn't understand why she hadn't spoken to him about it before.

She replied in a cool tone, as if she understood his pain but didn't care. "I love you but love isn't everything, I need something more than that, Rahul. I have to take this chance, I don't know if you can ever give me what he has to offer. I can't wait forever. It's my life, I am sorry," she said and she walked away, not looking back once. He slumped down on the bench. She was gone.

Every time Ma asked about Ayesha, he made up silly excuses. She asked if they had fought. And he came up with more excuses.

"Don't lie to me. I know something is wrong. When did you learn to lie to me? You have lost her, haven't you?" she asked in a frail voice.

"She was never mine to lose, honestly. Here, drink up and go to bed. You shouldn't waste energy on such stupid things," he said.

Rahul had been too busy taking care of Ma to think about Ayesha and he didn't like her name being mentioned. It made his stomach go woozy; it made him feel an emptiness within that he knew he could never fill. It caused a deep pain inside his heart; it reminded him that his heart was broken and he didn't want to mend it. "She came to say goodbye to me," said Rahul. "She said she was going away. I asked her to wait till you came home but she said she had already said goodbye to you."

"So? What happened?"

"Go to bed, Ma. Things happen for the best. Didn't you always tell me that when I was a kid?"

"Come here." Ma held him and comforted him. Her hands had stopped trembling; they gave him strength. That night he had slept in his Mum's lap, just like he had a decade ago when there was no Ayesha. And he felt the pain resurface.

Sixteen hours to go....

Chapter 6

Waking up late, mid-afternoon shopping trips, lazy evenings with iced tea and gossip were all a part of the whole new world Tanya had set out to discover. She wasn't thinking about work or about targets or presentations and for a change, she felt good about herself.

Her office had frantically tried to get in touch with her. Her boss had even sent a messenger boy to her place and left an SOS note. Anita was patiently handling it all. The people at work were pissed off that Tanya had disappeared. They were even more upset when their emails to her bounced. Anita hadn't told Tanya how badly her boss had been trying to get in touch with her. She wanted Tanya to enjoy the peace and quiet that she had missed out on for so long.

Tanya was lying on the terrace watching the sunset when she heard the phone ring, but she was too lazy to go and get it. Thankfully, Anita answered the phone. Though she didn't want to leave the seat, Tanya had to get dressed immediately if she wanted to be in time to meet Gia for drinks. She hadn't seen Gia since Ravi's birthday party and was really looking forward to seeing her. She stretched as if she was going to touch the sky and walked into the living room. Anita emerged from her bedroom.

"It was your office," Anita said pointing to the phone, "They wanted to know if you were...."

"Alive? Hope you told them I wasn't.... Can't imagine walking into that place ever again," Tanya said as she walked towards the bedroom.

"They wanted to know if you were all right. And I told them you were stressed and were taking some time off." Anita followed Tanya.

Tanya turned around in shock. "Taking time off? why did you tell them that? Now they will expect me back in there!"

"No they don't." Anita threw a turquoise blouse and a pair of jeans on the bed, "They said that if you had wanted to take time off, you had to take permission. They told me you will be fired if you do not have a valid medical document."

What Anita hadn't mentioned to Tanya was that her boss was willing to ignore that little HR rule if Tanya could resume work by Monday. They really needed her.

Tanya kept looking at Anita who was now looking through a jewellery box.

"I said we don't have it," she smiled at Tanya.

"So you got me fired? I could have resigned," Tanya shrugged.

"Yes you could have, but then you would have to serve the notice period. Did you really want to go back there for a month?" Anita asked.

Tanya picked up the clothes and walked to the bathroom, not caring that she'd just been fired. "Smart! What would I do without you?"

"Now get ready; let me call Ravi and check where he is. I hate his guy nights. He always ends up drinking too much."

Anita had been talking to Tanya's boss for an entire week. He was ready to bend over backwards for Tanya. Anita had finally convinced him to let Tanya go, because she had a nervous breakdown and it would be 'detrimental to the company's future if her position remained vacant for so long'.

The boss appreciated Anita's honesty and promised her that as soon as Tanya was back on her feet, she would be welcomed back with arms wide open. Tanya didn't need to know this. All Tanya needed right now was time to heal, time to breathe and time to smile.

* * * * * *

Rahul reached the Cee office an hour early. The receptionist was busy with the phone again and she had the same fake smile on her face. There was no hint of recognition on her face as Rahul approached the desk. "How may I help?" she asked with a tired expression.

"I am here to see Mr. Menon," Rahul said confidently.

"Do you have an appointment?" An uninterested cold look and a waft of the same old pungent fragrance hit Rahul.

"I am seeing him at six," he snapped without so much as glancing at her.

"I see. It's a bit early. Let me speak to his office. May I have your name please?"

"Arrogance works," he thought as he gave her his name and waited for a response. He got another fake smile as she waited for a response on the phone.

"You're here on important business," Rahul told himself.

"There seems to be no answer. What's the purpose of the visit?" she asked.

"Business," he wondered whether it was the pungent perfume or the receptionist that made him want to be so arrogant. He realised it was a bit of both.

"Let me see what I can do. Could you wait right there?" she said pointing towards a glass door behind her desk. Rahul nodded and went in.

The waiting room was empty, except for an elderly lady sitting in one corner. Rahul flashed a smile at her and sat down on a sofa in the corner. He wondered what Menon was going to offer him. He wondered how he was going to earn the next month's rent. He wondered if this was a stepping stone to realise Ma's dream.... A stern-looking woman walked in and called out Rahul's name. Rahul was startled, but he didn't show it.

"Here's your pass. Twelfth floor, fourth door to your right. Sorry about the wait. Mr. Menon's in a meeting until six, but he will see you immediately after the meeting," she said in a monotone.

Before Rahul could thank her, she stormed out of the waiting room. Rahul shrugged. He didn't like how self-centred people in the organisation were. They just did their job and walked off. Warmth, the warmth that he had always felt at OneStop was missing and it had been replaced by the cold, dry waft of breeze coming through an air-conditioning shaft, carrying a touch of an artificial deodorant. This cool breeze was a pretence. It was a reminder that this was a world where selling false dreams, not caring and blatantly lying to people were considered virtues.

An empty desk and a leather sofa greeted Rahul as he entered the fourth door to his right on the 12th floor. He looked around, but when he couldn't see anybody, he just sat down on the soft chair. How had he ended up here in an empty office, completely helpless and uncertain about what the future held for him?

When Ma had died, there was nothing left for Rahul in Goa. He had carried nothing but a few memories with him. Considering they were the only legacy Ma had left behind, he couldn't leave them behind and they wouldn't leave him alone either.

He had not slept at all on the train to Mumbai. As soon as he stepped off the train, he took in the warm humid Mumbai air. A characteristic scent of stewed sugary tea, over-fried spices and over-used cooking oil greeted him. Within those pungent scents, he sensed a scent he could not define, but the scent made him want to smile. He walked past the busy bodies and managed to find an auto-rickshaw. He asked the rickshaw to take him to a cheap hotel.

As the rickshaw coughed and puffed through the bustling market, Rahul closed his eyes and took in the scents of the city. Leaking petrol from a car, fried garlic from a roadside Chinese stall, the stench of hundreds of chickens in a poultry shop waiting to be slaughtered, a salty scent of fish, a grassy, earthy scent of freshly-washed vegetables.... There was another scent overlying all these — the scent of Mumbai, the scent of the people belonging here, these people who seemed too busy to stop and take in the chaos around them. Rahul became one of them the day he felt a rush to earn money and walked into a mall, looking for part-time work.

He told himself that this was his option only until he found a real job. The newly-opened mall was running short of staff and the manager, without much thought, assigned the perfume store to this rather inexperienced boy. It was to be a temporary arrangement until he found an experienced person. Rahul was so good at selling perfumes that the manager didn't see the point of finding an experienced perfume salesman. Until someone reminded Rahul of the dream that had been left behind, he was content to merely exist in the city of dreams.

The thought of Menon shook Rahul up. As he looked down at the coffee table, he spotted Menon smiling back at him from the cover of a magazine. Rahul grabbed a magazine from the pile to flip through while he waited for the man who unsettled him so much. It was a while before a lady walked in, smiling.

"Mr. Rajgopal?"

Rahul recognised the voice from the telephone conversation the day before. The voice was the same but the cold, uninterested tone was gone; there was a hint of friendliness in her voice today.

"Gosh! Did I speak to you on the phone yesterday? You sounded like a twenty-year-old!"

"Oh!" She blushed under the old-fashioned foundation she wore. She touched her dyed brown hair as she took the desk. "I am Mr Menon's secretary, Nina Mathews. He's still in a meeting; he will be with you shortly."

"Is that musk?" Rahul asked, sniffing the air.

She was clearly taken aback by the question "Yes. Why?"

"Sorry, but I figured someone like you would wear something more subtle, like maybe Cool Water," he said cautiously.

Rahul could see an eyebrow shoot up behind the golden rims of her glasses.

"Why?" She had taken on an interrogating tone.

"That smells more like a gentle and a warm person. Sorry if that offended you," he added just to make sure he was within his boundaries.

"Oh no! No sir, that didn't offend me, it just surprised me. Cool Water happens to be my favourite fragrance, but someone gifted me musk and I just want to finish it," she said, laughing. "But how did you know?"

Rahul just smiled. Ms. Mathews smiled back and Rahul knew he now had a friend in Menon's office.

"Nina, make sure the concept notes for the new shows are on my table first thing tomorrow."

Avinash Menon walked in, preoccupied with his Blackberry. He looked up and glanced at Rahul and then at his watch. "So you are here on time, Mr. Mall. Great! Come on in. Nina, this is my last meeting for the day."

"Right, Mr. Menon." Nina smiled and nodded.

"You could call it a day then. I'll see you tomorrow."

He walked to a silver door at the other end of the room and Rahul followed him. Before going through the door, Rahul waved a goodbye to Nina. She stood there, smiling, long after the door closed behind Rahul.

Chapter 7

They walked into an enormous room with a huge glass table and swanky black chairs. Behind the table was a glass wall overlooking the crowded street and in front of the table was a wall filled entirely with flickering television screens. If the lobby was a spaceship, this ought to be the control room, thought Rahul.

"Sit down. What's your name?"

"Rahul, Rahul Rajgopal." Rahul tried to sound as confident as possible, but the knot in his stomach seemed to get the better of him. His voice sounded like the voice of a nervous boy.

"How far would you go to be rich and famous?"Avinash asked Rahul with a piercing gaze.

Rahul shifted in his chair. "I… I don't know. As long as it feels right, I'd do anything." He tried weighing his words before they came out but he didn't want to take too long to think.

"Good. Before I say anything else, you'll have to sign these." Avinash pushed a bundle of papers towards Rahul, who eyed them uneasily.

Avinash continued, "It's just a formality; it says that nothing mentioned in this room will ever be mentioned outside and that the ideas discussed here belong to me and my network and you will be sued if you try to discuss this conversation with anybody without the channel's or my permission."

Avinash got up and walked to the window. His silhouette

against the orange sky outside the window would've made a pretty picture, Rahul thought. With a rather shaky hand, Rahul signed the papers.

"Good. Now are you ready to give me six to nine months of your life?"

"Excuse me?" Rahul stuttered. He didn't know what to make of the question.

"I ask the questions. You answer them."

"I... why six months?"

"It may go up to nine months." Avinash was back in his chair and was playing with a remote control, staring at a screen behind Rahul.

"But what for?"

"Yes or no? I ask the questions."

"Depends on what you need them for and what I get in return." Rahul managed to organise the words buzzing around in his head to make sure they made sense.

"Smart. Okay, this is what it is: you will be trained, groomed and presented in a television reality show. All expenses will be borne by the network for the period. Over and above that, you will get a salary equivalent to your current salary. You will live the life of a multi-millionaire. And then we will find you a wife."

Rahul's jaw dropped. He stared at Menon in utter disbelief. "I... I don't understand."

Menon continued speaking as if he were reciting a poem, his gaze fixed on the panel of televisions behind Rahul. Rahul hated the lack of eye contact.

"I am offering you a chance to live the life of a multi-millionaire, meet pretty girls and get a salary. Think about it. I am presenting the idea to a core team and a few people from the headquarters tomorrow. After that I could explain the whole deal to you. Can you be here at 10 a.m.?"

Rahul could only nod.

"Good then, see you tomorrow."

This was the second time he had met Menon and Rahul had

again ended up feeling unsettled and nervous. The man knew how to put random, intense thoughts in Rahul's head, but this time, the thoughts had a hint of optimism.

* * * * * *

Rahul could hear the phone ring in his apartment as he turned the key. He didn't run to answer it. It continued to ring as Rahul took off his shoes and stared at the phone for half a minute before answering it.

"Where are you, men?"

It was Rosie.

"Hey Rosie!" He felt glad she'd called, although he hadn't expected it.

"You've been missing for three days! Boss was trying to call you frantically. What the hell are you doing? Want to get fired or what?"

He could hear the heavy traffic. "Where are you?"

"I should be asking you that, you idiot. You can't take leave without informing, men. What is the matter with you?"

"Rosie, I am thinking of quitting."

"Bloody fool. Quitting! Let me meet you… I am reaching your house in ten minutes."

"Rosie you don't have to. I have made up my mind."

"Shut up. Something's wrong with you."

"Who'll make dinner for your Savio?" Rahul laughed.

"You don't worry about that. I have to come and see you. Bloody tiring day managing your counter I've had," she replied angrily before hanging up.

He tried to tidy up a little, while thinking of an explanation. He wasn't allowed to say anything about what he might be getting into; he wasn't even sure if he wanted to get into the deal with Menon. He had to figure out a way to keep the job till he could make up his mind.

He opened the door as soon as the doorbell rang. There stood

Rosie, her cheerful face loaded with make-up and genuine concern. "Hi man! This is where you live?" she exclaimed walking into the tiny room.

Same old blunt Rosie, Rahul thought. "This is Mumbai. This is the best I could get, given my budget," he shrugged.

"Ok Ok. Sit down now. No jumping topics. Why you want to quit?"

Her funny lingo always amused Rahul.

"I have decided to move on," he said as calmly as he could.

"Move on to what? You got another job or what?"

Rahul shook his head.

"So why are you quitting before you get another job? This is Mumbai. Jobs are not easy to find, you idiot."

"Rosie, I am…."

"What is the use of breaking my head? You won't listen!" Rosie sounded dejected. "But Rahul, man, you are so good and all. If anyone else had done this, no, that devil, that manager would have fired him. But they know, there's nobody they can find to fill your place. That's why they have been calling to check on you. Don't let it go."

"Rosie, did they ask you to…"

"No. I came because…," she hesitated a little, and said, "I came because I care for you. I don't want you to quit the mall. I am so selfish, man. You can do better, but that perfume counter needs you. I need you. Just come back."

"I… I don't know what to say, Rosie."

"Are you coming back?"

"Can you do me a favour?" Rahul had spotted a chance to have his cake and eat it too. "Will you tell the manager that I had to leave town and that it was an emergency. Which is why I could not contact them… will you tell them that?"

"But you are sitting here!" She had a confused look on her face.

"Rosie, darling, I want you to lie."

"JESUS CHRIST! Why would I lie? No. I won't lie."

"If you don't lie they might fire me. Do you want me back?"

"If you know that, then go and tell them yourself, na. Why you making me lie?"

"Rosie, I need to think. Please. Please, just lie this once for my sake. Please do this for me?"

"What should I say? What reason should I give them?"

"My mother is ill and I have gone to take care of her. I couldn't get in touch with them at the mall so I called you on your cell."

"Shameless! Telling lies about your mother! I will not lie like that." Rosie was enraged.

Rahul wanted to tell her that it was his mother's dream that he was trying to fulfil by telling a lie about her. "She died a long time ago, Rosie. It's all right."

"I will only say some emergency came up and you went to take care of it. I will not lie. When should I say you will come back?"

"A week or two." He hugged Rosie.

"My poor Savio must be hungry at home. See you soon."

She got up to leave and pulled Rahul's cheeks just the way he always pulled hers. Rosie was the only real friend he had. She had agreed to lie in the hope that Rahul would be back at the mall and he knew that he was going to let her down.

Chapter 8

Rahul felt completely out of place in the Cee office. While everyone was dressed like Agent Smith, he was dressed in a simple Tantra T-shirt and jeans. He had to wait a long time before a few Agent Smiths got up and shook hands with Avinash.

One of them said, "We trust you to do whatever it takes to get the TRPs going."

"I appreciate that. Thank you for being here today."

Avinash was looking at Rahul out of the corner of his eye. He escorted the Agent Smiths to the elevator. He muttered something to Nina after he came back and signalled Rahul to follow him.

Avinash took a seat and started doing something on the smallest laptop Rahul had ever seen. Rahul remained silent out of anticipation. Avinash, however, didn't find it necessary to speak to Rahul. He did not even exchange pleasantries.

After what seemed like an eternity to Rahul, he snapped shut his laptop and smiled at Rahul. "I've shared what I have on my mind with the key members of the board. The channel is going to go ahead with this entire concept."

"Which is?" Rahul tried hard to keep his voice from trembling. He realised that Avinash meant serious business and he wanted Avinash to know that he was serious too.

"It is common knowledge that our channel's TRPs have been dropping. What we really need at the moment is a sensational new show that gets us the eyeballs we need. You must have observed that there are many reality shows on Indian television. Kaun Banega Crorepati, Indian Idol, Popstars, Gurukul, Sa Re Ga Ma Pa. The audience is sick of all the talent hunts and the so-called game shows that are inspired by American TV. We need a fresher concept; something that sells a dream.

"The show I have developed over the past couple of weeks is somewhat on these lines — a saleable dream and the length people could go to make it come true."

He paused to look at Rahul and continued. "Every girl dreams of meeting the man of her dreams and we are going to create just that — a man of every girl's dream — the ultimate Mills & Boon hero, the knight in shining armour. He's rich, he's handsome and all they have to do is get him to fall in love with them."

Avinash got up from his seat and began walking around the spacious office. "The only catch," he continued, "is that the guy is an illusion. He seems perfect but is not really perfect. He's a perfume salesman."

He pointed to Rahul.

Rahul was beginning to see where Avinash was going but he wanted to be sure before he reacted.

Avinash continued. "He is an ordinary guy, selected and groomed by the channel to pretend he is 'Prince Charming' or 'Mr. Right'."

Avinash spoke excitedly. "Think about it. What does every Indian girl or for that matter every girl want? She wants a rich, well-mannered, romantic husband, who loves her. What do her parents want? A cultured man from a good family, rich, if possible, well-known as well. The man we create will possess all these qualities. Just for the duration of the show, of course. He will be the most eligible bachelor. Thousands of girls will want to marry him. We'll just get those girls on the show as contestants. They will go through a beauty contest-like short-listing process. The finalists will be eliminated by our bachelor using a combination of dating, games and tasks. We are working on those details."

Rahul was straining to catch every word as it flew out of Avinash's mouth.

"The truth will be announced to the final three contestants after our man has made his choice. If the chosen girl doesn't mind the fact that he is an ordinary, poor man, you've got a brand-new fairytale. And this fairytale happens on national television!"

Rahul just sat there, gaping at Avinash, not knowing what to say.

"I hope the idea is clearer now. You have time to think about it, Rahul."

Rahul wasn't listening, his mind was buzzing with thoughts. What was he getting into? Why had Menon chosen him to play a rich bachelor? Would it be right to cheat thousands of young girls? Rahul shook his head and got up. He walked to the massive window and looked out at the city that was somehow supposed to help him realise his dream. Was this his dream? Playing someone he was not, someone he was never going to be.

He turned around and looked at the television panels. Rahul thought of the first time he'd come into the building; he remembered that emptiness the trip had induced. He remembered how he had left the building feeling incomplete and unimportant. He wanted those robots to know who he was but was this the way?

Avinash was back in his seat, tapping the table with a remote control, "Your thoughts?"

"How are you going to pull this off? People have seen me, the people at the mall, my landlord, my colleagues, the receptionist down there, Ms. Mathews. They will see me and know I am...."

"So, you are up for it."

"I didn't say that!"

"If it was a no, you'd have said that outright. You are trying to reason with me which means you want to be a part of this. Good!"

"I... okay but answer my question...."

"Do you really think you're that important? The receptionist sees thousands of faces everyday, why should she remember yours? The people at the mall will forget about you in a month's time. By the time the show goes on air, we will have your personality changed. You'll undergo a, what did she say... ah, yes, a makeover."

"Is it that easy?"

"So I am told! But, that's a risk I am taking; what have you got to lose? It's a paid adventure. You are getting paid to enjoy a luxurious life. You are getting paid to be surrounded by pretty girls who are fighting to be with you. You are going to have all the good things in life and what do you pay?"

"Nothing?"

"Exactly! If you were to have those things I promised you for a day you'd have to put in all your savings so far and much more. What I'm offering you is a great deal...."

"Superficially maybe, but something doesn't feel right."

"If it is nervousness, don't worry about it. If you want to turn me down, by all means do; as long as you don't discuss this outside, I don't give a damn. We can easily find a replacement. Think about it; it's an exciting once-in-a lifetime deal."

"I need time to think," Rahul said in a voice of bewilderment.

"I understand, but in my business, time is more important than money. I can't wait for you to make up your mind while a competitor goes and grabs those TRPs. I'll give you until this evening. If you want to be a part of it, come see me at J.W. Marriott at 8 p.m. or simply call and leave a message with Nina. No pressure!"

Rahul nodded and got up to leave. He smiled at Nina on his way out, but she sensed something amiss in his smile. He made his way to the lift. As the lift doors opened, a huge crowd of robots made their way out, walking past Rahul as if he was just a piece of furniture standing in their way. Many more robots walked in and out as the elevator made its way down the building. Each one of them preoccupied with cell-phones or with papers. Some of them spoke to each other, but in a language too fast for Rahul to grasp. Some people just looked at him with a cold gaze until his eyes met theirs and forced them to look away. By the time he got to the ground floor, he felt that now familiar sinking feeling in his stomach again. The one he had felt the first time he had come to the office. Rahul couldn't wait to get home.

By the time Rahul was out of Cee, he knew he was going to take up the offer. He was a graduate with modest marks; his only contact with the working world had been selling perfumes. He couldn't get anything better than what Menon was offering.

He still had his doubts about the show, but evening found him making his way to the Marriott. Maybe this was a lesson for girls like Ayesha who chose financial security over love. Maybe they'd finally know how it felt to be let down. Maybe they would realise that love doesn't consider money important. Maybe they would be humiliated.

Rahul walked into the plush lobby of the Marriott and looked around. He didn't know where to find Menon. He didn't have to look very hard, Menon signalled to him from the other end of the lobby. There was an elegantly-dressed woman standing next to him. She waved to Rahul and smiled. Rahul walked to them and shook hands with Menon. "It's too tempting to reject, isn't it? Anyway, meet Sarita Menon, my wife. Rahul is the boy I spoke to you about."

"Sherry Menon," she corrected Avinash as she shook hands with Rahul.

"Let's get to work then. The conference room?" Avinash asked Sherry, who guided them through the lobby.

Rahul saw Sherry flash her perfect smile at a few people. A senior member of the hotel staff was waiting by the door, smiling. On the table sat a vase of fresh white roses, a fresh pot of coffee and some cookies.

"Ah! My favourite flowers." Sherry smiled at the man at the door. "Thank you, it was very thoughtful of you, Ashok."

"Pleasure, Mrs. Menon, I'll be at the reception if you need me." He closed the door and left.

Sherry poured the coffee for everyone as soon as they settled down in the cushy chairs. Avinash started speaking, taking control of the conversation. "This is our first official meeting. I don't want you to be seen at the office anymore. You'll have to quit your job, leave your apartment and tell them that you are moving to another place. You should cut off all contact with people as soon as possible. That is, until we think you're ready, of course.

"This is a contract that states the terms of employment, details about your pay and everything. You can go over it later." He pushed a booklet towards Rahul. Rahul looked at Sherry; she was observing Rahul but she had a warm look on her face. There was something very comforting about her face. "Sarita... Sherry is here to help us groom and train you for the show. Do you want to take over, darling?"

Sherry cleared her throat. "Well, Rahul, you'll be going through a makeover. I am responsible for devising a plan to bring about the necessary changes in your personality over the next few months."

"Next month," Avinash corrected her.

"Yes, we'll try Avinash," she said. "Rahul, you are going to be taken care of by people I have chosen. You will be in safe hands. You're a fantastic guy, but we are going to make you stunning!"

A vibrant smile surfaced on her face. Rahul was amused by the variety of smiles she could flash. The Burberry Brit that had seemed an odd choice to Rahul earlier seemed to be the perfect scent for her now. Under the perfect make-up that Sherry wore, there was a layer of eccentricity and excitement. Rahul smiled back, realising he hadn't spoken a word all evening.

"So where am I going to live?" he mumbled.

"For now, you will be at our farmhouse. It is isolated. I don't want anybody other than us seeing you through the transformation phase," Avinash answered.

"Except for my team of little helpers, of course. You will have experts from their respective fields working on your makeover. We have a gym, a swimming pool, a river view. It's just fantastic there," Sherry announced and clapped her hands together noiselessly.

"We'll figure out how to move your belongings," Avinash said.

"I'll just have a backpack," Rahul declared nonchalantly.

Sherry looked at him with surprise and pity. Avinash, however, seemed very unconcerned. "Brilliant. So when do you think we can move you?" he said.

Sherry gave Rahul another compassionate glance, almost apologetic about her husband's apathy.

"I think about two days should be more than enough for me to wrap up things. By when do you need this?" Rahul was holding up the booklet Avinash had given him earlier.

"Saturday. Welcome aboard," Avinash said, smiling triumphantly.

"Do let me know if you need any help with the packing. I could arrange something," Sherry offered.

"Thanks, Mrs. Menon, I think I'll be fine," Rahul said returning her smile.

"Call me Sherry."

Avinash looked at his wife with a hint of surprise. Outside the Page 3 circle Sherry was Mrs. Menon and an ordinary perfume-seller could never have called her Sherry. "Sherry, darling, we're getting late."

Avinash didn't like surprises, they made him uncomfortable. "Rahul, I'll see you on Saturday at this address," he said and handed Rahul a card. "That's my house address. My mobile number's on it, just in case you want to talk to me about anything."

"See you on Saturday then," Rahul said as he walked out of the room.

He walked through the lobby, feeling excited. The last time he'd felt this mix of excitement and nervousness was when he had left his hometown to come to Mumbai. He didn't know what was in store for him next, but he could hardly wait. He walked out and was startled to see the face he always loved thinking about. He thought he was imagining it and it took him some time to realise it was really her. There was something different about her though. She was smiling as the breeze blew strands of hair on her face.

She was busy tucking the stray strands behind her ears. In a typical Bollywood moment, her eyes met Rahul's for a split second, his heart started to beat faster, but then she looked away without a hint of recognition.

'It doesn't matter. I am not going to be at the mall anymore to keep seeing her,' he told himself as he stared at her. He hated thinking about deserting his perfumes, Rosie and the mall, but the pain of not seeing Tanya's face every now and then stung him harder than any of those things.

* * * * * *

Gia thought she had seen it all when it came to the crazy concept notes her boss sent her way, but as she read the one he'd just sent in, she realised that Avinash Menon had outdone himself easily with this one. She read through the concept note again. An entrepreneur based in London wanted to find a bride. Gia was supposed to handle all the pre-production on this show. The concept sounded outrageous to her, but she had a good feeling about it. She started making notes of the things she needed to do before her meeting with Menon. She was one of Menon's blue-eyed babies at the network because she was always well-equipped with ideas and POAs before the meeting. She decided that they should get the marketing guys to work on a teaser campaign to create a buzz. She started scribbling ideas into her little notebook and smiled. She loved Menon's outrageous ideas because making ideas happen was what she thrived on. Suddenly, Gia didn't care that her plans to hit the bar early had to be scrapped. She was going to rock the latest concept Avinash had sent her way.

This however, did not stop her from feeling nervous. No matter how confident she was, a meeting with Menon always made her jittery.

Chapter 9

Tanya had been to Vie Lounge a couple of times before on business. She had never taken the time to notice how beautiful the place really was. She walked across the creaky deck past the bar towards the sea. The water shimmered in the pure white moonlight. It took Tanya back to something nostalgic; she couldn't figure out what it reminded her of, but she knew the warmth she was feeling. She knew it from a long time ago. She turned around and saw Anita smiling and looking towards the bar. Gia was at the bar chatting up a foreigner.

Tanya and Anita both shook their heads and laughed. They took a table on the deck. They didn't fancy the loud music or dancing that the indoor seating offered. Anita noticed that Tanya couldn't take her eyes off the moon.

"What would you like Tani? They do good martinis. And the…." Tanya was still staring at the moon.

"Tani, would you like the moon?"

"Sorry?"

"You are mesmerised by the moon. So I figured you might want it."

"This place is beautiful. Look at the moon. It's so romantic…"

Anita nearly choked on her water and said, "I didn't know that word even existed in your dictionary."

Tanya gave Anita a 'not-again' stare.

"Sorry. Sometimes you do shock me! What does the moon remind you of?"

"I don't know," Tanya replied. The smile was gone.

Anita realised what had happened. She tried to control further damage by changing the subject. "Let's order us some drinks," Anita said, pretending to be lost in the drinks menu, "What would you like? Their flavoured martinis are good. I am thinking of getting the blue cheese chicken starter. What say?"

"Yeah, sounds good. I'll have a red wine, maybe," Tanya muttered without interest and looked at the moon again.

Anita noticed a shiny layer of unshed tears form in Tanya's eyes, but before Anita could say anything Tanya blinked them away along with the memories the moon brought. "Excuse me. I need to use the restroom," and Tanya hurried to the bathroom.

Anita realised something was wrong. She decided to get Gia to join them. She was still laughing and giggling at the bar with the *gora*. Anita interrupted the conversation. "Gia!"

"Anita! Err.... What are you doing here? Gosh, how are you?" Gia screamed in a plastic accent. The *gora* watched them in bewilderment as they hugged and air kissed before Gia pulled Anita aside. "What was that Anita? I was having the best conversation of my life...."

"I am sorry for interrupting, but how else was I supposed to tell you we were here?"

"You guys were late! Don't blame me if I found me some entertainment."

"Yeah, if you'd taken your eyes off that stranger, you'd have seen us walk in more than twenty minutes ago!"

"He's cute and we seem to click. I couldn't help it!" Gia was making a baby face.

"I am sure you clicked, but I wish you'd notice the ring on his left hand," Anita said as she signalled towards the foreigner.

Gia noticed the white-and-pink hand that held a glass of scotch, and she noticed the gold wedding band. The baby face disappeared and she frowned. "I'll say goodbye then. Men are really like toilets. The good ones are taken and the remaining ones are full of shit!"

Anita couldn't help but crack up. "I'll see you over at our table. Tani is waiting. Don't take too long," Anita said through bouts of laughter and went back to Tanya who looked visibly depressed. "What's the matter, Tani?"

"Can we take a table in the indoor lounge? It's a bit too cold out here."

Mumbai was trying to deal with a heat-wave and Anita knew that it wasn't the temperature that was bothering Tanya.

"Sure we can!" Anita turned to a waiter. "Excuse me, could we get a table inside please? It's a bit uncomfortable on the deck for my friend here."

"I'll just check Ma'am," he replied politely.

"Thanks."

Anita felt guilty for the sudden shift in Tanya's mood. She realised that something was bothering Tanya, but she didn't want to dwell on it too much. Tonight was all about showing Tanya a good time. The waiter came back with an apologetic look. "I am sorry Ma'am, the indoor section is booked for a private party."

"No problem. In that case, would it be possible for you to cancel our drinks? We'd like to leave."

"I most certainly can. And once again I am really sorry."

"Don't worry about it. Thanks very much."

Anita turned to Tanya. "Let's go somewhere for dinner instead. What say?"

Tanya nodded.

They both walked along the creaky deck to Gia who was on her way to them. She looked at Anita in confusion.

"We are going to eat something. It's going to be an early night. Come on," Anita announced.

"Where do you think should we go? Tani, your call, after all you are the guest of honour!" Gia said while they waited for the valet to get the car.

"I don't know Gia, I rarely go out. I have no idea about the good things in life," Tanya said.

Anita remained silent out of guilt.

"Oh don't be so hard on yourself. You'll learn about them fast enough with me around. Let's go to the Marriott; they're hosting an Italian food festival and I love Italian!" Gia said as they got into the car.

"Food or men?" Tanya asked.

Gia and Anita stared at Tanya.

"Come on, I can crack a joke. I am Ravi's sister, remember?" Tanya giggled.

Peals of laughter filled the car and the mood was restored. Tanya took over the music system for the five-minute ride, while Gia called a friend who worked at the Marriott to get a table without a reservation.

"Done! The Italian is meeting us in the lobby and he's got a table for us!"

"So you were in the mood for an Italian, after all?" Tanya joked as they got out of the car.

A sudden gust of wind blew strands of hair all over her face. It made Tanya laugh, and she discovered the joy of laughing just like that.

Chapter 10

Sherry greeted Rahul and his backpack at the door. She welcomed him into the luxurious apartment with enthusiasm, even though it was early Saturday morning. "Hi Rahul! How are you? Isn't it a lovely Saturday? Come on in, have some tea?"

"No, thank you. I am fine," Rahul lied. He felt anything but fine. The paintings on the walls seemed like a psychedelic blur of colours to him. It was a big house, but somehow it made him claustrophobic.

"May I use the bathroom?" he asked, his voice shaking.

"Sure! This way," Sherry said, but he hadn't heard a word.

He was trying hard not to get sick on the sparkling clean marble floor.

Inside the bathroom, he looked at the mirror. His face was drained of colour and his red eyes were begging for sleep.

"Breathe, breathe!" he told himself. Rahul was hoping an alarm clock would go off somewhere and he would wake from this dream in time to get dressed to go back to his perfumes at the mall. But all he heard was a faint knock on the door.

"Rahul, are you all right?" Rahul opened the door and saw Sherry's face, dripping with concern.

"You'll be okay. You're just nervous. A cup of tea will do you good. Come on."

Rahul followed her into the living room.

"Avinash wants to have a word with you before we leave." She handed him a mug.

Rahul smelt chamomile and mango, and thought of how wonderful it'd be as a perfume.

"Lovely isn't it?" Sherry asked.

"What?" Rahul asked, still in a daze.

"The tea. Let me get Avinash." Sherry left the room.

It was just about nine and Sherry was dressed like a catalogue model. Rahul took a sip from the mug, and its contents surprised him. He had no idea something tasting like this could be called tea. The water was tasteless and except for the aroma of chamomile and mango, there wasn't a hint of sweetness to it. No milk or sugar either.

"How are you, Rahul?" Avinash Menon walked in and sat down across him.

Rahul looked up from the mug and said, "I am ok. A bit nervous, but ok."

"Good. So all set?"

"Yes. I guess so."

"What have you told your family?"

"I have none."

"Your friends?"

"I have one friend and she thinks I am off to Dubai for work."

"Work? Dubai?"

"Yeah! I had to tell her something. So I told her that I was going there to work for a perfumer."

"Hmm... Is she your girlfriend?"

"Oh, no! She's just a colleague, a friend at work."

"Good. What about the Mall?"

"I asked her to take care of it. I told her I'd lose this opportunity if I had to serve the notice period. She told the management that I went to Dubai to meet a sick relative and won't be coming back for a long time. So they let me off, asking me to re-apply when I get back."

"So, there will have to be a safety phone call every once in a while to your friend?" Menon spoke without looking up as he typed something on his Blackberry.

"I guess if I don't want her to think I disappeared, yes. She might guess it's me on the show if I just disappear."

"Oh I don't think anyone can recognise you after my training." Sherry had entered with a surprisingly big handbag that matched her outfit. He could smell lavender today. "Are you done with your little legal chat, darling?" she asked her husband.

"I will be in a bit, why don't you sit down till then." Menon turned to Rahul again. "Did you read through the contract?"

"Yes, I tried, but by the tenth page, I figured I didn't understand it that much."

"It says that you are now an undercover employee of Cee Networks. You will be cast in a show and there are a few clauses regarding your behaviour and the nature of your job. The game rules haven't yet been formulated; once they are, they will be presented to you. Other than that," said Menon as he skimmed through the fat bundle, "you are going to be employed for a year, but if needed, you are legally bound to extend the contract by six months, getting paid double the salary you get currently. It's mostly in your favour and to protect the secrecy of the show."

Menon put down the document and lit a cigarette.

"Ok," replied Rahul and took another sip. "This tea tastes funny!"

"It's a herbal infusion. Good for relaxation," Sherry announced.

"Oh, didn't know there was a tea like this. Smells good." Rahul took another sip. "The only variety of tea I drink is *masala chai*, cutting and… actually that's about it!" He laughed.

"Well, then that's your first lesson. There are different teas, depending on the places they're grown in. And then there are herbal infusion teas like the one you are drinking now. We'll talk about them in the car. We must leave if we want to get there by lunch. Shall we?" Sherry got up.

Menon had a surprised look on his face. He expected the contract would be discussed for a longer time but once more, Sherry had left him surprised and uneasy.

The drive to Karjat was uneventful. Avinash was preoccupied with his Blackberry and Sherry was making notes. Somewhere near the outskirts of Mumbai, Rahul drifted off to sleep. He woke up when he sensed the car engine die. A sprawling house stood in front of him. Trees and bushes in a million shades of green surrounded it.

"Here we are! This, Rahul, is going to be your training ground," Sherry gushed proudly.

"It's huge!" Rahul gaped at the house as he got out of the car. He followed Menon and Sherry into the house.

Sherry took a very sleepy Rahul for a guided tour of the house. Rahul didn't notice much but he followed Sherry through the lounge, bedrooms, the patio, the garden, the poolside and several rooms for which Rahul didn't know the right names. He had tuned out Sherry's running commentary. "This is your room with a river view and the big balcony. This is the second-best room in the house."

"Thanks. I really like it," Rahul said, looking around, but not noticing much.

"Good, this is going to be home for a while. Make yourself comfortable. It's way past lunch time. Let me organise something. I'll see you in the dining room."

"Actually, I think I'll skip the lunch."

"Ok don't worry. I'll have something sent here. You get some rest."

Rahul took a deep breath and sat down on the bed. The bed was much softer than his modest couch, but he missed the hardness that caressed his back at the end of a tiring day. He missed the creaking of the spring each time he turned; he missed the chipped ceiling and the noisy fan that comforted him through hot summer nights. He was too tired to continue to miss his modest room. Rahul drifted off to sleep in the middle of the day, something he hadn't done for a long time.

Chirping birds and the sound of splashing of water roused Rahul from his deep slumber. He didn't realise he wasn't in his tiny apartment until he looked around. He sprang up from the bed and walked down to the living room. He heard Menon and Sherry chatting with someone on the patio.

"There's our guest of honour!" Sherry put the cup down as everyone turned to Rahul.

"Meet Sudha Ranjan, caretaker of this house." Menon pointed to the third head curiously eyeing Rahul through her horn-rimmed glasses.

"Sudha is the boss around here. If it weren't for her, this house would be a wreck," Sherry said.

"Have a seat. Some tea?" Sudha got up and poured some tea into a cup before handing it to Rahul. He cringed at the light brown liquid in the cup.

"Could I have some milk please?"

"Oh milk doesn't go well with that one. I think he'd like some conventional tea." Sherry winked at Sudha.

"Yes, of course. *Masala chai*? Ginger?" Sudha was on her way to the kitchen.

"Yes please." Rahul was glad he didn't have to drink the fancy *chai*.

"Down to business now. I am leaving tomorrow evening. Sherry and Sudha will be in charge. You will meet the rest of the team tomorrow," Menon announced.

"Oh yes," added Sherry reading from a small pocket diary. "We have it all worked out. There is a physical training schedule that we must get you started on immediately. Simultaneously, we'll start lifestyle training where you'll learn about literature, art, food, culture... all the 'good' things you need to know! We'll give you a makeover: you know, work on changing your hair, clothing but that's for later. There will be etiquette, hobby development and loads of other things."

"I am excited." Rahul didn't know what half those things meant, but they sounded intimidating... and interesting at the same time.

"Good," said Menon. "Your point of contact to me is Sudha or Sherry. Sherry will of course, be in Mumbai most of the time, but she will visit you more often than I will. Three weeks from now, I hope to see a whole new version of you." Menon turned to Sherry. "I expect quite a bit to be done by then. We can't waste any time."

"Of course, there'll be changes honey, but we need some time to transform him." Sherry gave Rahul an understanding nod.

Menon was about to say something but his phone rang. "Excuse me." He walked towards the pool.

"We are in no hurry. You take your time with all this, Rahul," Sherry reassured Rahul, who was anxiously looking at Menon in the distance.

"Don't worry Sherry Ma'am. I'll try my best," Rahul promised.

Sherry smiled at him.

"Just Sherry! We have to work as friends. You're free to ask me questions, because I want you to understand everything. And, listen, no pressure, okay? These things are best learnt at your own pace," she explained gently with another one of her smiles—this time it was a serene smile. Sudha arrived with a cup of tea.

"It's not a perfect *masala* tea. I haven't made one in ages. Sherry prefers tea bags and infusions," she said placing the cup on the table in front of Rahul. He promptly reached for the cup and took in the fragrance before sipping it.

"It couldn't be better, Sudhaji. What do you drink then?" Rahul asked.

"I try to enjoy the infusions with her," replied Sudha.

"She's a big filter coffee fan," Sherry told Rahul.

"Yes, it's hard to stop liking something you have enjoyed for almost half a century."

"Now I know your real age Sudha!" Sherry turned to Rahul. "She never reveals her age. She doesn't look like she's lived for half a century, does she?"

"Absolutely not, I'd say she was forty. Not a day older."

"You've missed the target by twelve years. I never hide my

age. Sherry prefers that I hide it so that she doesn't get reminded that she is just ten years away from my age," pat came the reply.

"That's enough mathematics, Sudha." Sherry swerved the conversation from age to tea again. "Well, *masala chai* is quite a rage in England right now. My friend, the famous socialite Liz McGrath, can't stop raving about it. So, we could pass this off as a classy choice. We have to develop your other choices. I know you like perfumes, but we need to create hobbies for you, and classy ones at that."

"Apart from perfumes I haven't developed an interest in anything. So...."

"We'll introduce you to a couple of hobbies then." Sherry scribbled into her notebook again and then handed Rahul a small notebook. "Could you write down your daily diet in there and hand it over to Sudha? Also, mention any allergies and food preferences. Sudha, we have to hand this over to the diet consultant. She'll be here tomorrow afternoon with the others. We have to start with the fitness ASAP."

"We'll have the gym ready on Monday," Sudha assured Sherry.

"Great, it's a lovely evening, so let's forget business, shall we? Anybody fancy a walk?"

"Oh, I am going back to my book." Sudha picked up a book from under the coffee table.

"I'll just fill this thing up in my room, if that's ok?" Rahul said holding up the diary.

"Great. I'll get my husband to join me then. See you!" Sherry walked towards Menon who was still on the phone. Rahul took Sudha's leave and went to his room.

His ears longed for the noises from the street below his flat, but all he got was the song of the river flowing and the slight rustling of leaves. A gust of cool wind greeted him as he walked out into the balcony for some fresh air.

This was his new room and the beginning of his new life.

Chapter 11

It was the busiest Sunday morning the Menon farmhouse had ever seen. Sudha and Sherry were literally running around the house along with the domestic help, constantly giving out instructions. Their helpers were busy executing the orders. The dining room, however, remained untouched by the chaos. Menon sat peacefully at the dining table poring over the newspaper.

"You look bewildered." Menon observed as he lowered the newspaper to peer at his latest find — his ticket to pleasing the powers-that-be in the parent company that funded his channel.

"It feels like they're trying to organise a wedding in a day," chuckled Rahul.

"The wedding's far away. They are just organising the making of a perfect Mr. Right," Menon said as he went back to the newspaper.

"Good morning, Rahul." Sherry waltzed in with a flower vase and turned to her husband as she placed the vase on the dining table. "Honey, the Operation Prince Charming team has left Mumbai."

Before Rahul could say anything Sherry yelled in the sweetest manner possible, "Laxman, get some *masala* tea and breakfast for Rahul."

"Rahul, what would you like for breakfast?" Sudha hurried into the dining room with a heap of towels in her hand as Sherry ran out calling for some Tiwari.

"Anything's fine, really." A nervous boy placed a cup of tea in front of him.

"This is Laxman. Just ask him if you need anything. Laxman, get some toast butter and ask sir what jam he'd like. I'll see you in a bit Rahul. It's a bit chaotic, as you can see." Sudha left the dining room apologetically.

Rahul wondered where the calm of last evening had disappeared as he bit into the warm toast that lay in front of him. Sherry walked back into the room and sat down at the table. "I apologise about the chaos. I really do. We've never used all the rooms in the house before. There's so much to get done. I wish my husband had given me some more time. How am I supposed to get all this done in three days?" Sherry answered Rahul's unasked question as she pushed around papaya cubes on her plate.

Menon left the room without excusing himself.

"Who's coming?" Rahul felt relieved now that Menon was out the room. He could ask questions.

"The whole team — the physical trainer, the public speaking trainer, the stylist, the dietician, a chef, some staff for the house," she said all in one breath.

"Wow!" He nearly choked on his toast. They were all coming for him — the useless, ordinary man amongst the robots.

"I never thought this house would ever get so full," Sherry said.

There was going to be a house full of people just to tend to him. That's being special, he tried to convince himself.

"I have set up the study to be a mini entertainment room for you. It is right next to your room. There's an Internet connection, a television, the works. If you need anything at all, just ask Sudha, she will have it organised." Sherry sipped some green liquid from a glass. "You see, Prince Charming, everyone here is at your service."

"Come on! I am just an ordinary salesman. You know that." Rahul was feeling a bit overwhelmed. He wasn't comfortable with the attention.

"Wrong. From now on, forget that you're an ordinary salesman. If you don't think you're special, you won't convince anyone. It's all about the attitude, darling."

"Right... I'll be in the study if you need me." Rahul excused himself from the dining room and went straight to his bedroom. He was startled to find Sudha coming out of his room.

"I was just putting some fresh flowers in the vase. You hardly have clothes. I will talk to Sherry about that. I have had your clothes taken down to the laundry. They'll be back in the wardrobe by this evening."

"Thanks. I am not used to this. It's a bit awkward."

"Your highness, there's absolutely no need to be awkward!" Sudha curtsied and laughed, "If you need anything there's a bell, right here. We are at your service."

"Please Sudhaji!" Rahul felt a little weird being treated this way. "Where is the study?" he asked

"It's right across the passage. Let me show you." Sudha took him into a huge room, complete with big windows and a large desk close to the window overlooking the river.

"Everything is grand in this house!" Rahul exclaimed.

"The Menons believe in living life king-size! I'll have to take your leave. There is loads of work to be done." Sudha hurried off as Rahul muttered a thank you.

Rahul walked around the room, peering at the bookshelves filled with encyclopedias, classic English literature and magazines. Most of the books looked unopened. He seated himself on the creaky chair and looked out of the window; it was a nice day to be out for a walk, but he was glad to be indoors. He focussed his attention on the computer.

Rahul had heard about the wonders of the Internet, but he had rarely used it except every odd weekend to check out new perfumes to order for his section. The popular things about it like chat and email never interested him. As soon as the computer started up, Rahul went to his favourite website, perfumeworld.net and looked at perfumes old and new. He read the top, middle and base notes and recreated the fragrance in his head. He tried personifying the fragrance. He remembered how his manager used to rush him when all Rahul wanted to do was spend time reading about the perfumes. And here he had the computer all to himself, for however long he wanted.

He wandered through the world of perfumes, his head spinning with the new fragrances that he read about. The yellow-brown study was forgotten as a multi-coloured haze of fragrances started building up around him.

"Sir, sir?" A faint voice dissolved the haze and brought him back to the musty smell of the old books in the study. "Madam is calling you, in the living room," Laxman muttered in Hindi.

"*Aata hun*, I am coming." Rahul felt like an insomniac who had just been woken up from a perfect nap.

In the living room, Sherry and Menon were discussing something with a couple of new faces. Rahul went unnoticed for a bit but as soon he saw Rahul, Menon signalled him to sit down. "Rahul, meet your team."

Avinash pointed to a burly guy. "Asif, your physical trainer. Shruti, your diet consultant." She was a tiny woman who could have used a little more weight herself.

"Pervez, public speaking expert."

Pervez was prim and proper; clean shaven 'good-boy' straight out of a Std. I English textbook. He got up and shook hands with Rahul, quite formally.

"Everyone, this is Rahul. His fate lies in your hands. Sherry will be in charge of the entire makeover and when she is not here, Mrs Ranjan will take care of things. Is everything clear?"

Everyone nodded.

"Good, now have you brought signed copies of the contracts?" Menon asked

Like good pupils each one of them got up and handed a bunch of papers to Menon.

"A stylist and a hobby specialist will join the team soon."

Menon turned to Sherry. "Do you want to take over, Sherry? I have a few calls to make."

"Well, to begin with, please, make yourselves at home," Sherry started warmly, as Menon left. "We can start from tomorrow. Rahul has already filled out the diary you had requested, Shruti. Each one of you will get a timetable to follow with Rahul on Tuesday. We have to work as a team and get to know each other well, for which we have all of tomorrow. Sudha and I are here to help you. Don't hesitate to ask us if you need anything."

Sherry made a 'thumbs up' gesture before concluding and wishing the team luck.

Menon walked back into the room and glanced up from his Blackberry. "All of you can become celebrities with the success of this show, remember. So give it your best shot."

The whole team seemed to be a bit nervous except for Pervez who immediately started speaking. "Thank you for giving us this opportunity, Mr. Menon. We won't let you down," he said.

Rahul's meek 'thank you' was lost as Sherry announced it was time for lunch. Rahul walked towards the dining room in a daze, feeling slightly overwhelmed.

Lunch was Sherry's way of breaking the ice with the new people. She enquired about things related to their fields and they replied. These people were here to transform him, to take him out of his mediocrity and make him a 'suitable boy'. They were here to prove how good they were at what they did. Rahul was just another project for them. Rahul was silent through lunch and wondered what they knew about him except that he was selected by Menon for this show. Rahul was already missing his perfumes and his ordinary life.

Chapter 12

Meanwhile, Tanya's life had changed dramatically. She found herself running on the treadmill next to Anita, getting manicures, meeting Anita's friends over lunch and at parties; and to her surprise, Tanya found it all very enjoyable. When she wasn't following Anita around, Tanya was watching movies, listening to music, writing her journal and revisiting memories she had locked up in a dusty corner of her mind. They would come rushing back to her when a certain song played on the radio or when a familiar line popped up in a book she was reading. The memories had never deserted her, but she had stopped paying attention to the little, insignificant memories and tried not to dwell on the significant memories for too long. Now that she had the time, the memories she had ignored had started re-emerging. She sat in the guest room, staring at the man in the picture kept there, her father. She hadn't seen it in ages and now as she wiped the dust off the photograph, her anger left her.

She missed him, and she admitted it to herself the first time after his death. She wanted to sit next to him in his large study. She wanted to listen in on his silence while he read, slowly rocking his favourite rocking-chair. She wanted to talk to him, reach out to him. Tanya picked up another frame from the bedside table. Tanya felt a strange sadness grip her as she looked at the woman in the picture. The woman in the picture looked so much like Tanya, it was almost like she was looking into a mirror. Her Mum must have been around Tanya's age when this picture was clicked. Tanya smiled at the sparkle in her Mum's eyes — the grey-green eyes she had inherited.

Tanya always wondered why she never missed her Mum, but then how does one miss somebody who's never been a part of one's memories?

Tanya had been a toddler when she lost her mother in a car accident. She remembered nothing of her Mum and Tanya's father never talked about her. Tanya would wait eagerly for Ravi to come home from boarding school, because with him he brought stories of Mum. She never understood why tears flowed from Ravi's eyes when he talked about their mother.

"Because I miss her," Ravi would say whenever Tanya asked about the tears.

"Am I a bad girl?"

"Why?"

"I don't miss her," she would put her head down and say. "I don't know why!"

"Don't be silly, Tano. Of course you miss her. You just don't know it."

"How is it like to miss her?"

"Some things can't be explained. You'll understand."

She did understand as she grew up. She missed Ravi when he was at school, she missed her doll when she went to nursery school, she missed the warm summers during the cold winters, and she missed home when she went off to boarding school but she never missed Mum. Tanya came to understand, as she grew older, why she couldn't miss Mum, but she couldn't understand why Dad never missed Mum. One day she summed up the courage to ask him, "Do you miss Mum?"

"Of course, why do you ask?"

"You never talk about her."

"Talking about her serves no purpose. Eat your vegetables. You shouldn't talk while eating."

And they went back to eating in silence, the ticking of the giant grandfather clock the only sound in the room.

Tanya spent most of her teenage years struggling to please the two most important people in her life. Her father and her brother were two opposites. Her father hated showing any emotions. He expected strict discipline and wanted Tanya to be the son he couldn't find in Ravi. Tanya and her father barely spoke about anything beyond school and studies and ate most of their meals together in silence.

Ravi, however, liked reading poetry to Tanya. He would speak to Tanya about various things he felt. They spent hours discussing music, literature and films.

Tanya loved the warmth of her brother's outspoken love but she also liked the chilly winter of her father's unexpressed love. As she grew up, the difference in their personalities led to a distance between her brother and her father. Ravi moved to Mumbai to work as a photographer, much to Dad's dislike. From that day, Ravi, like Mum became a banned topic at the dining table. Tanya started hating the weekend trips home from boarding school. The silence in the house irritated her. She longed for her Ravi Bhaiyya's voice, telling her stories about college, films and his friends. She loved her father but she couldn't deal with the emptiness in the house. She still went home to endless hours in the study with her father. She started missing her father when he was sitting right next to her. She looked at him for hours on end, for an appreciative smile or a loving hug and she was always disappointed.

One weekend he surprised her by starting a conversation.

"What should we do next weekend, Tanya?" he'd asked her.

She was surprised at the thought of next weekend being something special.

"Don't you want to make some special plans for your fifteenth birthday?"

Tanya had forgotten all about her birthday. She always looked forward to her father kissing her on the forehead before saying happy birthday. How could she forget?

"I think we should invite your friends from school home for dinner," he announced.

Tanya wanted to spend it with just her family or what was left of it, but she didn't argue with him. "Will Bhaiyya come?" she asked in a low voice.

"No, he will not. He has left this house and this family. Don't ask about him again," and her father walked off.

Tanya felt the tears well up but she didn't want to cry. She wanted an explanation but she had been told not to ask about Bhaiyya again. A birthday without Ravi Bhaiyya and his silly gifts was unimaginable. At the same time, a birthday without her father's kiss on the forehead was unimaginable.

From that day, Tanya's brother and father became two separate, parallel strands of her life. Her brother sent her long descriptive letters. She'd sit by the lake and read them out to herself, again and again. The stories about his assignments, college, Mumbai and his landlady fascinated her. She longed for his occasional phone call just as much as she dreaded going home every weekend. The distance had strengthened Ravi and Tanya's bond and weakened her relationship with her father.

The lake near the school was her haven, where she escaped to with all her worries and fears. This was where she learnt of a world beyond her home and boarding school, through Ravi's letters.

Tanya went for a walk on the beach that evening. She found that the sea soothed her spirit. She climbed up the rocky steps to the promenade. Tanya sat down hugging her knees and resting her head on them. She started thinking of her teenage years again.

As Ravi got busy with his work in Mumbai, the frequency of his letters reduced. They came once a month but they were still descriptive and elaborate. She imagined his struggle to get to work every day in the overcrowded trains, his trysts with his unreasonable clients and his late night adventures on the empty streets of Mumbai. Ravi would visit her once in a while.

Whenever they met, they spoke about everything but their parents.

Tanya's grades spoke of her lack of interest at school. The letters, some books and a small diary were the closest friends she had made. It didn't surprise Tanya when the headmistress wanted to see her one day. She knew she was in trouble, but Tanya didn't care about school. She had barely passed in her exams and was in trouble with her attendance in class. That was reason enough to spend that evening seated in the headmistress' office. The crackling flames in the fireplace made leaping shadows on the opposite wall.

The Headmistress sat down and smiled at Tanya. "How are you enjoying your time at St. Martin's, my dear?"

"I... it's a great school." Tanya shrugged as she looked around with awe at the wonderful books that the headmistress kept in her office. The leatherbound books with mellow gold writing on them looked beautiful in the yellow light.

"I am glad you like it," she said as she got up to offer Tanya fresh cookies from the bakery classes. "They are lovely. The class is right below my window."

Tanya reluctantly picked up a cookie. She was waiting for the marks issue to come up.

"That one's my favourite. There's nothing like a cinnamon and almond cookie to cheer you up on a cold winter night," she smiled at Tanya.

"I am sorry, Ma'am. I picked it up just like that. They aren't my favourite," Tanya explained.

"Oh! Then have another one. Ginger or maybe choco-chip?"

"This is just fine." Tanya bit into it. "It's nice."

"Indulging in your favourite things is very important, my child. It helps you feel better, you know."

"I don't think it works though."

"Not always... but most of the times it does. Try it the next time."

"I can't think of things all the time!" Tanya's gaze was focussed on the fireplace.

The headmistress came around the table and knelt down next to Tanya and held her hands. She smiled at Tanya and Tanya knew that she had a friend in the school. Tanya smiled back.

"You must come around more often. I get fresh cookies every Tuesday!"

Tanya remembered being surprised at the fact that the headmistress did not even mention her marks or her attendance. She remembered that after her visit to the headmistress, she began to develop an interest in studies. She started paying attention in class. She spent more time working on her favourite subjects.

Tanya would visit the headmistress often, not for cookies but to discuss things she read in the books. When her grades started improving, the whole class looked at her in awe. She became a favourite with the teachers who once complained about her performance. Tanya got addicted to the feeling — the feeling of being the best at whatever she did.

Ravi noticed the change in Tanya and tried talking to her about it. "Marks are not everything, you should always have fun doing what you do. That's the most important thing. Are you having fun, Tano?" he would ask her every time he called.

She still loved his letters but her letters to him were short, concise and yet, full of questions. Tanya knew Ravi was worried about her, but her father was happy with her performance. She could only keep one person happy and she had never seen her father happier. He was thrilled when she got into the best college in Delhi and he was even more thrilled when she got into one of the best business schools in the country.

Ravi noticed how his sister was becoming performance oriented but he let her be. He didn't want to nag her. Every once in a while he would ask her if everything was all right, to which he would get a monosyllabic response.

Right after her board exams, Tanya didn't join her friends on trips to exotic locations or hobby classes. She signed up for Vedic maths. Ravi wondered if it was something she really wanted.

"Tanya, what's going on?" he asked her while they walked in the school yard. It was her last week at school and Ravi had to meet her before she went home for the summer.

"Nothing much. The board results will be out soon, I am hoping to be on the merit list." She wasn't looking around like usual, her gaze was fixed on the ground.

"I don't care about that. I meant, what's going on with you. Your letters are short. You hardly ever talk about things other than studies. Where are all the questions my sister had?"

He stopped and turned to her. "What happened to all those long conversations about the books you read? Where is my sister?"

"You know how it is. Homework, revisions! I just don't get enough time." Tanya shrugged.

"You used to have homework and revisions then too. Since when did they become so important?"

"Since I started enjoying it."

Tanya knew that with Ravi, 'enjoy' was a key word.

"As long as you're enjoying it, it's all cool." Ravi put an arm around his sister. "But I want my letters. Homework or no homework. Deal?"

"Deal!"

Tanya smiled and hugged her brother.

Of course, she broke the deal. In her quest to be the best, Tanya stopped asking questions, wondering or daydreaming. For her there was just one dream, to be the best at whatever she did.

When she returned from her walk, she noticed that Ravi and Anita were having a cosy chat on the terrace. She looked at them both and smiled. As she made her way to her room, Tanya realised that Ravi and Anita were everything that a couple should be. They were happy when they were together.

It hadn't taken Anita long to befriend Tanya back then.

"Hey Tano, this is my colleague Anita," Ravi had said as they walked around his office.

Tanya was visiting him during her summer vacation from college.

"Ravi tells me you're here on a break." Anita had sat her down as Ravi disappeared to answer his phone.

"Yeah, I am applying for an internship with an ad agency in Mumbai," Tanya muttered. "I want to get into the best agency before their interns quota gets full."

Anita and Tanya had a long conversation and Tanya found herself talking with ease. She decided that she quite liked Anita.

Ravi later told Tanya that he had a crush on Anita but she was way out of his league. Tanya had understood nothing. But two years later, she was a witness at their registered marriage. They both threw a grand party afterwards to celebrate 'Ravi's imprisonment'. She had never seen Ravi so happy.

"Tano, you're back! We're going out for dinner, get ready fast." Ravi's voice brought Tanya back to the present.

She ventured out into the living room, and hugged Ravi. "That's a surprise! What's going on?" He kissed her forehead and asked her.

"Just felt like it."

Tanya's eyes welled up. Ravi held his little sister, just like the old times. "I'm sorry, Bhaiyya, I broke the deal we made. I didn't write as often as I should have. I am so sorry."

"It was a decade ago, kiddo. Relax, you made up for it in your own special way. Now, come on, get ready for dinner." He pulled her cheeks and hugged her again.

Chapter 13

The bell rang in an urgent musical rhythm. Tanya found herself opening the door to a very tense and frustrated Gia. Gia forced a smile at Tanya and continued speaking into her cell phone. She did look livid from the way she was clenching her jaw. "I'll see what I can do."

Gia clicked the cell off and took a deep breath. She looked at Tanya, gritting her teeth angrily. "Damn these bosses! They don't own me, you know. They just call up anytime they want!"

"Calm down. What's the matter?"

"I need a hug." Gia pulled Tanya into a hug, "Work has been so, so stressful lately. I wish I could just be like you."

"The grass is always greener on the other side."

Tanya motioned Gia towards the couch.

"No. I am serious. We have this new show planned and they have put me in charge of screening the entries and one chick backed out. I need to file thirty names with this AD, assistant director you know, who has to hand them to my boss tomorrow. I don't know what I am going to do!"

"Relax, just give a dummy name."

"It isn't that simple Tanya," Gia said as she answered her phone. "Yes, I know. I will find the missing name by tonight. I said I will. Now, leave me alone," she snapped and clicked the phone shut.

"Whoa! You're a bitch to work with."

Tanya offered her a glass of water.

"These kids assisting on the show don't understand unless you yell. Let's talk about something else. How's the sabbatical going?"

"It's going okay. Although, I am kind of getting bored." Tanya sat down on the couch.

"Why don't you go back to work then?"

"I can't imagine working there again. I am looking for excitement. Something different from what I have always done." Tanya pulled her legs up and leaned back.

"We all look for excitement, Tanya. Nobody likes the same old stuff. And life isn't always as exciting as you want it to be," Gia said.

Anita, who had just come into the living room, shot a well-shaped eyebrow up on hearing Gia utter such sensible words. "Tani! You aren't dressed yet? Why are you sitting around chatting?"

Anita pulled Tanya out of the couch and pushed her towards the bedroom.

"Gia, can I offer you something?" Anita was known to be a good host.

"Vodka neat! I'm kidding, a glass of water please."

"What were you screaming about?" Anita asked as she remerged from the kitchen with two glasses of water.

"Work worries, what else?" Gia replied. She sipped some water and took a few deep breaths, a technique she'd recently learnt from her celebrity yoga guru. "We are coming out with a show; you must've heard about it."

"It's crazy, that show!" Anita exclaimed, but soon realised that Gia needed to vent. "Sorry go on."

"It is crazy. Unfortunately, I am in charge of getting the contestants together." Gia gulped down some more water.

"One of the contestants backed out. And I have to give the complete list of names by tonight."

"Isn't she contract bound?"

"She hadn't signed it. I screwed up," Gia admitted. "Now I am going to be fired."

Gia stared into nothing. Anita had never seen Gia look so morose.

"Try explaining it to your boss." Anita offered a simple solution. Gia just looked at Anita with such helplessness, that Anita just had to get up and hug her.

As soon as Tanya emerged from the room, the trio set out for a friend's birthday party. Gia was still down in the dumps. When they got to the party, which was an intimate affair on the lawns of a spacious Andheri bungalow, Anita mingled, while Tanya and Gia disappeared somewhere. Anita didn't notice this until she heard loud laughter from the other end of the garden. Gia had chosen to drown her stress in alcohol and lots of it and Tanya had decided to keep her company.

"I think you girls have had enough to drink." Anita said, trying hard to hide her embarrassment.

She slipped the glasses out of their hands, and spoke in a low tone, "We are going to say bye and you two will wait by the gate while I go and thank Sharmila."

"Yessssssssssss!" they both sang out.

Anita hurried back and helped the girls into the car. Now that they were out of the party, she allowed embarrassment to flush her cheeks. "Girls, are we very drunk?" she asked with a stern look that was lost on the girls.

"Yes, we are!"

"God! We need coffee," said Anita and zipped out of the parking lot.

The coffee shop at Land's End was empty, but Anita still preferred a table in the corner to make sure that the girls didn't create a ruckus. As soon as they sat down, Gia's phone started to ring. "Hey, do you know what time it is?" she yelled, then paused for a reply. "I know. I am trying to find someone for the show. Yes, I am on it. Now you wait for my call and stop irritating me," she screamed into the phone.

"I am sorry about all the noise!" Anita apologised to the waiter who had shown up to take their order.

"Don't worry about it Ma'am," the waiter said and almost reading Anita's mind he asked, "Shall I get you three strong coffees?"

"Yes, as quickly as you can, please."

"How the hell am I going to find a girl???" Gia yelled again and turned to Tanya. "Shhh... I just lied!!!"

"Liar-liar! You told that man you were finding a girl." Tanya slapped Gia's arm.

Anita sat across the table frustrated, waiting for the coffee.

"Unless you think Anita is going to enrol?" Tanya laughed out loud.

"The show is for unmarried girls, sillllly!" Gia's voice was beginning to slur. Anita looked around, hoping the waiter would hurry with their coffees.

"I guess I am your only option then... Better be nice to me!" Tanya giggled again, but Gia's face became serious.

"You can save my cute butt, you know?"

"Really? I can?"

"Of course, you can also kill your boredom. We'll kill two birds with one stone!"

"Okay!"

"Should I call my AD then?"

"Maybe!"

"This is madness!" Anita muttered as Gia started calling, but she didn't stop Gia.

"Hello, dude! Problem solved. I have that name. You can stop sucking my blood now," Gia sang into the phone, "The name is Tanya Kher. Media professional. I don't have photos right now but she will bring them tomorrow. Don't you dare call me back now."

Anita sipped coffee in silence as Gia and Tanya giggled, ignoring the mugs in front of them. She didn't have the energy to babysit them.

* * * * * *

When Anita woke up next morning, Gia had already left for work and Tanya was just walking out of her room. "Oh my God, I had too much to drink last night, didn't I?"

Anita looked at Tanya, and looked back into her newspaper. That look was enough for Tanya to know that she had pissed Anita off with something she did.

"What did I do?"

Anita looked at her again, shook her head and sighed. She meticulously folded her newspaper and got up from the couch and walked away.

* * * * * *

Gia walked into her office with a heavy head and wobbly knees. She'd had way too much to drink, and even though she was no stranger to hangovers, this hangover was the worst she'd had in ages. She saw the AD walk to her with a file. "Oh no! The contestant!" she thought to herself.

"Hey Gee! The list is with the boss. You got the photos and the profile?"

"You gave him an incomplete list?" she shrieked at the youngster. "And whose profile are you talking about?" She opened the door to her messy office and signalled the AD to follow her.

"No. I gave him the complete list," he reassured Gia. "You gave me the missing name last night. And you also said that you'll bring photos and the profile later."

"I gave you a name? When?"

"Yesterday, wait I'll tell you her name." He flipped through the notepad. "Ah! Tanya Kher, Media professional..."

"I gave you that name?"

"Yes!"

"Oh shit, I need to sit down!" She held the table as she nervously sat down in the chair. She grabbed her head like she was about to cry.

"What happened?" The AD came forward, worried that he was going to witness Gia cry, or worse, throw up.

"Tanya is a friend of mine! We were drunk. I must have given you the name, but I didn't mean it! She's not going to actually come on the show!" Gia held her head in her hands.

"You know that the Boss approved the list and it is with the whole team now." The AD tried to hide his panic unsuccessfully.

"I know! And Boss won't be happy to know that I have done something this stupid. I better pack my things."

"Try explaining it to him!"

"Are you crazy? Avinash Menon doesn't like explanations. And he does not tolerate nonsensical drunken acts!"

Gia sat at her desk holding her head tight. She couldn't remember how Tanya's name got in. There was no way she could change the name now. An email from Avinash Menon blinked on her computer screen.

'Gia, thanks for the names. I have forwarded the list to the team. They will be ready with contracts and details for each girl. The first meeting is in a week.'

She cringed. The whole team would know how she screwed up. She was known to be a star producer who was always on top of her game. It was all over for her now. She looked at a picture on a crossed form and took it in her hands and crumpled it into the bin. "Stupid Sheila! If it wasn't for her and her orthodox family, I wouldn't be in this soup!" She kicked the bin and grabbed her bag. She had to go see Tanya.

"Gee wait, wait.... The last name on that list, we can't find the form for her." A production assistant ran towards Gia.

Gritting her teeth in frustration she turned and smiled at the assistant. "Yes honey, we misplaced the form. I am going to just speak to the girl and get a duplicate filled. Worry not! I have to run now. Bye!"

Gia ran out of the office before anyone else could catch her.

* * * * * *

Anita was typing out an interview on her laptop when the doorbell startled her. She was even more startled to see Gia outside her apartment, in the middle of a working day. Anita looked down at the tattered pajamas and worn out T-shirt that she was wearing and looked up at Gia, apologetically.

"I'm sorry. I should have called. But can I, like, come in?" Gia hadn't noticed the sorry state of Anita's clothes. She was busy trying to salvage her career.

"Sure, come on in." Anita looked around at the mess in the living room.

"Thanks. Is Tanya around?"

"She's gone out to buy something." Anita collected the scraps of paper she had spread around the couch.

"Oh. I wanted to speak with her." Gia looked dejected.

"Is this about last night and the list?" Anita stopped clearing and looked at Gia.

"Yes." Gia shrugged and held her head again. "I am sorry, Anita."

"Oh no, don't be. It was good fun. Don't apologise."

"I've got Tanya involved in the whole thing and I know she won't participate. And now I could lose my job…." As she finished her sentence, something dawned upon Gia.

She turned to Anita with an accusing look and hissed, "You were totally sober! Why didn't you stop me?"

"I understand that Tanya Kher is your latest contestant." Anita sat down on the couch calmly.

"You didn't stop me? Why? You want me to be jobless or what?" Gia yelled.

"It's not that. You girls seemed to be pretty decisive about it. You suggested it as a great way to relieve Tanya of her boredom," Anita laughed.

"This is NOT funny. I have to give them Tanya's details. I can't change the name now. The whole team has the list of names. And if my boss knows about this, I am f****d!" Gia cried out in agony.

"Mind your language!"

"Sorry! But what can I do?"

"Talk to Tanya. You convinced a drunken Tanya, now convince the sober one." Anita walked to the kitchen. Gia followed her.

"What do you mean convince her?" She looked at Anita helplessly and then another realisation struck her. "You want her to go on the show!"

"It's good, what do you call it, 'time-pass'. Besides she isn't doing much with herself these days." Anita poured some juice out for Gia and pushed the glass towards her with a smile.

"Ah-ha! You think she'll come?" Gia was suddenly quite hopeful.

"If she's convinced about it, she might."

"How do I do it?"

"She'll be back in a bit. And we can talk to her."

"You'll help me?" Gia's eager smile made Anita laugh.

"Yes. Though what you did was stupid, I'll help."

"I promise I'll never trouble you again!"

"Don't make promises you won't be able to keep," Anita said. "Ok, I am stepping into the shower. Tanya should be here in half an hour or so. Think about how to pitch the idea to her," and with that Anita disappeared into her room.

Gia walked out to the terrace. The tiles were warm from the afternoon sun. She slipped out of her sandals and let her soles feel the warm tiles as she walked to the railing. It had been a long time since Gia had been on a holiday. She thought of the lavish palatial house in Konkan, the location for the show. She would love to be on the show. A handsome man to woo, a comfortable retreat in the middle of nowhere, good food, nice clothes, why wouldn't I want it, she thought. She knew how to pitch the idea to Tanya.

Tanya let herself into the house and immediately went to the kitchen to get herself a glass of water. Just as she walked back into the living room, she noticed the little figure standing on the terrace, looking down at the city.

"Hey Gia!" she shouted out across the living room.

Gia turned around and the warm afternoon breeze ruffled her short hair. She smoothed her hair as she walked back into the living room. "Hey! Wassup?"

Gia was trying a little too hard, but she was desperate. Tanya just shrugged as she sank into the couch.

"Bored again?"

"Yep, yep, yep!" She looked around the room. "Where's Anita?"

"She's in the shower." Gia sat down next to her.

"Oh. Listen Gia. Did we get too drunk last night?" Tanya inclined her head quizzically at Gia.

"Yes," said Gia starting to feel miserable again.

"Anita won't tell me anything about it. I think I am turning out to be this baggage around their neck." Tanya pointed towards Ravi and Anita's bedroom.

"Baggage? What's wrong with you?"

"I've been staying here for quite some time now. I am not doing anything spectacular with myself. As if that wasn't enough, I get drunk and embarrass Anita," Tanya said in a low tone.

Gia reached out and held Tanya's hand. "It's all right. You've been doing exceptionally well for yourself. This is your time off. Enjoy it. Don't think so much. They are more than happy to be here for you."

Tanya pulled her hair back into a bun and placed her palms on her eyes. She had stopped wearing her glasses on Anita's insistence. "I don't know. I can't take them for granted. I guess I should move back into my apartment." She looked at Gia and shook her head. "I hate being alone though. I like coming home to Bhaiyya and Anita."

Gia couldn't stand to see her so helpless. She forgot her own problems and offered Tanya some advice. "Look, what you need right now is a vacation. So you can forget all these things for a while," she suggested.

"I've considered it, but being alone in a strange place with nothing to do! The thought scares me."

Gia took a deep breath, and took the plunge. "Tanya, yesterday I did a stupid thing. But it doesn't sound all that stupid right now."

Tanya stared at Gia, almost dreading what she was about to hear. "What?"

"You were saying you were bored." Gia cleared her throat. "I was having trouble finding a contestant for my show and I suggested that you help me, and that the contest will be a good way to spend your time. So I put your name down for it."

She felt relieved to be out with it, but she didn't anticipate Tanya's reaction.

"No! You did not!" Tanya shrieked.

"I am sorry. I was a bit tipsy and I didn't realise that your name had figured on the final list."

"Giaaaaa!" The softness of Tanya's features disappeared as her nose grew red and her eyebrows shot into her forehead.

"I said I am sorry. I came to apologise. I might lose my job when I tell them the truth. But you could use this contest Tanya."

Tanya was pacing the living room. "Is this for that weird bride hunt show?" she asked Gia who nodded and cringed at the same time.

"Are you crazy? How could being on a TV show, trying to hook the perfect bachelor, be called a holiday?" Tanya held Gia's plump yet tiny frame, and shook her. "Are you out of your mind, seriously?"

"No. Listen to me. Calm down."

"Gia, I think you need help if you think that this whole thing makes sense, and don't even think I am going to agree to it. You can forget it."

"Look, I'll withdraw your name if you aren't convinced. You're my friend!"

"Then why are you even trying to convince me?"

"Tanya, you just said you wanted a holiday ...."

"Holiday does not translate into making a fool of myself on

national television."

"Let me complete," Gia yelled. "You said you want a holiday but hated the idea of not doing anything or not being around people. Well, here's your chance. It's a palatial retreat in the Konkan, amazing ambience, loads to do and all you have to do is meet this guy. He is not bad looking at all. I have met him. He's a decent guy. I am not asking you to win it. The camera won't be on you 24 hours! You can do your thing and get out in a week or two. Trust me, you will feel better and I will get to keep my job!"

Gia had not met the guy, but she knew Menon liked him a lot. She could tell a white lie, to save her career and it wasn't harming anyone!

"I don't think this is a good idea. You're all for it just because you want to keep your job." Tanya stormed to her room and slammed the door shut.

Gia walked to the door and knocked. "Tanya, I admit I came here to try and get you to accept to save my job, but then I heard you and felt that this could really help you. I am sorry."

Gia left.

Anita heard the last bit of the conversation and she was convinced that Gia wasn't lying.

Chapter 14

In Karjat, things were in full swing. Sherry and Sudha were all set to work on the first stage of Rahul's makeover along with the new team.

In a meeting with Pervez, Shruti and Asif, Sherry had chalked out a timetable. According to this timetable, Rahul should have woken up half an hour ago. Sherry was pacing up and down the corridor outside Rahul's room in a designer track suit, wondering whether or not to wake him up. Her social sense said it was rather rude, but she needed him to be on track with the timetable. She walked towards Rahul's door with a decisive step and knocked.

"It's time to rise and shine!" she said in a sweet voice completely devoid of any anxiety.

She heard a bit of stirring in the room.

"Good morning! Should I have some tea sent to you?" She spoke in a high pitch to make sure that Rahul could hear her beyond the door.

"Morning! It's okay. I'll come down in a bit," Rahul replied groggily as he pushed away the sheets and forced himself out of the bed.

Half an hour later, Rahul was at the breakfast table. Pervez was busy struggling to eat a *paratha* with a fork and knife, while Asif was discussing something with Sherry and Shruti. "Good morning, everyone."

Rahul was still groggy as he took a seat at the dining table. Everyone stopped and they turned to him with a big smile. He responded with an awkward smile.

"Rahul, we have made some changes in your diet. You will have a protein shake to start your day, since you don't like eating a heavy meal right in the morning. After an hour, you will be served a breakfast which I will specially plan out for you. Today, we thought of serving you a mushroom omelette, if that's fine," Shruti said.

Her tone made it clear that even though she was checking with him, her decision about the omelette was made.

"Yeah, anything is ok." Rahul shrugged as Rekha, another one of Sudha's helping hands placed a big glass of yellow liquid in front of him.

"That's your shake, Rahul. I thought you'd like the mango flavour." Sudha peeped out from the kitchen and signalled Shruti to join her.

"Asif, my dear, why don't you talk to Rahul about his training schedule while I go for my walk?" Sherry waved to Asif and left.

"Rahul, have you ever worked out before?" Asif asked Rahul as he bit into the *paratha*.

"Nope," Rahul said, eyeing the protein shake.

"Okay then, we will start with getting your weight and body mass. We'll also measure you, so that we have something to compare your success to," Asif explained.

"Okay," Rahul said gulping his shake down. It wasn't as bad as he had expected.

"I will be helping you with your public speaking, hobbies and lifestyle training," Pervez said giving up on the *paratha* halfway through.

Asif ignored Pervez and went on. "Initially, we will start with yoga and stretches combined with light weights to prepare your body."

Rahul nodded at Asif and smiled at Pervez. "And when do we start the training?"

"Ten minutes after you're finished with your shake," Asif answered.

"And Pervez, when do we start the hobbies and speaking courses?"

"I think Sherry has allotted me some time after your breakfast," Pervez replied almost jumping up with excitement.

"Great! I'm excited." Rahul gulped down the last of his shake, his sarcasm lost on the group. There was nothing else to do but to get up to follow Asif into the gym.

"We have 10 minutes, sir. Let me quickly explain." Asif pointed to a body chart and then marked parts on it. Then one by one he pointed to different machines and explained which part of the body they were going to tone up. Rahul nodded along, his mind on the strong citrusy scent mixed with the smell of phenyl topped by the strong deodorant Asif was wearing.

"So, should we start, sir?" Asif was walking to the centre of the gym floor. It was a huge room with mirrors for three walls, a treadmill, stationary bike and some machines. It was awfully well-equipped for a weekend home meant for two.

"Sure. And Asif, please call me Rahul."

Rahul followed Asif to a set of matching mats that lay in the middle of the room. They spent the next forty-five minutes attempting different twists and stretches that were to bring Rahul's body to a 'supple' state, as Asif had called it. Supple or not, Rahul's body was definitely sore and every step Rahul took after the work-out reminded him of the existence of his hamstrings, pecs and shoulders.

A hot shower later Rahul sat down, glad that he was going to eat breakfast. Pervez and Sherry sat next to him, and from their impatience, Rahul knew they had something on their mind. An omelette which had no traces of *mirchi* or *masala* arrived with brown bread on the side. The sight of brown bread almost killed his appetite. "Sudhaji, may I please have white bread instead?" he called out.

Shruti emerged from the kitchen to answer the question." Rahul, we'd like you to stick to brown bread. Wholegrain will give us better results." She gave him a smile that suggested the topic had been closed.

Rahul tore apart the bread and scooped up one corner of the mushroom omelette in the piece of bread and stuffed it in his mouth. It was nothing like the omelette he liked to eat, but Shruti had made clear that the results were more important than Rahul's preferences.

All eyes seemed to be on him, as he tore another piece of bread. He looked up to find Pervez smiling at him. Rahul stopped short of eating the second morsel. "Sir, we will now try to use a fork and knife to eat," Pervez announced picking up his own fork and knife.

Sherry got up and helped Rahul pick up his. "Knife in the right hand, fork in the left. Fork to pin the food down, knife to cut. Twist the fork to bring the food to your mouth. And..."

Pervez smiled like a winner as he silently munched.

Rahul placed his fork on the omelette and sliced through. He managed to cut the food but he couldn't bring it to his mouth successfully. His stomach rumbled for one more bite.

Pervez got up from his chair. "Here, let me help you." Pervez helped Rahul pile the piece of omelette on the back of the fork and bring it up halfway to his mouth. Rahul moved forward and met the fork halfway and munched on the bite with satisfaction.

"That was better. But always remember, you never go to the food, the food comes to you," Sherry said demonstrating the act of bringing food to your mouth with an imaginary fork and knife.

"I have always eaten with my hands," said Rahul, struggling with his third morsel.

"It comes with practice. Pin, now cut. That's it. Now bring it to your mouth. Uh-oh! Doesn't matter, you try again."

Rahul's third morsel fell on the napkin resting on his lap. After the napkin, his jeans and his t-shirt had been fed, Rahul realised that hardly any of the omelette had gone into his stomach. He stared at all the food fallen around him and let out a wistful sigh. This is what his job had become — pinning food down with a fork, cutting it with a knife and making sure that the food came to him. He was on the slow road to getting 'posh'.

"We already had a bit of personality development down there, with the fork and knife. Hope you enjoyed that," Pervez said as they entered the study.

"Trying to dissect my food? Loved it." Rahul's sarcasm cracked up Pervez.

"You've got a good sense of humour," Pervez remarked. He then opened a little diary. "Do you want to talk about hobbies?" Pervez was scribbling things in the diary.

"Sure. My one and only hobby, as I told Mr. Menon, is perfumes."

"Yes, he did mention that. Shall we begin with books and films, then?" Pervez sprung up from his seat without waiting for an answer.

Rahul turned around as Pervez raced to a pile of books. "Sir."

"Rahul, please!" Rahul stood next to Pervez.

"These are some books I have put together. Please go through them, and tell me if you've read any of them," he said politely.

Rahul looked through the pile. He recognised most of the books that he had read in his younger days. He tried to remember the last book he had read. Reading was one of the many things in his life that he had left behind in Goa. "Pervez, I am not an avid reader. I haven't read many of these," he lied.

"Not a problem. I want you to spend time with the ones you've not read and figure out which ones you enjoy." Pervez held out different books to Rahul. "Once we figure what you enjoy reading, we will give you more books of that kind. I will have them sent to your room and arranged on your bookshelves. Now films."

Pervez had rung the bell from the study and Kishore came running. Rahul was directed to a brand new table.

"Now sir, sorry, Rahul, can you pick out films you haven't seen and try and watch them. It's a mix of English, Hindi and World cinema. We'll see what catches your fancy."

There were many Hindi titles that he had watched and Rahul tried to block out the memories of Ayesha that came flooding back. He had seen most of the movies with her. "Pervez, I think I should see English films. They will help me improve my language too," Rahul suggested.

"Yes, that is, in fact, a brilliant idea. I will have a DVD player sent to...."

"No, I can watch them here. I don't want to be spending all of my time in my bedroom," Rahul sat on the love seat, taking in the smell of musty books, yet again.

"Great. Now music! I am going to give you this iPod, it has a variety of songs, considered very classy. I want you to write down the ones you like and the ones you don't." Pervez handed Rahul an iPod. Rahul was awed. It was the latest version that hadn't even come to the mall yet.

"Pervez, I like this hobby session. It seems to be a whole lot of fun," Rahul said as he fiddled with this new toy.

"It is meant to be fun. Anytime you stop enjoying it, we will have to change the format. This session is all about understanding and modifying your favourite activities."

Pervez handed him a book, saying, "Could you just mark the activities that you enjoy?"

Rahul nodded.

"And now we come to speaking skills," Pervez said, smiling.

As Rahul enjoyed his makeover, the hidden cameras captured his transformation. The camera crew was documenting the making of 'A Match Made in Heaven'. This was just the beginning of many deceptions, and he had no idea.

Days were flying by in what used to be the Menons' holiday home. It seemed like the house had woken up from its serenity to become the centre of activity. Everybody was busy, constantly trying to achieve something, but the focus remained firmly on Rahul. There were no afternoon naps or quiet teas by the river. Rahul spent a lot of time in the gym and when he wasn't in the gym, he was watching films in the study or reading his books by the river, noting down what he enjoyed and what he didn't. Initially, Rahul had hated the idea of writing these things down; they seemed to make the act of reading mechanical, some sort of school exercise, but as time passed by, he began to enjoy it. He would mark the words he liked, he'd scribble little things about a certain character he adored and after he was done reading the book, he'd go through his notes and smile as he remembered the bits and pieces from the book that had given him joy.

It had been a while since he'd taken a break and as he had a free spot in his otherwise busy schedule, Rahul decided to take a breather. Pervez and Sudha joined him, just as he snapped the book shut. He was due at the gym in an hour.

"You're a fast reader," Pervez said glancing at the book.

After many discussions about films, music and books, they had agreed that it would be great for Rahul to start playing the guitar.

"I used to read a lot when I was young." Rahul turned to look in the direction of the river. "Once I came to Mumbai. I just never had the time to read. I started reading perfumes instead."

"Now is a good time to get back to reading. You've got the luxury of leisure," Sudha said.

Even in basic jeans and a T-shirt, Rahul looked handsome. He had filled out a bit, his tense face looked a lot more relaxed and his hair had grown longer; and he was carrying it off with great style. "Sudhaji, this is not leisure. I feel like I am a part of a beauty pageant, where I am the only contestant."

They all laughed. "Sherry is coming tonight. I am sure she is going to be very happy with your progress. We've put through a request for a guitar teacher with her." Sudha put her glasses on and shook the evening paper open.

"All I need is a guitar." Rahul got up and stretched.

"Don't tell me you already know how to play the guitar!" Pervez exclaimed with surprise.

"Don't be so surprised Pervez, his past is like an ocean," said Sudha and looked up at Rahul. "Why don't you write your story, Rahul?"

Rahul just shrugged and replied, “Maybe someday, when I've come to terms with the drama of my own life.” He got up and walked toward the house.

“It is amazing how an ordinary man can be such an enigma to every person who comes across him,” Pervez said staring at the door through which Rahul had disappeared into the house.

“Well, that's exactly what makes him extraordinary,” Sudha replied.

When Sherry arrived at farmhouse, later in the evening, she heard splashing in the pool. Asif and Rahul were doing their swimming routine. She sat down with Sudha, Shruti and Pervez.

Sudha began to summarise the events of the last week. “The diet is working. We have seen a little weight gain and body shaping. The hobby classes are going extremely well. Rahul can almost eat an entire meal with a fork and knife. He has taken to writing in a journal. He also wants to start playing the guitar.”

Nothing that Sherry hadn't heard over the phone.

“The diet is working but not at the pace we need. I have, therefore decided to put him on a free diet. He can eat whatever he wants through the day. Here's the plan.” Shruti handed Sherry the diet list.

“Good. Pervez?” Sherry asked.

“Well, one must give credit to Mr. Menon. Rahul is not your ordinary salesman. He is a well-read, cultured man. He is rediscovering those things through our sessions. His choices are extremely classy. To be quite frank, he doesn't really need me here, Mrs. Menon. He already has a strong personality and even better, he has the ability to develop it,” Pervez admitted rather honestly.

“Pervez, he needs you to guide him. Sudha, I've asked Avinash's team to send in a guitar. Pervez, Shruti, thank you, we will see you at dinner.”

After making sure that the two had left the room, Sherry said, disapproval tingeing her voice, “And how are our secret residents doing?”

"They are doing just fine. They've been working from the garage. I don't approve of this. You are cheating the poor fellow. He's a very nice boy." Having made her point, Sudha left Sherry alone in the dining room.

Sherry didn't like the idea of secretly filming Rahul either. She didn't like the way Rahul was being used in this whole exercise. She had attended the meeting with the higher-ups at the network and she'd realised that for her husband, Rahul was nothing but a pawn in his quest to make Cee the most successful TV channel in the market. When all of this ended, the joke would be on Rahul, who would be forced to go back to the simple life he once lived.

The network would have its TRPs, Avinash would get complete control over the network, the people who trained Rahul would get lucrative contracts and the girls would go back to gold digging. But Rahul would go back to his dingy apartment and would be remembered as the salesman who pretended to be a rich businessman to find a suitable girl.

Nothing was going to be the same for Rahul, ever again. Sherry wondered how she was going to live with that. Had her husband thought this through? And in that moment, Sherry realised that her husband had designed a game that could only be lost!

The dining table was already set when Rahul came down for dinner. He smiled at the sight of the extra plate setting. It meant that Sherry was with them. He had come to think of the whole house as his new-found family. He missed Sherry when she was gone.

"My, my! I didn't recognise you. You have changed tremendously in ten days, Rahul!"

Rahul was expecting her to be in the dining room. He had sensed the sweet mixture of floral fragrances and musk right before he heard her voice. Even though it was a new fragrance today, Rahul knew that such a strong, delectable fragrance would be worn by nobody but Sherry.

"You didn't? Come on!" Rahul said as they hugged and air-kissed, rather formally but with panache. Another one of the superficial gestures he hated.

"You're almost ready for Avinash. Work on your wardrobe, hair and skin should start soon. I can't believe it!" She looked at Sudha, Asif and Pervez who had just entered the room. "Haven't we done a good job here?"

Rahul grinned. He was comfortable with the attention now, he was comfortable with these people and most of all comfortable with the lavish life he was leading.

"Sudha, next week, a fashion consultant will come in. I think another one month and we are ready to bring you out," Sherry gushed as they all took seats.

"I think with the new diet, three weeks is all he'd need. And the maintenance won't be that hard." Asif was smiling at Rahul.

"Right, all the painful push-ups and presses are going to pay off, finally," Rahul laughed as he dug into the salad on his plate. "And of course, the diet is finally going to show its magic." He winked at Shruti.

"And you'll go back to Mumbai and forget this lady who used to plan your day and make *masala chai* for you," Sudha said as she placed a plate of *tandoori* chicken on the table.

"Who could ever forget you? Will you marry me? After this show of course!"

"Silly boy, this is the hundredth time I'm repeating my answer, NO! Eat your dinner," Sudha admonished, laughing.

"Sudhaji, think about it, you wouldn't find a better match," Shruti joked as she passed along the bread. "*Roti* not for you, nah-ah!" she signalled to Rahul.

"Pervez you seem quiet, everything okay?" Sherry asked.

Pervez nodded.

"This house has never seen such merry times, has it, Sudha? You are such a magician, Rahul," Sherry said.

More laughter and conversation followed, as the evening progressed. It was obvious that Rahul Rajgopal's charm had touched each and every one in the house.

Chapter 15

Avinash Menon flipped through the photographs his wife had brought back from her recent trip to the farmhouse. He sat back and smirked. He had been right in picking the salesman. He had sniffed out an unsatisfied soul caged in the perfume store. Menon had known that the boy wasn't going to need much training. He also knew that Rahul would be on board the moment he handed him his visiting card. In the last couple of months, Rahul had been convinced he was living his destiny, but Menon was in control of that destiny and he needed to remain in control until this show was over. Rahul was going to give him what he needed to crush the competition, and for that, it was important to let Rahul think the show was all about him.

It had hardly been two months and Rahul had been transformed into the perfect bachelor.

The wheels were now all set to roll. Menon once again leafed through the concept file that had been shared with a selected few on the staff two months ago. The concept note was not full disclosure. He hadn't thought it was necessary for his team to get the whole picture. He had shown them a part of the picture and now that Rahul was ready to don the garb of Rajsingh, it was time to get things on the road. In that picture, Menon's trusted team saw a businessman of a royal bloodline who had been too busy to find a bride and now wanted to get married. They saw that this businessman trusted Menon to use national television to help him find the perfect wife. They thought Menon was a kind man to help his friend in need. Some might have thought the eligible bachelor was a kind friend to agree to such an idea to help out Menon. But nobody knew that the eligible bachelor was nothing but a salesman. He was being polished and packaged, not far from the city, to be the most eligible bachelor — the kind that you'd only find in fairytales. Except, Menon knew fairytales didn't exist and the happily-ever-after was reserved solely for him.

The partial picture had been enough for Menon's team to start designing the show packaging and advertising campaigns. They had already received applications from thousands of girls and the final 30 had been selected.

In three weeks, he trusted his team to go all out. In three weeks, Rahul could be brought back to the world as the man of every Indian girl's dream.

Menon looked out of the window. This was his chance to swing the TRPs into his basket, the chance he longed for with such impatience. This was his chance to beat the other channels at their soap operas and singing competitions. And this was his chance to rise above the debacles of Cee networks and establish himself as the ruthless media mogul he was born to be. Rahul was the horse he had bet on and he was fast approaching the finish line. The race was theirs.

Although Sherry had been by her husband's side as they attended the glamorous parties of the season, her heart was still back in the farmhouse. When they were alone, most of their conversations revolved around the events at the farmhouse. The events were like a story, and the hero of the story was Rahul. Every story has a villain, and Menon had a nagging feeling that his wife thought he was the bad guy in this one.

******

Rahul was surprised to know that he had received a call. Nobody ever called him. Nobody knew he was here. His surprise turned to nervousness as he heard Menon on the other end of the line.

"Make the 'I am doing well' phone call to your friend," said Menon. "Be careful about what you say."

Rahul opened his mouth to speak but Menon had already hung up.

"Hey Asif, you have your mobile on you?"

Asif who was passing by the living room, looked puzzled. "Yeah, here," he handed it to Rahul.

Rahul dialled Asif's number. The cell-phone started to ring and the caller id flashed 'Private Number'.

"Perfect. Thanks!"

After Asif had left, Rahul picked up the phone and dialled a number.

"Yes?" a formal voice said over the phone.

"Rosie, it's me, Rahul." Rahul spoke in a cool and composed manner, trying to unlearn all the manners and the voice culture he had learnt from Pervez.

"Rahul! Man! How are you??" Rosie shrieked.

"I am okay. How are you?"

"Same old, men! But I tell you, I am bored without you." One could tell from her voice that she had a smile plastered on her lips as she spoke. "They have put me in charge of the perfumes counter. Everyone misses you!"

"I guess they do." Rahul felt guilty to have abandoned his perfume haven just like that. "How is everyone at the mall?"

"They are all okay, men. You have been gone for so long and now you call?"

"Sorry, just been so busy with things in Dubai."

"Yes, yes. New friends and all, you can't remember old ones," sniffed Rosie.

"No, Rosie. No one can take your place, but it's just that...," he replied, unsure of how to reassure her about something that wasn't going to happen. "How's your Savio?"

"Savio is good. He's got a new job and everything."

"Good. Glad to hear that."

"Rahul, when are you coming back? What are you doing there?"

Rahul had dreaded this very moment. "It will be a while before I do," he said. "That's why I called you. I am going to take some more time here."

"Okay, I have to go," she said and he could hear she was upset. "You take care. Give me your phone number, I will call you sometime."

"I don't have a phone. I am calling you from a public phone."

"Okay, keep calling."

"I will. You take care," he said and hung up feeling guiltier than ever. He was lying to the only friend he had in the world. Why? What for?

* * * * * *

The producers and coordinators settled in their chairs at 7 pm sharp. Menon started speaking about the concept, his ideas and how he knew this show was the next big thing.

"If this is all clear, I would like to see all of you individually tomorrow to discuss your plan on taking this further. It is something different, something refreshing and it will put us not only back in the race but right onto the first spot. Questions?" Menon asked as he concluded his monolog.

A lot of questions were thrown at him in the boardroom but Menon was prepared for them. Right from 'Where did you meet him?', 'Is he ugly?', 'Is he sponsoring the show?' to 'Where is he at the moment?', 'Why does he need national television to find a wife?'

Menon batted out answers to all the questions with practised ease. Lying through his teeth was an art Avinash Menon had mastered the moment he had set foot in the media business.

"I met him in London at a social gathering. He is your typical, suave, good-looking businessman. He is closing a business deal in South Africa right now. He wants a modern Indian girl and has no time to find her the traditional way. He isn't sponsoring the show."

He didn't care about lying to his employees. They were just the executors of the idea. The decision makers already knew the truth and they knew that Menon's lies were going to rake in the big bucks for the network soon.

* * * * * *

Rahul, according to everyone, was ready to face the world in his new avatar. Rahul himself wasn't so sure, but once Menon had decided it was time, Rahul knew it was time and he had better start ignoring his own judgment. Even as a cold, chilly sensation gripped the nape of his neck and slowly engulfed his spine, Rahul maintained his public face. The guy who fitted his clothes couldn't tell how naked Rahul felt, even though he was fully clothed. The girl who managed his daily diet didn't notice that Rahul wasn't interested in what was put on his plate lately. The hair stylists working on his hair and the beauticians working on his face didn't understand just how low his self-esteem was. But in the confines of his room, Rahul knew exactly how he felt. Rahul looked into the mirror. His slightly overgrown hair had been trimmed and styled. His face was glowing thanks to all the different kinds of treatments it had been subjected to. His face was unrecognisable, even to himself.

Rahul pulled on the designer suit, brushed his styled hair to look neat despite the 'bedhead' look that he'd been given. He slipped on his expensive watch and rings. He was ready for the world. Just as he turned around, Sherry walked in with a box and held it out to him. For the first time since she'd met him, he saw a genuine smile on her face. "Thank you," the card read.

"I don't know what to say Sherry. You shouldn't have!"

"Oh! I had to. Look at you! I am so proud of you,"

"Well, Sherry, I owe all of this to you. You believed in me right from the start. And I wouldn't have believed in myself if it wasn't for you," he confessed to Sherry.

The sweet simple aura of Elizabeth Arden's 5th Avenue surrounded her in all its elegance. It just spelt out Sherry's persona. "Won't you open it?" she asked.

Rahul tore apart the red and silver packaging. What he saw underneath the package touched him. Nobody had bought him a perfume, ever. He always wore the scent of the many perfumes he sold at his counter. It was a maddening mix of sweet, spicy and elegant scents that Rahul carried around himself. He helped people choose perfumes for their loved ones and today, he held a fragrance chosen for him: Polo Blue. For the first time ever, he held a fragrance that belonged to him.

"Do you like it?"

"Of course." He was overwhelmed. He had never thought of choosing a fragrance for himself but as he held the box, he realised that this was his fragrance. The fragrance he loved the most, the fragrance he could now identify with.

"I found it really unacceptable that the perfume-man did not have a bottle of his own. Go ahead, spray it on." Sherry came forward to help him tear open the package.

Rahul sprayed on the fragrance, a bit uncomfortably. "Let's go," he said as he took in his own scent.

Rahul transformed into a businessman of royal descent effortlessly as the camera clicked away. In his head, he kept replaying the international accent he had been learning. He had to start feeling comfortable being this character. Just when Rahul got comfortable with the idea of being who he was not, Menon walked into the study, clapping. Rahul was taken aback. He hadn't expected Menon to walk in unannounced. After months of not seeing Menon, Rahul had forgotten the effect that this man had on him. Even as Menon gave Rahul an appreciative glance, Rahul felt edgy. Rahul waited for the appreciative glance to turn into a smile and yield words of encouragement, but Menon just smirked.

"I almost didn't recognise him," he said, turning to the others standing in the corner. "You've all done a fantastic job."

"I think when I say the credit goes to Rahul, I speak for all. After all, had he not given it his hundred per cent, we would never have achieved our goal, right?" Sherry looked at the team.

"Three cheers for Rahul!" yelled Asif and the team responded with cheers.

Rahul beamed. He finally had somewhere he belonged. The smile faded away as Rahul met Menon's eyes. Menon was an outsider within this environment that he had created and Rahul knew from the cold look in his eyes that Avinash Menon was not happy being an outsider.

Menon cleared his throat. "Now," he said and clapped his hands to tone down the pandemonium. "Let's talk business. The pre-production is almost through for the show. Rahul has to be introduced to the team. We will go all out with our teaser campaign soon. His training will continue, and we'll call it acclimatisation before he sets out to find his perfect Indian bride. Rahul, you will now be known as Rajsingh Jaiswal. It has a royal touch, the name. Nobody will be able to link you to Rahul Rajgopal. Rahul Rajgopal should not even be mentioned, you understand?"

"What? Now you want me to fake an identity?" Rahul said in his newly-acquired accent.

"We agreed on that before starting," Menon continued. "A lot has gone into your transformation. Your identity has to be changed. We aren't faking an identity. You're playing a character on the game show," Menon explained.

Rahul knew that he had to pretend to be rich, but to pretend to be a person who didn't exist!

"But... the girls will think I am for real!"

"Don't think too much, Perfume Boy. That's not your job."

With those words Menon shattered the brand new glass walls Rahul had built around himself and walked off.

For the first time in months, Rahul was beginning to realise the magnitude of the farce. An awkward silence crept into the room with Menon's exit. The newly-acquired muscles, fancy suits and chic haircut didn't matter. Rahul was suddenly aware that no matter how much he changed, he would always be the perfume boy, but for now he decided to focus on being Rajsingh Jaiswal.

Chapter 16

Rajsingh's life was spelt out in the rule book. Every page told Rahul exactly what was supposed to happen to Rajsingh Jaiswal and when. The channel had got thousands of entries from girls who hoped to marry Rajsingh Jaiswal, a blue-blooded bachelor who was also a multimillionaire. The applications had been whittled down to a shortlist of 30 finalists. The 30 girls were to come down to a palatial retreat in Konkan. They would be cut off from the outside world as they met the man of their dreams to woo him. What Rahul hated about the show format was the way he had to go about dumping girls like they were toys that didn't amuse him anymore. What decent girl would agree to be treated this way? Why would she even want to marry a guy who thought this was a way to choose a bride?

The first round of dumping would happen within the first two days at the retreat. He'd have to pick five of the least compatible girls and kiss them goodbye. Every girl would then spend the next week immersed in a task, terrorised by the thought of Rajsingh's rejection. She would struggle hard to make sure that she wasn't one of the two contestants leaving the show at the end of the week.

By the third week only twenty-one contestants would remain. These twenty-one girls would go through even more rigorous tasks and activities and try hard to avoid being one of the six girls to go home over the next three weeks.

According to the rule book, at this juncture, the show would get interesting. The remaining girls were going to date Rajsingh over the next few days. This would help Rajsingh get closer to knowing which of the girls was 'The One'.

Even though Rahul detested the way these girls were going to be treated on the show, he decided he liked feeling he was in charge. Rahul, an ordinary perfume salesman had the power to decide which girls disappointed him and which ones pleased him. The girls' future on the show depended on him. And if the girls were ready to be treated this way, why was he feeling so bad for them?

He went back to reading what would happen over the final couple of weeks on the show. The girls would be given tasks that would test their ability to prove that they had it in them to be the perfect woman Rajsingh was looking for. The two girls that didn't impress him at this stage would have to say goodbye to their dream.

Talent shows, parties, managing homes, compatibility tests, dates, celebrity visits and more would follow. What struck Rahul was that throughout the show, these girls would be trying hard to please him, to win him over so that they could have the honour of being his wife. He was going to develop a rapport with the girls, he was going to have a unique relationship with them, but in the end, he got to call the shots. He was the most important person on this show; he was ordinary no more.

The competition between the girls would get fiercer with each week. The game was now going to be all about the relationship that each girl had developed with Rajsingh. The girls that had so far impressed Rajsingh, would have to try harder, much harder. A lot of drama would follow as one by one, Rajsingh would eliminate the girls he liked the least. The channel hoped that the girls would go to any length to convince Rajsingh to choose them to be his wife. The channel hoped for catfights, groupism and a lot of *masala* that would spell additional TRPs for the channel. And then, the final three would remain — the three girls that impressed Rajsingh the most, the three girls who were most likely to be Mrs Rajsingh Jaiswal. And then Rajsingh would pick his favourite — the one.

Once the girl was picked, the channel would disclose who Raj really was. This would be the time for Raj to disappear and make way for Rahul Rajgopal, a simple perfume salesman. What the girls would not know was that if the girl he had picked chose to marry him in spite of him being someone ordinary, Rahul would get the Konkan property, a car, ten million rupees in cash and a perfume shop of his own.

Some of the details of the game were to be reworked but this was the gist of the game Rahul was to play. Menon had created a game Rahul was bound to lose. Why would a girl who dreamt of marrying a millionaire ever agree to settle for a perfume salesman?

Rahul Rajgopal and Rajsingh Jaiswal knew that they were trapped with each other until the end of the show.

'Que sera sera!' thought Rajsingh Jaiswal and retired to bed.

* * * * * *

It was a beautiful day on which Raj came back to the city that Rahul left months ago. Rahul left Mumbai to find a dream, and Raj returned to the city to find his dream bride.

'It's weird,' Rahul thought to himself as the car approached Mumbai, 'how the city smells different when you're a millionaire.'

As they drove through the busy streets of Mumbai, Sherry briefed him on what he was supposed to do when they reached the apartment they'd rented for him. Rahul tried to pay attention but something was bothering him. He could smell nothing. The smells of rancid oil, sweat, tea and petrol that embodied Mumbai in Rahul's head were not a part of Rajsingh Jaiswal's Mumbai. The rich are probably meant to be insensitive to those aromas.

He tried to search for the scent of a rich man's Mumbai and all he could smell was the frigid air in the new car and a faint musk, probably from Sherry.

Sherry stopped at a red light and turned to Rahul. "Aren't you excited? Back after three months, how does it feel?"

Rahul was still trying to identify the fragrance, so he didn't hear Sherry.

"Rahul? Are you all right?"

"I thought, from today onwards, I was Rajsingh Jaiswal,"

"Oh! I almost forgot that. To me though, you're always Rahul Rajgopal," Sherry said. She knew that giving up his name was a big shock for Rahul. "So are you excited?"

"As Rahul, yes I am, and as Raj, not really; this is supposed to be my life isn't it?"

They both laughed as they swerved into another lane, a familiar one. Rahul could see the markers pointing out the way to OneStop. Sherry obviously didn't notice the huge glass and concrete structure approaching to their left. She drove past OneStop and Rahul craned his neck to look at it. He didn't feel anything at all. Rajsingh Jaiswal had nothing to do with OneStop.

As Sherry's car glided up Mount Mary Hill, Rahul couldn't help but remember Rosie. She would take lunch breaks to quickly go and pray at the Church. He reminded himself again, that he had nothing to do with Rosie. He was Rajsingh Jaiswal. Finally, the car pulled into a high-rise residential complex. The watchman opened the door and Raj stepped out, regally. Rahul Rajgopal was left behind. He walked to the elevator leading Sherry like a gentleman would.

As soon as the elevator doors opened on the twelfth floor, Sherry urged Rahul to go ahead. "I'll just join you in a moment," she said looking into her bag for something.

He walked along the corridor to an open door. He glanced in to see Menon with a couple of other people.

"Welcome home Raj! How are you?" Menon came up to shake hands with him.

"Not too bad. How are you?" Raj asked in his plummy accent.

"I am all right, thank you. Good to be home?"

"Well, yeah, it's been a long time," he said as he looked around the living room arrogantly. Sherry, who'd entered the room was amused by Rahul's elegant demeanour. She was shocked to see that Rahul had adapted so well as Rajsingh Jaiswal.

"This is Ms Gitanjali Shah, the producer," said Menon introducing a short girl.

She came forward and extended a ring-laden hand to Raj. Her short hair was ruffled and she looked as if she was suffering from a hangover.

Menon pointed to a tall, lean guy with a signature *filmi* stubble and dressed in a crumpled *khadi* shirt. "This is Ashutosh Joshi, the director for the promotional video."

Menon waited for Ashutosh to shake hands and exchange pleasantries with Raj, then said, "Gitanjali will be in charge of the pre-production and will coordinate with you about any involvement necessary from your side. Right, Gitanjali?"

The girl's round eyes were fixed on Raj. She had to tear them away to look at Menon. "Absolutely, I will be in touch."

She was smiling from ear to ear. Rahul could smell Nina Ricci's L'air Du Temps on her. He held her gaze, and said, "I look forward to working with you Gitanjali, and you too, Ashutosh."

Rahul spoke as Rajsingh Jaiswal would have.

"I guess Mr Jaiswal you've had a long flight; we should leave you to rest a bit," said Gitanjali in her musical voice.

"Shall we meet at say 6, to discuss the show, Avinash? I'd like to catch up on all that you guys have been doing while I wasn't here." Rahul stared into Menon's eyes.

Menon wasn't expecting Rahul to call a meeting. "Of course, of course," he nodded.

For a change, Rahul was comfortable and Menon wasn't. Sherry stood silently in the room, her face glowing with pride. "I'll see you folks at 6, at a pub or something. I could use a drink," he said to Gitanjali, who smiled radiantly.

"Great, there's a nice bar at the Land's End. It's a five minute drive. That okay?" Gitanjali looked around for approval.

The pub at Taj Land's End was agreed upon. As everyone went out, Rahul glanced at his watch. He had two hours to get ready for the second act.

The flat had a huge drawing room with a bar in one corner, and sliding windows overlooking the bandstand and the sea. There was minimal furniture, according to Sherry, but for a man who had lived with a single multitasking couch, this was supremely luxurious.

There was a black leather couch, the kind that you could sink into and there was a large glass and steel coffee table. On one of the walls was a unit that housed a DVD player and a state-of-the-art music system and above the unit was a large new-age TV, the kind that he'd seen in the mall. It was all perfect for Raj, but a bit too much for Rahul. There was no space for Rahul Rajgopal in this sprawling apartment.

The other wall was adorned with posters of some classic films from around the world. The door to the left of the main door opened into a bedroom which doubled as a study, going by the big bookshelves next to the bed. There was another door next to the poster-adorned wall, which happened to be the kitchen and a dining room with a small terrace. The master bedroom was across the hall, with its own terrace and a bathroom. He stepped into the master bedroom rather timidly, awestruck by its size. It was something like the bedrooms one saw in a typical Bollywood film — a king-size bed with a soft mattress and silk sheets, a huge wardrobe with full length mirrors covering it to one side of the bed and glass doors on the other side that opened onto the terrace. There was a smaller LCD television, strategically positioned to be watched while lazing in bed.

Next to the wardrobe, was a frosted glass door leading to the huge bathroom, fitted with a weird tub with knobs and round buttons. The bathroom was as big as Rahul's tiny apartment. Rahul smiled at himself in the mirror next to the bathtub. This was his room. He was going to be the one lazing in the silk sheets while watching television; he was the one who would be taking long baths in the shiny bathtub and he had a feeling he was going to like it.

He came out into the living room and sat down on the couch, thinking about the life he had stumbled upon.

"I see you have made yourself very comfortable in the shoes of Mr. Jaiswal?" Menon's voice startled him.

Rahul stood up.

"Anyway, I came back to tell you that Kishore from the Karjat house will be catering to your needs in the house. Pervez, Shruti and Asif will be back tomorrow to help you out too. Sudha is going to be staying in the guest room. She will supervise all the details. Let me brief you about the meeting tonight."

Menon was not as cordial as he had been in the company of the others. He made it clear that right now, Rahul was Rahul and not Rajsingh.

"I don't need to be briefed, Avinash. Rajsingh Jaiswal knows what he is getting into. Now, if you'll excuse me, I'd like to get ready for the meeting we have this evening." Rahul liked the authority Rajsingh Jaiswal had over Avinash Menon.

"Rahul, let me brief you," said Menon, a bit startled with Rahul's response.

"Avinash, Rahul was left behind in the Karjat house. If you want me to act like Rajsingh Jaiswal, you have to treat me like Rajsingh Jaiswal." With that, he stormed off into the master bedroom. Menon stood still in the huge living room for a couple of minutes before he shook his head and decided to indulge Rahul.

Rajsingh had taken control of all the meetings. He'd told the Cee team what sort of a bride he wanted and he'd refused to be a part of the promotions. There was just a photograph of his that could be circulated. Menon felt that it would be a disaster but he could not go against his special friend's wish.

Sherry and Sudha were busy taking care of this special guest. Menon felt helpless against this monster he had created.

The press gathered to interview the bizarre man who wanted to select his bride in such a weird manner.

"I don't want to talk to the press," Rajsingh said, much to the horror of the PR department.

"What do you think you are doing, Rahul?" Sherry asked once they were alone. "You need the coverage."

"The more you refuse them, the bigger the enigma you create, and of course, the more the press wants you." He smiled as he poured himself water. The accent was now a part of his persona.

Sherry admired the fine gentleman Rahul had turned into but it was starting to scare her. Was the show wiping out the existence of the real Rahul?

Chapter 17

The evening was unusually quiet. There were no parties to dress up for, no shopping trips, not even any guests to entertain. It had been a while since the Kher household had been this quiet. Anita was hoping to speak with Tanya over dinner. Tanya finally came out of her room and sat at the table. She seemed visibly disturbed. "I am so upset with Gia," she said after a long silence.

She picked up a plate and slammed it on the table. She then went on to slam the bowls into the plate with a clang. The noise made Anita wince but she tried to ignore it. Tanya flung food angrily into her plate, spilling some as she went about it.

"I never expected her to convince me to do something this outrageous just to save her job."

Tanya sat down and looked at Anita, scanning her face for a reaction. Anita took a sip of water and laid her cards down carefully.

"Considering I was the only sober person at that table, I have to tell you this. You are the one to blame in this drama."

"What?" Tanya screamed, her nostrils flared.

Anita knew that Tanya was enraged and whatever it is that she wanted to say, had to be put across rather carefully. However, Anita had no patience for diplomacy this evening. As Tanya slammed a spoon into her plate, Anita winced again and decided to ditch diplomacy. "Stop screaming and banging things. I don't like it. And yes, you heard me right. You were the one who came up with that idea."

Ravi's jokes would have defused the angry silence that followed. Anita found herself missing her husband terribly. She wondered why he had to travel, that too at such a crucial time.

"How can you say that, Anita? I was drunk! You're not supposed to be taken seriously when you're drunk," Tanya said, as she broke the silence.

"You're mad at Gia for having put your name in, even though she was drunk when she did that," said Anita biting into a slice of cucumber.

"No, that's not the reason I am mad at her. I am mad at the fact that she's trying to save her job by convincing me to go on that stupid show."

"I heard what she said to you. She may have tried to save her job, but she meant well. Try and think about it. What have you got to lose if you go on the show?"

Tanya found it hard to believe that Anita was defending Gia. She was convinced that either she was going insane or everyone around her had gone bonkers! Anita was her guardian, her friend, her family and she was supposed to know what was right. Then why was she convinced that Gia meant well?!

Tanya felt betrayed, angry, frustrated all at the same time. She wanted to throw something at the wall to express her rage, but she had already been warned by Anita. She closed her eyes and tried to count to ten in her head. Just then a little voice whispered to her, "Why don't you go? It would be fun, you know."

She felt betrayed yet again, this time by a voice inside her own head. It had to be a conspiracy.

"Tanya, think about it. Seriously, what do you stand to lose? Gia will lose her job if she decides to 'fess up. Do this as a favour to her. She could lose everything she has worked so hard for. You know what it feels like to lose it all, don't you? I know she'd stick her neck out for you if she had to. All you have to do is go on this short holiday. Can't you go on a small holiday for her?"

"I've got to try and win some businessman's heart on that show. It would cost me my sanity. I am not interested in that guy for God's sake!"

"You don't have to win anything. Just be yourself, have a good time and then get out when the time comes. Didn't you want to do something wild? Here's your chance..."

"Anita, I don't understand why you and Gia are convinced this would be cool for me," said Tanya feeling much calmer. Though the rage was gone, confusion continued to make her feel miserable.

"Think over it objectively. I called Gia. She's going to talk to her boss at noon tomorrow. If you change your mind, call her. I don't think she's getting any sleep tonight."

Anita left her sister-in-law alone with her thoughts. Tanya paced up and down, a million thoughts racing through her head. She wanted to help Gia, she really did, but she didn't want to make a fool of herself on national television.

Yet again, a small voice in her head spoke up. "You were a fool. A self-centred, hardworking fool who may have won many awards but hardly made any friends.... A fool who was young and attractive but to whom nobody was attracted to."

Tanya stopped where she was. Of course she was a fool. Tanya had set off at a superfast speed on a road leading to the wrong destination. And now here she was, letting go of a chance to help a friend who needed her. Yet again, she was proving to be a fool. Tanya was going to sit back and watch her only friend lose her job because she was afraid she'd end up looking foolish. What did Tanya have to lose? She wasn't going to cry, she wasn't going to be angry, she was going to go with the flow and she was going to do something adventurous.

Tanya picked up the phone and dialled Gia's number, but there was no answer on her home number and her mobile was switched off. Tanya called Gia's office. She heard the musical clock in the living room. It was 10 p.m. Tanya expected the answering machine, but a tired voice answered the phone.

"Gitanjali Shah." Gia's voice sounded empty without her usual enthusiasm.

"Gia, it's me."

"Oh Tanya, again I am sorry, don't worry. I will go in and cancel your name tomorrow."

"I called to tell you something." Tanya was trying not to think about what she was about to say.

"Tell me…"

Tanya took a deep breath and in a soft but decisive voice she said, "I am ready to go on that show. Bring the papers over, I'll sign them."

Gia froze in her chair. "What? Are you serious? Tanya, are you all right?"

"I am. I thought about it, a lot. I've got nothing to lose, but you could lose your job."

"I could just call one of the earlier rejected contestants; it's not so bad. I might have to resign, but it can be rectified Tanya. You don't have to do this for me."

Tanya was about to say something, but she paused a minute, took a deep breath again and said, "I am not doing this for you. I am doing this for myself. It's very selfish. I want to go on the show. I want to do this crazy thing."

"But Tanya, you haven't even applied. How can I pull this off? I thought about it all day. If what we are about to do gets out, I really will lose my job and my reputation."

"Come on, this afternoon you were convinced it could work. Make it work. Nobody will have to know that you screwed up."

"I don't know how to pull it off!"

Tanya could feel the rage rise again. After convincing her to get on the show, Gia was trying to reason her out of it. What did she want from her?

"I am on the list, everyone has the list and it will be very embarrassing for you to change all of that. Think about it Gia. You can do something."

Tanya hung up and went to bed.

* * * * * *

None of the three women slept that night. There was one other person who couldn't get any sleep that night. Rahul stared at the list of thirty names faxed to him. Tanya Kher was going to be on the show. He tossed and turned in his silk sheets. He wanted to see her again, but would she recognise him? He was scared and yet he felt hopeful. The thought of seeing her again put a smile on his face. He hoped she would save him from becoming the ghost of Rajsingh Jaiswal.

* * * * * *

Gia took all the precautionary measures to hide the fact that Tanya's entry form had reached her well after the last date of submission. She was the only one who had the list of entries for the show. She made sure that the paperwork was perfect, in case somebody checked. Tanya had filled out the application form as honestly as she could.

Why did she want to marry Rajsingh? She was tired of taking care of herself and now wanted to be taken care of. Why did she think Rajsingh would want to marry her? She didn't know and the question would be better directed to Rajsingh. What was her profession? At age 28, she was a retired media planner. What was her ambition? It changed everyday, right now it was to be on the show and have some fun.

Gia laughed as she read through Tanya's form. She was sure that she'd have selected Tanya to be one of the thirty finalists solely based on her responses. Tanya was frank and it was refreshing to see her answers after all the pretentious, sugar-coated answers Gia had been reading on the other forms.

The D-day was in a week, she told Tanya. All thirty finalists were going to be taken to the mansion in Konkan.

Within two days Tanya received her welcome pack from the network. The girls were to report at the Cee headquarters early Saturday morning.

Ravi was back in town and the big news had to be broken to him. Tanya was out shopping, when Anita and Gia decided to talk to him.

"You've got to be kidding me!" Ravi yelled.

Anita had expected this reaction. "Tanya could use this experience. It could be a good break for her," she tried to reason with him.

"My sister is going to try and woo a man on national television. And not just any man, a moron who decides to use television to find a wife. Can you imagine what sort of a skunk he might be? Couldn't find someone in real life so came to India to find the wife of his dreams through a nationwide talent hunt?" fumed Ravi glaring at Anita. "Are you kidding me?"

"And you, Gia, what were you thinking? Tanya is not going to be a part of this. You may bloody well tell your boss that tomorrow."

Gia was shocked. Nobody yelled at her like that, ever. Ravi was going to be no exception. "Look, Tanya signed the papers. She is bound by the contract. And she wants this, she really does. Please speak to her before you yell at me," she replied rather angrily.

Anita made an apologetic face at Gia, on behalf of her husband. "If you're threatening me with the papers she signed, I don't give a shit. I'll sue you. How dare you take advantage of my sister? That too when she's emotionally disturbed? She isn't going anywhere," he yelled back at Gia.

In his anger, Ravi did not notice Tanya walk in.

"So, you think I am emotionally unbalanced?" Tanya

demanded.

Surprise replaced the anger on Ravi's face and his features softened. He looked at his sister tenderly. "No, no Tano. Don't get me wrong. I was just telling Gia, that she can't..."

"Never mind," Tanya said, despising the pity she saw in her brother's eyes. Tanya Kher didn't need pity, especially from her older brother. "Ravi, I am not your kid sister anymore. I signed those papers. And Gia is right, I want to do this."

"Tano," Ravi pleaded with his younger sister, "do you really want to be a part of this reality television crap?"

"Yes. I want to do something crap for a change," Tanya said calmly, "I am sick of doing the right things. I am sick of being the girl who topped school, I am sick of being the girl who topped college. I am sick of being the employee of the year."

Tanya spoke with a sense of calm purpose that surprised everyone. "Just let me do this one crazy thing, Bhaiyya."

"Tanya, you can do what you want; it's your life and this is your time to explore," said Anita breaking her silence. "Ravi, I am sorry, I should have told you this before.... Maybe she is right. Doing something crazy might help her. She is not emotionally unstable. In fact, this is the most stable I've seen her since I've known her."

Ravi looked at the two women he loved. He shrugged and smiled at Tanya. "Maybe you'd like to take some of the things I got for you from England on your telly-holiday!"

* * * * * *

The waiting room in the Cee lobby was swarming with good-looking girls. A few Cee employees were speaking loudly to each other. Tanya felt slightly daunted by the amount of activity around her. She'd been used to this chaos in her earlier life, but the calm of the past few weeks made her want to run away from it now. Tanya entered the waiting room and her heart sank a bit. She was supposed to compete with these girls. These girls were very pretty, they were impeccably dressed and they all seemed to be confident.

"I am not here to win. How does it matter?" Tanya tried to tell herself. She made her way to the back row and sat down rather timidly. This was strange for Tanya Kher who wasn't used to feeling intimidated. She hardly paid any attention as Gia addressed the girls. Gia introduced a certain Deepak Makhija. Deepak was a tall, skinny guy who looked like an overgrown school boy. Tanya wondered what Deepak was going to do. Apparently, Deepak was going to be on location with them and would be in charge of the show.

"If you girls need anything at all, you can go straight to him. Be careful though! He cannot arrange for make-up and diet food," Gia said and the girls laughed in a rhythmic chorus. Tanya pretended to smile. Deepak smiled at the girls and Gia continued to talk. This was followed by an introduction session, where each girl stood up and introduced herself. Tanya giggled and suppressed the urge to laugh out loud. She pictured her school's kindergarten uniform on every girl introducing herself. When it was her turn to speak, Tanya looked at Gia for support but Gia looked away.

"Hi, I am Tanya, I am here to have fun," she said rather softly.

The other girls laughed, which made Tanya rethink her words, but it was too late. The girl sitting next to Tanya turned to her.

"That was brave. You really think this is going to be fun? We all are fighting for one guy, and you want to have fun. Awesome." She flashed a perfect pearly white smile at Tanya. "Good luck with that!"

Tanya noticed how beautiful the girl was. She had a fair, porcelain-like complexion, small bow shaped eyebrows, light eyes and a straight nose. "Like Aishwarya Rai," Tanya thought. Tanya didn't remember the girl's name from the introductions but she knew that there was plenty of time to find out later.

Chapter 18

Rahul arrived like royalty in a convoy of three cars. He wanted to get to Jaiswal Mansion well before the girls did. He figured he could use the time to get acclimatised to the house without having to stress about the contestants or the crew.

The house was elaborately prepared for the arrival of the millionaire. Pradeep, the caretaker of the house, was waiting by the entrance to receive Rajsingh Jaiswal and his entourage. After quick introductions, Rahul was taken on a personal tour of the mansion. Right after the tour, Ashutosh was waiting to brief Rajsingh on a montage he wanted to shoot. It was going to be a busy morning.

"Ashu, if you don't mind I'd like to take a break for a bit. It's been a tiring journey and there are some emails I need to answer."

"Not an issue. I was just briefing you about what we need. We could shoot this later in the day if you like. We shot some footage of your arrival and we have bits of your tour. Just make sure you hang on to this look, for continuity you know." Ashu grinned and adjusted his baseball cap. In addition to directing all the promos, Ashu had managed to give Rahul a crash course in film-making jargon.

"You got it, mate!" And Rajsingh made way to his 'chamber'. He entered the study which was well-equipped with books, a small desk and a couch. Rahul remembered how Pradeep had excitedly said that this was where Rajsingh could 'entertain his guests' and laughed. It was a colonial mansion, complete with antique furniture. However, the whole place reeked of paint and vinyl. Of course, colonial architecture wasn't that popular this side of the Konkan and the house had been redone recently to host the show. Although the interiors looked extremely authentic, Rahul felt like he was watching a movie with a completely mismatched soundtrack.

He walked to the other end of the study and opened a heavy wooden door that led to the bedroom. The massive king-sized bed was extremely tempting to a sleep-deprived Rahul. He took a closer look at the bed-linen just to make sure that it didn't belong to Louis XVI. The bedside lamps, their lampshades, the mirror, the dresser — it was all ornate, but not jazzy. Rahul decided that he preferred Raj's Mumbai apartment. He moved away from the bed and took a moment to catch his own reflection in the full-length mirror by the dresser. Lately, Rahul had taken to enjoying looking at his reflection in the mirror. Even though he'd often felt like he was staring at a stranger, he liked reminding himself that he really was Rahul. He was afraid that Rajsingh Jaiswal might drown him out. Rahul didn't mind that he looked taller than he used to because of his physique, he didn't mind that his usually unkempt hair was now neatly styled. Rahul didn't care that his face looked radiant and that his body was fuller. Underneath the expensive designer shirt, one could tell that the once skinny Rahul now sported a well-chiselled body. Rajsingh didn't look like Rahul Rajgopal, the king of the perfume world in a Mumbai mall. But Rahul never wanted Rajsingh to forget that he had Rahul Rajgopal's eyes. And that was never going to change, he told himself.

* * * * * *

After the orientation, the girls were ushered into a luxury bus. A video crew was setting up as the engine of the bus whirred into motion. After all the girls had settled in, a familiar looking woman got on board. She was dressed rather funkily and sported kilos of make-up, which was a bit much for a long bus-ride.

"You all recognise VJ Tangy? She's going to join us on this bus journey. She's doing a special episode for her viewers and wants to interview each one of you," Deepak explained.

Tangy smiled at the girls and waved out before turning to the camera crew. Tanya was quite amused by Tangy. She didn't walk. She danced and pranced around the bus. She didn't even stand still while speaking into the camera. Together with her bright clothes and messy hair-do, Tangy looked like a teenager. Only when you looked closely did you see the lines around her eyes that gave away her age. Tangy fidgeted with loose strands of hair that fell on her face while speaking to people and flashed a bright smile at anyone who made eye-contact with her.

"Hello girls!" she chirped as the bus driver jerked the bus to a start, "Are we excited?"

"Yes!" all the girls replied in a chorus.

This trip was going to be quite a back-to-school experience, thought Tanya.

"Good, I am going to come around and talk to each one of you, so wait for your turn!" she chirped.

Tanya relaxed in her seat which was right at the back of the bus. It was going to be a while before Tangy got to her. Tanya wondered what this Rajsingh fellow would be like. She was convinced that this guy was going to be like any other rich businessman with pots of family money — rude and chauvinistic. She had met and dealt with quite a few of them. The thought of having to woo someone like that made her uneasy, but by now Tanya had learnt that no matter what she did, she could never shake off the uneasiness.

* * * * * *

Rahul decided to take a walk and explore the gardens that surrounded the Jaiswal Mansion. The large garden leading up to the house was nothing when compared to the huge garden at the back. Small circular terracotta tiles marked a path across the garden. The path led up to a beautifully-fenced green enclosure. He peeped in, curious as to what could lie beyond such a marvellous topiary gate. It was a rock garden complete with a small pond, trees and stepping-stones in the water to enable one to cross over to the other side of the pond. The pond, Rahul realised was actually the swimming pool that Pradeep had bragged about. Rahul was glad that he had skipped the swimming pool during the tour of the mansion. He realised that this was going to be his special place in the whole mansion. This was where he'd hide from the cameras, contestants and the attention when he needed to. He loved the sound of the flowing water, the green of the trees that guarded the sitting area from the sun and the smell of freshly mowed grass. A faint grumbling disturbed the serenity that Rahul was experiencing. He looked around then discovered that the sound was coming from his own stomach. Rahul made his way back to the patio which was set up to be the outdoor dining room at the back of the mansion.

Menon and Sherry were enjoying a late breakfast with a familiar looking man. “Rahul! Meet the host of our show, Karan,” Menon said.

Rahul was surprised by the fact that he was addressed by his real name. After about a minute, it suddenly struck him that he was standing face to face with THE Karan Kapoor! Karan Kapoor was always the rich boy who fell in love with a girl from a much lower socio-economic background or vice-versa. He sang with the girls through dream sequences on the snow-frosted peaks of Switzerland. He smiled as he thought of Karan Kapoor dancing around the trees as clouds descended upon the couple to give them the privacy to kiss. Rahul remembered those wedding dances and festive songs in which Karan would dance and let the whole world know that he was in love. Every girl growing up in the 80s dreamt of marrying Karan Kapoor. And here he was, a whole lot older, impeccably dressed in trousers, a crisp shirt and an air of confidence that comes with a few years of living in the limelight.

"Hello Rahul, I must say you have done a great job. The girls are going to go mad fighting over you, young man." Karan Kapoor's voice was the same voice that had eternalised many a monologue on love and its greatness. Rahul was still confused about how Karan knew his real name.

"He knows," said Sherry answering Rahul's unasked question.

"Karan knows you are a perfume salesman, and he is here as a mediator between you, the girls and the audience." Menon smiled warmly at Karan Kapoor.

"Since you are somewhat like the fantasy I created in the 80s, I was the ideal choice to host the show." Karan Kapoor's face had changed with time but his style still remained distinct.

"Sir, the girls might change their mind and marry you!" Rahul joked and grabbed an apple from the fruit basket.

"My dear boy, the girls fancy a Karan Kapoor without wrinkles. You're the one they'll be fighting for, I assure you."

It felt a bit surreal. Karan Kapoor was calling Rahul every girl's dream. Rahul was still unsure. Who could hold a candle to the man who had defined romance for more than a decade, a man who had received fan mail written in blood?

"I know what you are thinking. Unlike many of my co-actors, I am aware of my age. That's why I've chosen to play the father in all my recent films. It's fun being the liberal father, who supports the love birds. Now, I am here to help you. It's like life's come full circle," Karan said as he sipped from a mug.

Menon's cell phone rang. "Excuse me."

He answered the phone and hung up immediately. "They've left Mumbai and will be here in a couple of hours," Menon announced.

"I'd better run along and get ready then," said Rahul as he got up from the table, biting the last of his apple. "Pleasure meeting you, Mr Kapoor."

Karan Kapoor turned to Sherry. "Interesting fellow. Where'd

you find him?"

"He used to sell perfumes," Menon replied before Sherry could open her mouth.

The crackling tension between Avinash and Sherry was evident.

* * * * * *

The bus pulled into the driveway as Tanya finished her interview with Tangy. She could sense surprise in Tangy's eyes every time Tanya opened her mouth. Tanya was brutally honest and uninterested. She was different. Tanya was glad the interview was done with and looked out the window. The mansion looked gorgeous. "This is where he stays, the lucky bastard," she thought.

The girls were led into a huge drawing room. They walked through to a slightly larger room which was lined with thirty chairs facing a small dais. The girls found their seats. Tanya went straight for a chair in the corner of the last row. As soon as the girls settled in, a large group of people walked in and seated themsleves on the dais. Tanya recognised Karan Kapoor, as did most of the girls.

Tanya also recognised Avinash Menon, who she'd met at quite a few parties she'd attended for work. She also recognised his wife, Sherry who sat like a princess, with her legs crossed and authoritatively touching her husband's arm every time she spoke to him. Even in a simple suit, Sherry looked gorgeous. Deepak shook hands with them and introduced Tangy.

"Good afternoon," Karan Kapoor said into the microphone, his face exuberant.

"Good afternoon!" the girls replied in a chorus.

Tanya chose to just mouth the words. She was still busy observing everything around her.

"Welcome to Jaiswal Mansion!"

A round of applause followed, Tanya reluctantly clapped as

she glanced out at the garden.

"We all know you girls are here to win his heart, so let's get straight to business. Ladies, let me present to you, Mr Rajsingh Jaiswal."

Another round of applause followed. Tanya turned her attention back to the dais and saw a tall man walk through the door. He greeted everyone on stage before coming to Karan Kapoor. His eyes scanned the crowd as he smiled, showing off his dimples.

"Good-looking," Tanya admitted to herself.

His eyes lingered on her for a moment. Tanya shifted in her seat uncomfortably. He looked at her as if he knew her from before. His eyes said something to her but before she could hear it, the girls started clapping again. Rajsingh sat down. Karan Kapoor continued to speak about him, but Tanya wasn't paying any attention to what he said.

Rahul felt uneasy as Tanya's grey-green eyes continued to stare at him. He looked for a hint of recognition, but he saw nothing. Karan was done introducing Rajsingh and Rajsingh got up to speak.

"Good afternoon, ladies," he said and the girls went into another clapping frenzy.

Tanya couldn't take her eyes off him. Rahul noticed. In a way, the fact that Tanya hadn't recognised him was comforting and flattering.

"Thank you for the kind words, Karan. Thank you, Avinash and Sherry, for being so kind to me and helping me find my soulmate. I am as anxious as I am excited about this journey to find the woman I'd like to share my life with. You girls are here to figure out if I am the man you'd like to share your life with. Good luck to all of us," he said and grinned. "I feel lucky, to be surrounded by such beautiful people."

Rahul stared back into Tanya's eyes as he finished his little speech. She was the only one who was not interested in what Rajsingh had to say but he could tell she was fascinated by something about him. Tanya stared at Rajsingh as he looked into her eyes and then looked away thinking, "Bloody charmer."

Karan Kapoor noticed the exchange of stares between Rajsingh Jaiswal and a girl right at the back of the hall. Karan noticed that this girl was very different from the other girls. She hardly wore any make-up. She wore a simple white shirt. Her hair was straight, brushed back, falling on her shoulders. She looked ordinary but there was something attractive about her. She was the only girl among the thirty who was unimpressed by Rajsingh. Karan wondered why she was here if she wasn't impressed by what Rajsingh had to offer. But from the way Rahul looked at her, Karan was pretty sure that she had caught Rajsingh's fancy.

All through the orientation, which went on for quite some time, Rahul stole glances at Tanya. She still seemed indifferent to what was going on around her. Rahul found her nonchalance adorable. The girls in his line of vision thought he was checking them out and started touching their hair and smiling back at him.

Throughout the orientation, some girls took down notes, some listened carefully, but everyone gasped toward the end as Karan announced that five girls would be ousted from the show within 48 hours.

Rahul wondered why they were so surprised, and looked at Sherry.

She whispered, "You know the elimination process, they don't. It will always be a surprise for them."

Rahul nodded.

After the introduction, the girls were directed to their respective rooms. Tanya was supposed to share with a Delhi girl. The name in the list read, Simran Arora. By the time Tanya found the room, Simran had already arrived and marked her territory. She had chosen the bed by the window and the bigger closet and had started drawing herself a bath.

"Oh hello, so you are...," she drawled.

"Tanya Kher, hi," Tanya said as she placed her suitcase on

the empty bed.

"I've already taken that bed, and the wardrobe. Please don't move my things around."

Simran had slipped into a bathrobe, which was a little too short to be called a bathrobe, but it showed off her long, well-toned legs. Having made it clear to Tanya that they weren't going to be soul-sisters or best friends, Simran walked over to the dressing table and rubbed on a gooey yellow cream on her face. She had a lovely dusky complexion. Tanya stared as she applied it in a perfect circular motion till it formed a thick layer.

Simran caught Tanya staring at her. "What're you looking at? It's just a face pack!"

"Yeah I know," Tanya said as she busied herself with unpacking her things. She hadn't expected such a rude response but then staring was rude too.

Simran disappeared into the bathroom. Tanya heaved a sigh of relief and found herself staring into the mirror on the dressing table. Her complexion wasn't that bad and she wasn't wearing any make-up. Her wheatish complexion looked pale as compared to Simran's luminous, dusky skin. Tanya noticed the numerous bottles that Simran had brought and realised that she hadn't brought much make-up with her.

"Screw it, it's not like I want to win," she thought to herself.

She relaxed in the room for a while before picking out what she was going to wear to dinner. It was a while before Simran came out of the bathroom. Tanya rushed in and emerged in ten minutes, dressed in a simple cotton *kurti* and jeans. Simran was still dabbing things onto her skin. Tanya brushed her hair, and pulled it back in a pony-tail. She put on a pair of dangling earrings. As she wore her watch, she saw that she had another fifteen minutes before she had to get to the dining room. She found a kohl pencil in her purse and lined her eyes. She then fished out a lip gloss. She stood right behind Simran to look in the mirror to apply the gloss. Simran was just finishing her make-up.

Tanya noticed that Simran still had curlers in her hair and

hadn't changed out of the bathrobe. Tanya stowed away her clothes and shoes in the closet. Though it was the smaller of the closets, it was big enough to fit in Tanya's stuff. Just as Tanya pushed the suitcase under her bed, Simran started undoing the curlers.

"Stunning!" Tanya exclaimed.

Simran turned around, "What?"

"You look stunning!" Tanya confessed and she wasn't wrong.

Simran had a tall, lean figure with perfect curves that were well highlighted by the short dress she wore. "You don't look so bad yourself. In spite of the simple clothes, simple hair and lack of make-up, you look gorgeous."

Tanya opened her mouth to argue but Simran continued, "Naah, we are at war here. No more fishing for compliments. Let's go."

Tanya and Simran walked out into the corridor. They ran into Madhura. She was from Pune, a 'proper Maharashtrian' in her words and she claimed to be a distant relative of Madhuri Dixit.

'Brilliant,' thought Tanya as she remembered Madhuri Dixit's sweet, sensual smile.

Madhura had that smile. Madhura was exactly the opposite of Simran. She was sweet, always smiled and made you feel as if you had been friends with her forever.

Tanya noticed that Simran didn't like her much and as soon as they reached the dining room, Simran left her side and started socialising with the other girls. Tanya who still felt a little intimidated by the beauty brigade, decided to remain with Madhura.

"Enough about me. Tell me something about you?" Madhura flashed her Madhuri Dixit smile once again.

"I used to work for an advertising agency as a media planner and I quit my job recently." Tanya picked up her name tag from the table. Her serial number was 30.

"You quit your job to be on this show!" Madhura was taken

aback. "You're joking, right?"

"Long story… My job stopped being as exciting as it used to be. I wanted to do something crazy. So here I am…." Tanya was seated quite far from Madhura. She pointed to her chair and said, "That's me, I'll see you later."

She was glad to be far away; she wasn't comfortable with the idea of chatting with someone while eating. Tanya was seated next to Shehnaz Bharucha.

"Hi," she mumbled, feeling rather intimidated by Shehnaz. She was dressed in a designer halter dress and had a tattoo on her back. She was wearing minimal make-up but she had a pearl white glow on her face and she was busy talking to a girl across the table, whose badge read Aditi Karkaria. There were too many women and too many names for Tanya to handle. At this point, she started feeling sorry for Rajsingh Jaiswal. He had to date all these girls. Rajsingh Jaiswal entered followed by Karan Kapoor. Her sympathy disappeared as soon as she saw him.

"Think of the devil," Tanya said to herself.

Rahul couldn't wait to see Tanya again. She made him feel real, she made him nostalgic; he longed to sell a perfume to her, just to relive that evening, the only time he'd ever heard her voice. He knew she was not going out in the first round. She was his only link to what he really was and he wasn't going to let her go. There was no reason for him to feel that way considering she hadn't even smiled when she stared at him during the orientation.

As soon as he walked into the dining room, Rahul's eyes scanned the room for Tanya. He spotted her looking rather overwhelmed. She looked so vulnerable, so adorable sitting with her elbows on the table, hands cupping her face. He had to exercise great restraint to stop himself from going over and giving her a comforting hug. Their eyes met and she looked away. She no longer looked overwhelmed; she looked visibly annoyed.

Karan Kapoor was observant and it didn't take him long to notice that Rahul kept looking at Tanya, every now and then, slyly from the corner of his eye. It also didn't take Karan long to notice the disdain in Tanya's eyes. He wondered what was going on. Did Tanya know Rahul from before? He kept observing the two until it was time for him to make an announcement.

"Tomorrow, you will walk the ramp in a *sari*. Deepak will update you on the other arrangements. And yes, Raj and Mrs. Menon are very excited about seeing you all dressed up. Don't forget to dress to kill, both Raj and the competition."

There was a murmur in the room. Rahul looked at Tanya; she looked panic-stricken. Rahul knew what the problem was — Tanya hadn't brought a saree. In fact he wondered if she owned a saree at all.

Deepak was already shooting off instructions about the fashion show. "*Saris* will be provided by Naina Choksi Designs, but if the contestants want to wear their own, they can."

Rahul let out a sigh of relief. As Deepak continued to fire off some more information about the fashion show, Karan and Rajsingh got up and excused themselves.

Karan led Rahul to a private room. Though there were cameras rolling, Rahul could be himself in this room, Karan reassured him. This was the room where Rahul, the perfume salesman could talk about how he felt, what he observed while he led the life of Rajsingh Jaiswal. Karan started chatting with Rahul, very casually, but this was an interview.

"That was quite an impression Raj made out there. What did you, Rahul Rajgopal think of those gorgeous women?" Karan asked.

"It feels good to see so many beautiful people in one room, and that includes you Karan!" Rahul said.

"Ah come on, don't you flatter me. Anyway, have you considered which five girls you'd like to eliminate?" Karan asked, but he looked pleased with Rahul's compliment.

"If I could, I wouldn't send anyone home. They all look so wonderful, but one's got to do what one's got to do. I'll wait until the fashion show to make my decision."

"What about first impressions? Did you come across someone

who stood out?" Karan knew he was treading on a minefield with that question.

"Well, frankly they are all awesome, but there is this one girl who is very different from the others." Rahul stared into space and smiled.

"Interesting, so we know which one is definitely staying then?"

"I can't be sure, but yeah she seems interesting. Keep guessing Karan!"

Ashutosh decided that was all they needed and left with his crew to catch a few bytes with the girls. Karan handed Rahul an envelope from Cee. Rahul looked at Karan, confused.

"Change in the structure," Karan explained. "Instead of five first and then two each week, the first four weeks will see 20 girls packed off home."

Rahul shrugged. He didn't give a damn about who went home. He only cared about that one girl and he was going to make sure that she stayed.

* * * * * *

Rosie was walking back from work that evening. She walked past a huge poster promoting the new reality show, 'A Match Made in Heaven'. While she waited for the bus, she spotted the same poster on the bus stop across the road. The guy was extremely good-looking but he looked familiar. Those eyes, they reminded her of Rahul. She sighed and smiled. She wished Rahul was around so she could tease him about this bugger being his lookalike.

The posters had caught everyone's fancy. It felt like the entire country couldn't wait for the first episode. Some wanted to see it for the good-looking Raj, some wanted to follow the progress of a certain contestant, but many were just curious about the outrageous idea of finding love on television. The world outside Jaiswal Mansion was curious, excited, thrilled and very eager to find out what was happening within the four walls.

Chapter 19

A big hall within the mansion had been turned into a common room. As the hour of the fashion show drew closer, *saris* and accessories were handed out before the girls went into the green room to get ready. By the time Tanya arrived to make her selection, most of the girls were done picking their saris. Tanya looked through what was left. She finally settled on a simple blue-green *bandhani sari*. There were a bunch of girls representing the fashion house who handed out petticoats, blouses and accessories to go with the *saris*. Tanya took her packet rather reluctantly and moved towards the green room.

The fashion show was going to be the highlight of the first episode and everone was scurrying around to ensure that it was a hit. A small ramp was raised in the garden. Cameras were set up, lights were fixed and the team was ready to win the audience over.

In the chaotic green room, Tanya struggled to figure out where to start. A stylist approached Tanya and asked her to start with getting into a petticoat and her blouse.

"Are you comfortable draping a *sari* on your own or do you want me to help you?" the stylist asked.

The confusion and anxiety on Tanya's face was answer enough. She pushed Tanya into a changing booth. "Hurry up and wear the slip right below your navel and shout out when you're ready. I'll come and drape the *sari*, ok?"

As soon as she was done tying the aqua blue satin slip around her waist, Tanya got the blouse out of the package. She was shocked to see a halter-neck top with shiny straps instead of a regular *sari*-blouse. Tanya peeped out to talk to the stylist. The stylist was being harassed by four girls and Tanya couldn't help but feel sorry for her. Tanya decided not to add to the stylist's woes by moaning about her blouse and decided to wear the halter top anyway. After she had secured the halter-top's strings into a sturdy knot, Tanya made her way to the stylist, who pulled Tanya's slip further down, exposing almost all of her midriff.

"My back is almost naked! I don't think I am comfortable," Tanya said as she tried to pull the slip back up.

The stylist stopped her and smiled. "Trust me, this is going to look sexy, not slutty," she said as she started draping the silky fabric around Tanya.

Although Tanya had always considered herself quite slim, the washboard abs and toned bodies around her made her feel rather conscious of her curves. "I don't think I have a body to show off," Tanya said hesitantly and looked around her.

"Rubbish! You have the perfect curves for a *sari*. Look at that perfect butt," said the stylist and winked.

Her comment made Tanya even more uncomfortable. "This was a stupid idea," she thought to herself and decided that she would be very happy if Rajsingh eliminated her tonight.

"Here hold this for me," said the stylist handing some of the fabric to Tanya and holding the other end of the *sari*. "How do you want the *pallu*?"

The last time she'd worn a *sari* was on Ravi's and Anita's wedding day. It was a registered marriage, but Anita had wanted Tanya to wear a *sari*. Tanya had managed to wear a simple cotton *sari* and all she remembered of the experience was that she had been extremely uncomfortable. So far the stylist hadn't really been very happy with Tanya's inputs, so she decided to leave the *pallu* to the stylist. "Go with your instinct," Tanya said, "but I'd prefer the simple way."

The stylist pinned the *pallu* over Tanya's left shoulder and let the fabric glide over her arm. She gave Tanya some suggestions about holding the *pallu* 'to ensure the right fall' and then sent her on to the make-up artist, who intently listened to the stylist's suggestions on the make-up. The make-up artist asked Tanya to close her eyes and sit back. Tanya obeyed, realising that she had little say in how she was going to look. She felt the make-up artiste apply gooey and powdery things on her face. When Tanya opened her eyes and looked in the mirror, she almost didn't recognise herself. Her face had a brand new layer, her eyes had been defined with kohl and eye-shadow, her cheeks were blushing, and her lips seemed fuller and richer. The eye-shadow brought out the green in her eyes and her face looked a bit less round than usual.

"Do you like it? Or should I add a bit more blusher here?" The make-up artist asked pointing to her cheek bones.

"This is fine, thanks," Tanya replied with a smile as the hairdresser took the make-up artist's place. She brushed Tanya's hair, and then twisted and pinned it up in sections. She fixed curlers onto the sections.

"Please wear your jewellery and be ready. Your hair will be set in about half an hour," she told Tanya and moved to Shehnaz Bharucha's chair which was right next to Tanya's.

Shehnaz looked like a princess with her make-up. Her cream-coloured *sari* with a colourful border complemented her creamy skin. The hairdresser played with Shehnaz's long highlighted tresses as she flipped through a magazine. She looked up and caught Tanya's eyes.

"Lovely *sari*," she complimented Tanya.

Tanya was taken aback and reached for the earrings on the table.

"Thanks, but I really like yours," Tanya murmured while putting her earrings on.

"Thanks. It's Mummy's. It's a traditional *gara*. I'm Parsi," Shehnaz replied. "They tell me I look like a *pukka* Parsi *chhokri*."

Tanya's sapphire and diamond danglers were already in her ears; she slipped on the bangles, blue and green with sparkling dust. She practised walking about so she could get comfortable in her *sari*, but she could hardly let go of the *sari* and the thought of walking down the ramp was just plain scary. The first ten girls had already lined up backstage; the second ten were touching their faces up.

The hairdresser undid the curlers. The waved hair fell in place, just as it was supposed to. The hair, the make-up and the sari made Tanya look like a whole new person. She was escorted backstage.

Tanya waited for her turn impatiently. She wanted to get it over with. The girl standing in front of her turned. "Why are you wearing such a simple *sari*?" she asked.

Tanya looked at the girl's heavy traditional Gujarati sari complete with heavy gold jewellery. "I did not bring a *sari* with me. I am Tanya, by the way."

The girl put her hand on Tanya's arm, "Oh! I should've met you before. I have so many *saris*. No problem, next time you ask me, ok? I am Pallak."

She peeped out to see who was walking the ramp.

"Good luck, Pallak," Tanya said as just two girls remained in front of Tanya.

"Thanks," she said before going off.

"Tanya Kher," Karan Kapoor announced and Tanya walked out in the middle of the stage. She walked the ramp, rather conscious of all the eyes on her and suddenly she decided to enjoy the moment. She twirled on the ramp and waved out to Karan Kapoor with a big grin. She noticed Rajsingh Jaiswal staring at her. She wished he would look away.

Rahul couldn't take his eyes off Tanya. Her *sari* was simple, she wasn't wearing much jewellery and yet she looked stunning. She walked towards him, and as she stood on the podium, Karan

Kapoor read a few things out from her form. Rahul was riveted looking at the nervous Tanya who suddenly started grinning and walking with a bounce in her step. Ho could sense she was having fun. Their eyes met again and she hesitated a little and looked away, but this time with an attitude that made her look sexy. Rahul grinned. He thought she looked perfect.

"Tanya Kher used to be a successful media planner with a leading advertising agency. She recently quit her job to make her life a bit more exciting. She loves reading, music and occasionally likes to write poetry. Tanya is 28 and has an MBA from Bajaj Institute. Do you have any questions for Tanya?"

"Many," thought Rahul, but Rajsingh shook his head. Tanya was uncomfortable under his constant gaze. She walked off the stage. All the girls were back on the stage. Karan joined them.

"Good show girls! Nervous about tomorrow? We're nervous too. Which of you will bid goodbye to the dream of being the future Mrs Jaiswal? Keep your fingers crossed and bags packed. Goodnight ladies and thank you."

The girls were ushered back towards the changing rooms. Rahul sifted through the forms and Karan helped him.

The next morning was quite uneventful. The girls took a tour of the mansion, lounged around in the living room or spent time in the gym. The crew was interviewing the girls one by one. Tanya's interview was rather bland compared to the others. She walked to the garden. The other girls hoped to bump into Raj but were disappointed.

The house was too crowded and she wasn't in the mood for small talk, so Tanya walked towards the swimming pool. She rolled her jeans up and sat down by the pool, dipping her feet in the water. She loved how the water tickled her feet and she giggled a little.

"You should smile more often." Rajsingh Jaiswal had emerged from nowhere.

Tanya jumped, then looked flustered. "I had no idea I had company," she said, feeling naked to have been caught giggling by this strange man.

"I am sorry, I seem to have startled you." Rajsingh moved forward and sat next to her. Tanya looked at him, irritated.

"It's your house. You can startle anyone you want." Tanya wished he'd leave her alone.

Rajsingh had no intention of fulfilling Tanya's unspoken wish. "So, are you comfortable in the house? I noticed you're really quiet," he asked.

Tanya looked away and rolled her eyes in irritation. "No, yeah, I am okay, thanks," she said.

"I read your form this morning. It's very interesting," said Rahul realising that she was still the same rude girl he had encountered at the mall; he wished he hadn't spoken to her.

Tanya drew up her knees and hugged them.

"So, why do you want to marry me?" Raj's question startled Tanya and she lost grip on her legs and they slipped back in the water. Rahul laughed. He wanted to surprise her with that question and he had succeeded.

"What?" she asked with a frown on her face.

"Why… do… you… want… to… marry… me?" Raj repeated himself, slowly, teasing the rude, arrogant Tanya.

"What sort of a question is that, Mr Jaiswal?"

"It's Raj, call me Raj. And what's wrong with that question? You came on this show to get married to me, didn't you?"

Tanya saw that he had assumed that she, like the other girls, was eager to get married to him. How dare he assume she'd ever marry a man like him? She angrily pulled her legs out of the water and got up and looked down at a startled Rajsingh Jaiswal.

"Mr Jaiswal, let me make it very clear. I did not come here to marry you. I came to see what kind of a man would seek the love of his life through a reality TV show. Don't flatter yourself. I do not want to marry you." She stomped off, leaving a trail of wet footprints behind her.

Rahul was shaken by her outburst. He sat there for a couple of minutes and then got up. In her anger, Tanya had forgotten her slippers. Rahul picked them up and walked toward the house.

Tanya stormed into her room and sat fuming on her bed. As she thought about the poolside conversation, she realised that Rajsingh hadn't been wrong in asking that question. She felt rather silly about her outburst. Why did Rajsingh annoy her so much? Why had she lost her cool like that? Why did he induce such a strong urge to be rude?

There was a soft knock on the door. She opened the door assuming it would be one of the neighbouring girls, but she was startled to see Raj and in his hand were her slippers.

"Thanks Mr Jaiswal. I am sorry about...."

"Please don't apologise. You're right. This show is ridiculous in its own way, but I hope I can explain myself to you someday. You forgot these by the pool." He left her slippers by the door and walked away.

Tanya heard the other girls politely greet him as he walked through the corridor. She heard his voice, softly acknowledging the girls. He was a polite man. She felt terrible about the way she had treated him.

Tanya packed her things. After the poolside incident, she knew she wasn't going to stay for long. Anita had always told her that men found it hard to tolerate women who hurt their ego. Suddenly, she was glad that she had yelled at Rajsingh. Going home wouldn't be such a bad thing, especially now that she knew how much she missed Anita and Ravi.

Everything about the show had been well planned. The girls were to go in and see Rajsingh in groups of five. Rajsingh would disclose the names of those eliminated during this rendezvous. Tanya had two hours to kill. She picked up one of Simran's magazines. "May I?" she asked Simran, who was drying her hair by the dresser.

"Sure, help yourself. I've got a few more in my bag, in case you need them. I had to pack them in, but I have a strong feeling I won't be eliminated today," she continued twirling her hair in front of the mirror.

Tanya opened the magazine and a song started playing in

her head. She smiled as she remembered what song it was. 'I believe that beauty magazines promote low self-esteem...,' she couldn't resist singing aloud as she went through page after page of size zero dames with perfect hair and make-up. She went back to the contents page.

One article read, 'Keep him wrapped around your little finger, while he thinks you are wrapped around his — the art of getting things done your way without making him feel hen-pecked'. Another article read, 'Home remedies for a glowing skin'; another one, 'Where to shop to look hot'.

Tanya flipped through the magazine, bored by its contents. The only thing that interested her was the agony aunt section. One girl was upset because her boyfriend had admitted to an affair with an older woman. Another was very upset to find out that she was attracted to a younger man living in her building and a third that her boss was hitting on her. She wondered if people were really that screwed up or if all these letters were faked by the magazine.

"How do I look?" Simran demanded.

"You look really good," Tanya replied and she wasn't lying, because she really did look awesome.

"If you were Rajsingh Jaiswal, how bad would you feel letting me go?" she sang, as she twirled around.

"If I was Rajsingh Jaiswal, I'd rather die than let you go," Tanya said, laughing with Simran.

Five minutes later, Simran was gone and Tanya got up to get ready.

The two groups that went in before Tanya's group came out incomplete. Rajsingh had asked some girls to stay back. Tanya went in with her group, confident that she was getting eliminated. The study been transformed into a mini-studio complete with TV cameras and lights. Raj and Karan were deep into some discussion as the girls sat down on the big couch.

"Good evening, girls," Karan said. "Are we nervous?"

They all nodded and responded with a rather watery smile.

Tanya did neither.

"It's hard to let such pretty girls go, but I can't marry all of you," Rajsingh Jaiswal joked, looking at all of them, and fixing his gaze on Tanya. "I hope you understand."

He looked down at the paper while Karan read out.

"Shweta Modi? May we ask you to join the girls in the other chamber please?" Karan fixed his warm gaze on Shweta.

Once Shweta had left, Karan and Raj chatted with the girls for a bit. Tanya waited for the ball to drop. She waited for Karan to say, "You four are the girls we don't want!"

She looked at the other girls in her group. Pallak looked completely different in her non-*desi avatar*. Next to Pallak was the same girl who had been seated next to Tanya on the very first day. All the girls on the couch were extremely hot and any man in his right senses wouldn't let them go. Tanya then realised that she was staying and Shweta Modi was going out.

She couldn't understand why Rajsingh had chosen to keep her on the show. As she left the room, she turned around to look at Rajsingh Jaiswal. She couldn't help but smile. As expected, the topic of conversation at dinner was the elimination. The girl, who was a distant relative of Madhuri Dixit's was leaving with a couple of girls Tanya didn't know. Tanya felt bad for her, but she was still quite surprised that Rajsingh had chosen to let her stay and to her astonishment, she was really glad.

Tuesday morning brought a slight dip in the temperature, making it just perfect for a stroll in the garden. Tanya pulled a track suit on and set out to entertain herself in the lovely shades of green. She switched her iPod on and started exploring the huge garden. She was completely unaware that from a window, not too far away, someone was watching her.

Rahul stood by his bedroom window as he observed Tanya Kher. He could tell that she had slept well last night. She looked as fresh as a daisy and there was a bounce in her step.

"How can she be so relaxed?" he wondered.

Everyone around Tanya was restless and under tremendous

pressure, and Tanya was untouched by it all. She was always taking long walks and reading books as if she was on a holiday. He looked at her groove slightly as she walked and he grinned. He was glad she was here.

When Tanya got back to her room, Simran was still fast asleep. Tanya tiptoed to the cupboard and fished out a notebook and a pen. She got back into bed and started scribbling. The sound of her pen scratching the surface of the paper mixed with Simran's soft snores gave Tanya a rhythm to write to. She worked at what she had written like a sculptor, scratching out words that didn't fit, rewriting the lines that didn't rhyme and smiling when words just fell into place. When she was done writing, she smiled, content with what she saw. She softly read out the poem:

"Pain you are my truest companion,
Physically, you come rarely,
But you torture me through emotion.

You never leave my side
And I keep coming back to you.
In every happy moment of mine,
You have to be there too….

Sometimes you come to my eyes
And fall out as a teardrop,
And sometimes to feel you my heart cries,
You always bring me to a full stop.

No, I am not complaining,
Because I have no right to.
It's because of you I live,

Others crib about you.
They all are crazy,
Because they know not how good you are,
We're meant to be together,
Because I am not me without you…"

Tanya rarely felt proud of what she wrote but this poem somehow made sense to her. Ever since she could remember, an unexplainable, unquantifiable pain had always accompanied her. Of late, she hadn't felt that pain and its absence had been making her restless. The poem felt like a plea from her subconscious to look for that pain. The pain had been a reminder to Tanya, a reminder that she could feel.

Tanya flipped through the notebook, each page full of words, rhymes and ideas. Each poem she had written explored the idea of her own self. She was looking for herself through her poetry and she had been feeling quite numb for the last few days. There was nothing to feel in Jaiswal Mansion, perhaps, that was why there was no pain.

'Because I am not me without you.' The last line echoed in her mind. She had to get out before she got used to the idea of not feeling anything within. She hated the thought of going back to the Tanya Kher she had left behind in her office. She had thawed her frozen heart and she wasn't going to let a television show freeze it back to its coldness again.

The week went by pretty quickly for Tanya. She finally started to enjoy spending time with just herself for company. When she wasn't writing, she worked at their weekly task — putting up a dance performance along with Pallak, Simran and Janaki. They were asked to perform a Bollywood medley, and Pallak had volunteered to choreograph it. Tanya learnt all the *jhatkas* and *matkas* and other *filmi* dance moves, and to her surprise, she enjoyed dancing.

Having completed her dance practice, Tanya decided to take a stroll before dinner. She spotted a table in the garden, complete with candlelight. She walked a little closer and it dawned on her that this was Shehnaz's date with Raj. Shehnaz's face was glowing as she smiled in a coy, timid manner, occasionally touching her earrings or her necklace. Tanya felt envy raging within her. She felt jealous of Shehnaz's captivating beauty. She felt angry about something. She walked back to her room, bewildered by the complexity of her emotions. Back in the safety of her room, she felt angry, then calm, and then she felt glad. She was FEELING. She wasn't freezing! She went back out into the hallway, in a 'Eureka!' mood. For once, she was happy about the complex emotions she felt.

"Hey, Karan was looking for you. He said that you have a date with Rajsingh at 6 p.m. tomorrow," yelled Radhika, the girl from the room down the hallway.

"Ah! Thanks. Have you had yours yet?" Tanya asked her as they walked toward the stairs.

"Not yet. I'm having lunch with him tomorrow," Radhika said as she tucked a stray strand behind her ear. "I am so nervous, don't know what to wear and all. What are you going to wear?"

Tanya hadn't thought about it at all. "I don't really know. I haven't brought much stuff with me. I guess I'll just wear a *salwar kameez* or something,"

"No Tanya!" Radhika's big brown eyes went wide with horror, "You can't wear a plain *salwar kameez*. You have got to spice it up. Come to Devika's room with me. She is going to help me with some beauty treatment and then we'll talk clothes. She had her date this morning."

"Thanks. I think I'll just get some dinner. The rehearsals are too tiring." Tanya really wanted to be alone.

"Oh, cool!"

"Aren't you coming to dinner?" Tanya asked as she started walking down the stairs.

"I am on a fruit diet. You enjoy dinner,"

"You too." Tanya turned around and shouted out to Radhika, who disappeared into Devika's room. She carried on down the stairs. Rajsingh Jaiswal was running up the stairs, and they collided with each other. She tried to balance herself, but ended up collapsing on him instead.

He winced in pain as Tanya's elbow crashed into his chest. "Are you all right?" he asked shakily.

"I am so sorry… I am okay… are you… I am so sorry, I was…." Tanya looked mortified.

"Don't worry, I'm okay…. Are you sure you're ok?" He helped her get back on her feet.

"I am fine. I am sorry I should have been looking where I was going," Tanya said as they both straightened up.

"No, no. I shouldn't have been running like that…"

"We're both guilty then. You sure you're okay, I mean, I almost crushed your chest with my elbow."

"Don't worry I am fine. I was just looking for Shehnaz. I wanted to give her something she forgot. Did you see her going this way?"

"I'm right here!" Shehnaz's voice came from the bottom of the stairs. "I went back to the table when I found I was missing an earring, but I couldn't find it there,"

Tanya felt awkward. "Right, then, I am going to get some dinner. See you guys." She walked away as Rajsingh walked Shehnaz to her room.

Rahul thought Shehnaz was gorgeous, but within a couple of minutes, he had to fight back the urge to yawn. He was bored with the usual sweet and coy demeanour that all the girls had been feigning on their dates with him. He longed for something other than the usual, 'my family is important to me, I would like to keep my identity, and I want to do something good for the world'.

To Rahul, it was all shoptalk.

Of course, Shehnaz was shocked when he hadn't volunteered to escort her to her room. Rahul felt guilty. "A gentleman should always treat a lady like a lady." Sherry's words rang in his ear.

When he saw the earring shimmering on the chair Shehnaz had been sitting on, he decided to cash in on the opportunity and ran towards her room. He ran through the kitchen, which was a shortcut to the rooms and as he sprinted up the stairs he literally bumped into Tanya.

As she collapsed on top of him, he noticed Tanya's scent. She smelt of citrusy fruits and of basil. She smelt of freshly-cut grass and of a salty sea-breeze at the same time. He couldn't identify what perfume it was, but her fragrance stayed with him as he dropped Shehnaz to her room. He tried to put his finger on the specific fragrance she wore — its base notes, its top notes, but couldn't. This was a first in many years for Rahul, the best perfume salesman in Mumbai.

Tanya was halfway through her dinner when Simran came and sat next to her. "I'm starving. Do you want something?" Simran asked.

"I am okay," Tanya replied.

Tanya looked around. Hardly any of the girls came down for dinner. When they did, they ate bite-sized portions. She could never starve herself like them, even if it meant living with a slightly curvy body.

"So I heard your date is scheduled for tomorrow?" Simran asked as she sat down with her plate.

"Yeah, I met Radhika. She told me."

"Nervous? Don't worry, he is easy to please."

"Not when you've knocked him down and almost broken his ribs! But who cares?"

"You knocked him down and what?"

"An accident; he was running up, I was going down and...."

"Crash! Ouch! You okay, *na*?"

"Yeah, I'm fine. How was your date with him?"

"It was all right. He's cute. We took a walk through the garden, then we had some coffee, we talked about stuff."

"What kind of stuff?" Tanya bit into her chicken.

Simran looked at Tanya and shot her eyebrow up. "Uh, we're contestants. Don't try to pry out information on my date to make yours easy."

She pushed away her plate of salad. Tanya almost thought that Simran was mad at her, but something told her to change the topic. "That's it? That was your dinner? I thought you were starving."

"Too many calories, I am grabbing an apple from the kitchen and heading to the room. You done there?" she asked.

"Yup!" Tanya wasn't done, but decided to deprive herself of the small piece of bread and some chicken that remained. It would be her humble contribution to the starvation squad.

On the way back to the room, Tanya paused at the spot where she and Rajsingh had collided. Despite herself, she felt rather excited about their next rendezvous.

Chapter 20

Tanya sat in front of the mirror, trying hard to decipher the instructions on the box. She had splashed her face with water and pat-dried it. Now, with a hair band holding her hair back, she squeezed out the yellowish liquid which was supposed to contain 'orange extracts to rejuvenate, peach extracts to give you a peachy complexion and lemon extract to give you a refreshing glow'.

"Oh God, you're taking forever! Here let me do it for you." Simran snatched the tube from Tanya's hand and rubbed the liquid on Tanya's face evenly. A cold soothing sensation passed through her skin. "There you go, now you are just 35 minutes away from fresh, rejuvenated skin that glows!"

Simran held out the tube with a fake smile plastered on her face. Though she thought this was funny, Tanya wondered why she had let Simran convince her to go through with the elaborate beauty treatment. "I have drawn the bath and in 35 minutes I shall come to peel the mask off. Let's get you ready for the date!"

She pushed Tanya into the bathroom and shut the door.

Simran had been very excited about Tanya's date. When she saw that Tanya was a complete dodo at D-I-Y beauty treatments, Simran decided to step in. Although Tanya agreed to apply the face mask and soak herself in a rejuvenating bath, she had stood her ground with regard to the clothes she was going to wear. It was going to be a simple *salwar kameez*.

While Tanya stewed in the floral scents and essential oils that Simran had added to the bath water, Simran hurried to another girl's room to find some jewellery to go with the *salwar kameez*.

"Sorry, I couldn't wait to show you these," Simran said, bursting into the bathroom holding a pair of earrings. "I am not looking at you, don't worry, but aren't these perfect?"

One look at the diamonds with small orange stones that dangled in a dainty floral design and Tanya agreed that they were perfect. "They are beautiful. Now, how long am I supposed to stew in this?" Tanya was rather bored.

Simran held the earrings to her ear and looked in the mirror, "Twenty minutes. Are you excited?"

"Hate to admit it, but I am." Tanya drew up water in her palm and watched it trickle down her fingers, leaving a bit of foam and flower particles in her palm.

"Why deny it? Aren't we all here to date him?" Simran sat down by the tub, glancing through a magazine she had left there earlier.

"I know, but I was dreading the date. I wasn't very impressed by him," Tanya admitted.

"I was wooed by the money. But when I met him, I was kind of impressed. He's charming," Simran reassured Tanya.

"But why would you agree to marry for money, that too through a reality show?"

"Look who's talking! I am off. You have 15 minutes. You know how to peel the stuff?"

"Yep!" Tanya replied as Simran walked out the bathroom door.

Tanya wrapped herself in Simran's spare bathrobe. She wasn't sure if it was the mask or just an illusion but she could see her skin glow. Simran had left her make-up box open for Tanya to paint her face, but Tanya decided to ignore it. She blow-dried her hair, like she always did. She held the drier to her hair and straightened out the tousled hair. Within minutes, she was ready. She looked in the mirror and admired the well-fitted *salwar kameez* and she was glad Anita had given her this outfit.

"She always knows what would look good on me," Tanya thought, feeling slightly homesick.

She felt like something was still missing. She put on her shiny peach coloured lipstick and applied a hint of mascara and she was ready to go, but she was still early for her date. She strolled down the corridor, wondering what she could do to kill time before the date.

"Hi! What are you doing here? You should be getting ready for your date."

Radhika's voice startled Tanya. Radhika had a smug look on her face and Tanya knew that she'd had a fabulous date with Raj and she wanted to gloat about it. Tanya felt jealousy creep up yet again. "Oh, I am ready for my date. How was your date?"

Radhika silently stared at Tanya. "You have got to be kidding me! You're under-dressed. Come, let's do your make-up while we talk about my date." Radhika grabbed Tanya's arm.

"Thanks." Tanya glanced at her reflection in a window at the end of the corridor. "I think I look okay. Did you have fun?"

"Absolutely, we talked about friends, family, hobbies, likes, dislikes. Typical first meeting stuff, you know. He is so sweet. I mean, he is so not the snob I expected him to be."

"Good for you." Tanya wondered whether she'd be ever able to see that humble, sweet side of Raj. Would she ever be able to see in him what the other girls saw?

"We had a nice Indian vegetarian spread. He knew I was a vegetarian. So thoughtful!"

"It all sounds great, Radhika. Looks like it was a fun date!"

Tanya had heard most of the girls gush about their dates and it was starting to infuriate Tanya. She didn't want to play this game — his game.

Rahul hadn't been able to concentrate on his coffee date. He couldn't stop thinking about the upcoming dinner date with Tanya.

He freshened up and hurried into the living room. He was surprised to see that Tanya was already there. "I wasn't expecting you this early," he said.

Tanya smiled at him. Raj looked quite handsome in a slightly crinkled white shirt and linen pants. Tanya could tell from the way he looked at her that he was glad to see a face sans make-up, heavy jewellery and overdone hair.

Raj looked at her for a minute, taking in the simplicity. Rahul, however, stood captivated by the beauty of the face that was an enigma to him, even in his perfume days. Rahul was so glad to see her smile.

"Should we start early then?" she asked in a cold manner, as if she wanted to just get done with the date.

"Sure, this way...."

He enjoyed her sharp reactions but never understood why she was so unpredictable. He knew she wasn't rude otherwise, but why did she have such weird reactions to everything he said or did?

They walked through the dining area in the verandah towards the swimming pool. At the other end of the pool was a table for two. Tanya was impressed.

"Looks like you like it. Shall we?" Raj said, almost as if he'd read her mind. He offered her a hand. "You might want to take off those. We have to cross the rocks to get there." He pointed at her shoes.

In the control room, Karan Kapoor watched them closely. He knew this was going to be a very special date.

Tanya slid out of her sandals and picked them up with her left hand, leaving her right hand free to hold Raj's hand. They both tiptoed across the rocks onto the other side of the pool.

Rahul caught another smile on Tanya's lips as he held her chair out for her. He felt proud that he had made her smile.

"I've ordered some Italian food. I hope you don't mind?"

"Italian is all right." Tanya was impressed, but she didn't want him to know that yet. Raj uncovered a platter that was sitting on the table to reveal several breads and antipasti. He poured some infused olive oil into a dish from a trolley next to the table.

"This olive oil, with the focaccia is a match made in heaven." The food had been supplied by a five star hotel that was promoting its Italian restaurant through the show, Karan Kapoor read on the script.

Of course, Tanya didn't know this. She smiled at Rajsingh and bit into the bread. He was right, it was wonderful. She closed her eyes to enjoy the herbs. Rahul couldn't take his eyes off her face, while she enjoyed her bite of the bread.

"I am glad you like Italian food. I've ordered Sphagetti Carbonara, Penne Arrabiata, a salad and of course, wine and...."

"I am impressed! I thought you NRIs like to eat as much Indian *khaana* as you can, but you seem to be an exception," she said.

Raj wished she had let him finish the sentence. He didn't know how to slip in the restaurant's name now.

"No, I am not an exception. It's just that I've had an overdose of Indian *khaana* over the past few dates. I am craving for some continental stuff now and I had a feeling you'd like it too," Raj said, hoping it would melt her. Rahul looked for a hint of appreciation as Tanya took in the sight of the food.

"Can I have some more of that olive oil?" Tanya was clearly more interested in the food than she was in Rajsingh Jaiswal.

"There you go. Try the ham, it has been flown down straight from Italy. That's why I love Mezzo Mezzo at the Marriott. They have the most authentic Italian food in Mumbai. Forget your diet, go on try some," he said.

Tanya was looking at him inquisitively. She couldn't understand why he was talking about a restaurant miles away. "Bring it on!"

She grabbed a slice of ham and bit into it. "You had food delivered from Mumbai?" she asked.

"They sell ingredients. The best cheeses, cured meats, handmade pasta, everything you need to cook up an authentic Italian meal. It's all been cooked here," he said.

He was relieved that he could squeeze in the blurb about the restaurant. He tried to forget that he was Rajsingh Jaiswal when he was around Tanya. She was his only link to his reality, one that this show was threatening to wipe out.

They both devoured the antipasti before Rahul poured a glass of red wine. "What did you do before coming on this show?"

He hated this part, but he had been instructed to ask these common questions.

"Mister Millionaire," she replied as she sipped her wine, "you must learn to do your homework. I filled out a form where I've already answered that question, and I am not about to repeat myself."

"Miss Media Planner, I have done my homework. I know that you used to have great career in advertising," he said, biting into another slice of ham, "but I thought you would have something to add."

"That's pretty much it. Is this a date or an interview?" Tanya asked as Raj got up to get out some olives.

"A bit of both actually. Aren't first dates always a mix of both?"

"I agree, but I don't like this idea of following the trend. I expected you to be a trendsetter, Mr. PC."

"Mr. PC?"

"Prince Charming, the fairytale guy,"

"So you think I am the fairytale guy?"

"Nope, I never believed in a Prince Charming, but you know you are acting out the other girls' fantasy," she said before biting into an olive from the bowl Raj had put in front of her.

"You're right I am acting it all out," he replied as he served the pasta that had been brought over by one of the production assistants.

"So you admit that you are not a perfect man."

"I never said I was. I am just another guy."

"Then why are you here to find a wife?"

"Lack of time. I couldn't find a nice Indian girl and of course, to help my friend Avinash," he explained.

"You really think you could find a life partner?" She pointed at the mansion. "Like this, on a show?"

"I don't know how one finds a life partner but I am in it for love. I can't imagine being married to a woman I don't love,"

"I didn't expect a successful businessman to be this naïve."

"Naïve?"

"Do you really think these girls are here for love? It is money that they're here for. It's the chance to be a millionaire's wife that attracted them to this show. It's a chance for them to fulfil their desires. It has nothing to do with love, Raj."

"Have you ever been in love, Tanya?"

"Yes, I was married to the love of my life," Tanya said with a straight face, sipping wine.

Rahul was startled; she looked too young to be married and divorced. Had she lied on the form? Karan looked at one of the assistants and back at the TV screen.

"Don't look so horrified. I was married to my job. I loved it or so I thought."

"Come on Tanya," Rahul said irritably. "I asked you if you were in love with a man!"

Karan let out a sigh of relief.

Tanya paused and sipped more wine. She shrugged and shook her head.

"Then how can you tell me where to find and where not to find love?"

"I am being practical."

"Love has got nothing to do with practicality."

"Okay, looks like Mr. PC has been in love before."

Rahul looked away and then looked at her again. He smiled at her and said, "Yes, I might have been in love in the past and I lost her. I lost her because it was impractical. I lost her because the world decided that we weren't meant to be."

There was an awkward silence. Tanya didn't know what to say so she continued to eat and drink. "I really like the food," she said, hoping to change the topic. She felt guilty for bringing up Rajsingh's past, but she was starting to like Rajsingh. He was honest with her, he didn't pretend. She still thought he was naïve, though.

"I'm glad. More wine?"

Tanya nodded and he poured her some.

"I used to be a workaholic, to such an extent that I was the employee of the year, every year. People hated me. I didn't know how to live, but my life was perfect and 'practical'. I had a highly coveted job, a fat bank balance, an apartment in a prime location. I had everything one could dream of, but I didn't have people to share anything with. I didn't have any friends of my own. I barely made an effort to make friends with the people my brother and sister-in-law tried to introduce me to. When I quit my job, I realised that I had nothing, absolutely nothing to be proud of."

It was her way to let Raj know that he had earned her trust. Both of them had forgotten that there were cameras on them, capturing every moment of this intimate conversation. Tanya had forgotten where she was. She just knew who she was with, and she knew that she liked him.

"I am sorry to hear that." Raj really meant it.

"Hey! This was supposed to be a date, why are we talking about these things?"

"Then what do you want to talk about? Actually, you should be convincing me to marry you," Raj teased.

"I can't think of any reason why anyone would want to marry me," Tanya chuckled.

"So you can't convince me?"

"I don't see any of the qualities in me that could make me the perfect wife. The other girls are pretty, they know how to run a house, and they know how to please a man. I don't. Really." She took another sip of wine.

"Give yourself a chance. Don't compare yourself to the other girls," he said and leaning and looking deep in her eyes.

The way he looked in her eyes scared her. She picked up her glass again and took a sip, just to break eye contact.

"Anyway, so tell me, what kind of a husband would you make, Mr. Right?"

"I'd say I am the 'imperfect' Mr. Right."

"Interesting. And why?"

"Dessert?" He didn't want to explain. He wanted her to find out. He wanted her to read him.

"No space for dessert, too much wine, too much food."

She seemed to understand and didn't press for an answer.

"I hope you had a good time."

"Fab time! Really."

"Me too."

They both got up and walked away from the table. Tanya seemed a bit unstable. Rahul held her hand and pulled her close as they tread on the rocks through the water. He held her hand as they walked back to the house, and once at the bottom of the stairs Tanya steadied herself and turned to Raj. "Thank you, I had a great time and I mean it," she said because she knew there was no one else listening in. A tiny camera captured this stolen moment.

Although she began to climb up the stairs alone, Raj followed her to her room. Once at the door, she smiled at him again and entered and closed the door behind her.

Tanya was drunk, but she wasn't so drunk that she could ignore the tiny flutter in her tummy. She stood at the door, petrified. What was she doing?

Karan Kapoor sat still. Tanya was the one. The other girls' elimination was just a formality. The game was over. The imperfect Mr Right had fallen in love. He picked up the phone and dialled Menon's number. This couldn't wait till tomorrow.

Back in the safety of his room, Rahul tried reviving the scent of Tanya. She smelt of lemon, peach, lavender, roses, but he still couldn't tell what perfume she was wearing. He closed his eyes, imagined her smile, her gaze. He stayed up all night. Tanya wouldn't let him sleep. To Tanya he was Rajsingh Jaiswal, but if it wasn't for Raj, he would have never got that close to Tanya. What was he going to do?

Chapter 21

Avinash Menon arrived before schedule and disappeared into Karan's room. After hearing from Karan Kapoor, he couldn't afford to wait. As soon as he got into Karan Kapoor's chamber, Menon exchanged quick pleasantries and got down to business. Karan picked up a remote control and played a DVD for Menon. They both stared at the screen, taking in each image. The silence continued until the screen turned an unmoving bright blue. They exchanged glances before Menon broke his silence.

"This cannot be the end of the story," Menon said in a calm voice. "Ashutosh will repackage the second episode to highlight the hostility. There's time. Karan, fix this. Before we go on air, I want Tanya out of the picture."

Menon was frantically punching something into his Blackberry. Karan stared at him, silently, wondering what was expected of him.

Menon continued to speak as he typed something out on his Blackberry. "The audience has to see Tanya as this pretentious person who is the vamp of this game. She is blowing hot and cold to win Raj over. It can be done with some intelligent editing." Menon sank back into the chair and lit up.

"She genuinely doesn't care about him. That's the twist here; she doesn't care and yet, Rajsingh manages to charm her.

Whatever is going on is extraordinary and our interference would ruin it," Karan tried to reason.

"What is really extraordinary about this show, Mr Kapoor, is the money I have put in it. If something like this," Menon pointed toward the TV, "is going on, I'll make it work to my advantage. There is a lot of hype around this show in the country. If anything makes it predictable right at the beginning, the show is over."

Menon let out a cloud of smoke which engulfed him. Karan saw a different side to Avinash Menon through the hazy shades of grey.

The performance was set for the evening. The girls decided to squeeze in one last rehearsal. Tanya danced like a puppet; the steps were right but there was no soul to her dancing. Simran pulled Tanya aside. "Was the date that bad?"

"Sorry?"

"You look miserable since your date with Raj. You don't have that glow, the one you get when you've had a fantastic first date. Was it that bad?" Simran aped Tanya's worried expression.

Tanya wasn't amused but she reassured her roommate. "Oh that! Yeah, it was alright… I just don't feel very well."

"Oh! Want to go see the doc?"

"Nah, it's just fatigue from all the dancing," Tanya lied, clutching at straws.

"In that case, you should go up and rest. We don't want you collapsing in the middle of the performance," Simran said firmly.

Tanya nodded and began walking towards the room. When she was about to go into the room, she heard Radhika. "Tanya, I heard your date went on for quite some time. Did you enjoy yourself?"

"Yeah, it was okay." Tanya didn't feel like talking to anyone, least of all to Radhika.

"Hmm… how do your chances of staying on the show look, *yaar*?"

Tanya didn't understand what Radhika meant, but she felt irritated. "Frankly, I don't know. Why don't you go and ask Raj?"

Radhika whispered, "Talk has been that since you're the simplest girl on the show, you don't score very high on looks. Maybe you want to work on that."

Radhika gave Tanya a fake, sympathetic smile. Tanya gave her an equally fake smile right back. "I don't want to work on anything, Radhika. I'd rather be myself now, so there are no surprises afterwards. That's what marriage is about — being yourself with your partner. But how would you know?" she snapped.

Radhika walked off in a huff. Tanya went into her room, her last statement rewinding and replaying itself in her head. She had never been interested in winning this show. However, she was suddenly filled with a fiery desire to win.

"Not for his money, not for his good looks but for who he is," a voice inside her head said. Tanya sat down, stunned by the revelation. She was falling for Raj. One date. That's all it had taken for Rajsingh to win her heart.

Sherry arrived a little while after her husband. She was excited about her judging duties for the evening. Her outfit, her make-up and her hair were all, as usual, impeccable. She decided to take a look into the chaos in the dressing room before going around to say hello to Rahul. She could feel the heads turn in awe as she walked past the girls, smiling and enquiring after them. She stopped to talk to a hair stylist she knew from before, she took a moment to compliment a girl on her brilliant outfit. Sherry's beauty and grace were effortless.

Sherry walked around the house, checking on things, making sure that everything was running smoothly. She didn't have to, but it was her way of establishing her importance. With her grace and style she hardly needed to. She made her way to the garden and just as she turned to go back into the house, she saw a figure crouching by a tree in the corner. She smiled when she guessed who it was. Without a second thought, Sherry crushed the tiny shrubs and plants outlining the lawn under her expensive heels and walked across to the figure. She put her hand on his shoulder.

"Don't worry it's just me." She wanted to surprise, not startle Rahul.

"Oh, hi! Is it time, already?" She could sense turmoil in his voice, but in his eyes she saw relief.

"The show starts in an hour. Aren't you getting ready?"

"I was wondering if you could help me pick something to wear." He looked like he needed rescuing.

"Sure, I'll help you. Let's go through your wardrobe." Sherry directed him towards the house.

Rahul remained silent till they entered the room. Sherry knew something was wrong. "There are no cameras in this room Rahul. Tell me what's going on," she demanded.

"Tell you what?" Rahul was bewildered. He was still lost in thought. He wasn't sure if he could share what he felt with anyone at all. Sherry was his friend, but she was also Menon's wife.

"I can see it. You don't need help with your clothes. Something's on your mind, so speak up!" She grabbed a box of tissues from the dresser and began wiping off the mud from her heels.

"I think I am falling in love," Rahul confessed.

Sherry looked up, shocked and then straightened up and eyed Rahul for a full minute. The awkward silence scared Rahul. Then she casually asked, "Who's the girl?"

"One of the contestants. I know I can trust you, so I will tell you this. She used to come to the mall... She doesn't recognise me, I assure you Sherry." There was desperation in his voice, "I am falling for her. Hell, I have fallen for her."

He looked up at Sherry, his eyes shining with excitement. Sherry looked away, to hide the worry in her eyes.

"Rahul, do you understand what you're saying? The fact that she knows you from before could result in her disqualification." Sherry's voice was full of concern.

Rahul shrugged. "That's the only thing that is keeping me from telling her everything. I need her here, Sherry. I need her to save me from this monster. I need someone to save me from Rajsingh Jaiswal..."

Rahul felt much lighter after having said it out loud, but he also realised the intensity of the situation. "Sherry, she might fall for Rajsingh, but that's not who I am. When the show's over, I am just an ordinary perfume salesman. What have I gotten myself into? What do I do?"

"First up, stop feeling so helpless. Play along. Rahul, even with Raj's name, this is who you are. You're this wonderful guy, even though you're just a salesman, your soul is the same, and let me tell you, when it comes to love, it is the soul that matters. And yes, you need to protect yourself against a monster. That monster is called Avinash Menon."

With that Sherry got up and turned to the door. "Don't ask me anything else. Just be very careful."

Rahul searched her face for an answer but Sherry opened the door and left.

The dance show was a straight-out-of-Bollywood extravaganza complete with elaborate dance sequences, jazzy outfits and *filmi* music. The girls glittered and sparkled on stage, vying for Rajsingh's attention. Rajsingh pretended to be entertained by the performances, while Rahul struggled with his emotions.

Sherry smiled, cheered and seemed to completely enjoy the show. The truth was that she was extremely curious to find out which one of the girls had stolen Rahul's heart.

She had almost given up by the time the last group came up on the stage to perform. Rahul's face lit up, and his eyes followed one girl throughout the performance. He smiled when she missed a step, he grinned when she goofed up. This girl had to be the one. Sherry was glad Rahul had found a friend he could call his own.

When Tanya's name did not figure on the list of girls getting disqualified that week, she wasn't surprised at all. She was looking forward to her next date with Rajsingh Jaiswal. She wanted to figure out why she had butterflies fluttering in her stomach every time she thought of him. Tanya tried to focus on the qualifying task for the week. It was a simple task but it also seemed too beauty pageantish for her liking. Even so, Tanya was looking forward to her personal interview with Raj and Karan. All the girls had been preparing for their interview; all the girls except Tanya. She was scheduled for an interview on Wednesday evening and even though it was already Wednesday noon, she was completely calm.

"You haven't prepared for the interview at all," Simran pointed out.

"What's there to prepare?" Tanya looked up from her book.

"It all comes so easily to you, doesn't it?" Simran snapped.

Tanya had been sensing hostility towards her in the house for a couple of days. She couldn't understand why her friends in the house had changed their attitude towards her. They had all been a little distant with her since Sunday.

"Who do you think you are to judge us for trying hard? What's with the 'Oh-I'm-so-myself' attitude? Let me tell you one thing, you are a bloody bore!" Simran stormed off into the bathroom, banging the door shut behind her.

Tanya was shocked at this outburst. She tried to organise the thoughts in her head for a minute and stalked into the bathroom. Simran was drawing a bath as if nothing had happened.

"What was that about?" Tanya demanded.

"Later, I am busy," Simran snapped.

"I don't care. I want to know where all that came from!" Tanya demanded.

"I am realising you are a fake. And I hate fake bitches."

Just a couple of days ago, the same girl had drawn a bath for her, helped with her clothes and now she hated her? Now she thought Tanya was a fake?

"Look, I don't know what I did to offend you." Tanya sat down on the closed toilet seat. "But this is no way to talk to me. If there is a problem tell me in a civilised manner. Don't yell and throw odd taunts at me."

Simran refused to be drawn out.

Tanya got up to leave. "And about the whole 'being myself' thing, I am not afraid of being me and if that bothers you, I am happy to not speak to you again."

Tanya slammed the door shut behind her, climbed into bed, took a deep breath and started reading again, as if nothing had happened. A little while later, Simran came out of the bathroom. She did her make-up, dried her hair, picked out clothes, and all the while she kept stealing glances at Tanya, hoping Tanya would say something. Tanya ignored her. Finally, she walked to Tanya's bed and sat down. "I am sorry. I just flipped. You know, PMS!" She rolled her eyes.

"Don't do it again." Tanya was not going to accept an apology.

"No really, everyone's going on about how Raj is smitten by you. And we all are here to win aren't we?" Simran got up and walked to the window.

"Right! I forgot that we are contestants on this show. We are not friends. Or are we just contestants who pretend to be friends?" Tanya's voice was flat and cold, just like it used to be when....

"Don't get me wrong. You told me that your date with Raj was okay, but we can all see how he can't take his eyes off you. We're all trying so hard to get his attention and you're so chilled out. The pressure doesn't even touch you. It pisses me off that you have his attention without putting in any effort," Simran confessed.

Tanya felt quite excited by the idea of Raj being smitten by her, but she felt a little irritated that Simran had jumped to conclusions.

"What pressure? I am on this show out of curiosity. I don't want to win it." Tanya knew she was lying, but she liked Simran.

"Why are you here then? Don't deny it. We all want to win this one. And after all, you shared your strategy with Radhika."

"Wait! What strategy?" Tanya was bewildered.

"Something about being yourself."

Tanya suddenly saw everything clearly. The girls saw her as a threat. And clearly, they had been discussing her. "It was just something I said in retaliation to her annoying comment. You should know better than to trust Radhika." Tanya was a little annoyed. Why couldn't Radhika mind her own business?

"I am sorry." Simran meant it.

"You'll be late for your interview. Good luck." Tanya went back to her book. But all she could think of was Raj.

Rahul sat through interview after interview, playing the sweet and charming Rajsingh Jaiswal, but in reality he was bored out of his mind. The girls were ready with monotonous, sugar-coated answers. He didn't even know what the point of this task was. The girls continued to wear masks and flaunt their beauty. They almost never meant what they said. He could tell that they were all playing to win. As soon as Simran walked in, Rahul felt refreshed. She was frank, she was real and she was extremely outspoken. Even though her answers were not genuine, at least they weren't sugar-coated. Rahul glanced at the schedule as Simran's interview wound up and smiled. Tanya was due for an interview in 15 minutes. He fixed himself a cup of coffee while Karan Kapoor tucked into the food.

Karan reviewed the fixed set of questions, even though he knew them by heart by now. He knew this interview was going to be a long one. He looked up at Rahul, who was trying to hide his excitement while sipping coffee. The anxiety and excitement had resulted in restlessness. Caffeine wasn't going to calm Rahul's nerves, Karan thought.

"Some chips?" Karan held out his plate.

Rahul just shook his head. Karan continued to munch. "Tanya is the only one remaining. If you're tired we can do this tomorrow."

"No!" Rahul almost screamed. "I mean we have to stick to the schedule, right?"

Karan smirked, unable to hide his amusement.

There was a knock on the door. An assistant director announced that Tanya was waiting outside. Karan glanced at his watch. "She's early. She can wait. I'll just finish my snack," Karan said, completely ignoring Rahul. He continued to eat the chips, one chip at a time.

Rahul realised this snack was going to take a long time to get finished. “May I?” Rahul picked up a few chips. “They are good!”

“I told you so.” Karan was trying hard to control his laughter. He couldn’t believe how school-boyish Rahul could get when it came to Tanya.

Within minutes, with help from Rahul, Karan finished the plate of chips. He rubbed his hands together and rang the bell, indicating they were ready.

Tanya walked in, tall and confident. She wasn’t that tall, it was just the way she held herself that made her look tall. Unlike the other girls, she had paid little attention to what she was wearing, there was not a trace of make-up on her face and she was not smiling ear-to-ear.

She walked to the chair and sat down nodding at Karan and Raj.

“Hello, Tanya. How are you doing?” Karan asked, wanting to break the awkward silence.

“Very well, thank you.”

“Shall we start?” Karan looked at Rahul and Tanya and down at his list of questions. Rahul, who had been looking intently at Tanya, tore his eyes off her and looked at Karan.

“Absolutely.” He turned back to Tanya. Her left eyebrow shot up in a questioning glance.

“How does it feel to be on this show?” Karan asked.

“Before I give my answers, I want to know, from both of you, whether you want me to be frank or you want me to sugar-coat the answers?”

Before Karan could say anything, Rahul responded. “Frankly we have had enough sugar to give us diabetes.”

Both Raj and Karan laughed, but Tanya just smiled and answered Karan’s question. “The show is interesting to look at from the outside, but when you are on it, it’s a bit overwhelming.”

“Overwhelming?” Karan asked.

“One minute you think the contestants are your friends and

then you realise they are your competitors. You are trying to woo a man. This man can interview you, date you and you go all out to dress up and pretend to be perfect just so he likes you. I mean, what about us liking him? We deserve a chance to question him too, or does the channel assume we have no expectations from a life partner?" Tanya looked straight into Karan's eyes.

Karan had always thought of Tanya as a coy, quiet girl. But he could see now, how fiery her opinions were. She was assertive, she was powerful and she knew how to get her point across. This girl was a firecracker.

"The channel knows your expectations — an eligible NRI bachelor who is extremely well-to-do," Karan explained.

"You think that's all we want? It is important for us to know his attitudes, his preferences, his traits, his strengths, his weaknesses and so many other things. If all we want is a rich, good-looking NRI, then all Raj really wants is a pretty Indian girl, with great social skills. But Raj is trying to figure us out. He is trying to get to know us, isn't he? We deserve a chance to figure him out too. For all you know, he could be a phony, just pretending to be a millionaire."

Karan froze in his chair, while Rahul scanned her fiery eyes for something she had remembered and hadn't shared. "That is a serious allegation. What makes you think he might be a phony?"

"Ok! I am exaggerating. Sorry Raj, no offense but you could be psycho, you could be depressive, you could be an alcoholic. Come on, this picture you paint, it's too good to be true. If you want to share your life with one of the girls, you've got to put what you've got, good or bad, on the table." Tanya had regained her boardroom confidence.

Rahul took a moment and tapped his pencil on the table. "I could try to put it on the table, and you girls will see right through it. All of you are blinded by the life I promise to give you. I bet you, you would accept me even if I was a pervert," Rahul said rather smugly.

"Sorry Raj, that's a disgusting attitude to have. But what else can one expect from someone who has to depend on a TV show to find himself a wife." Tanya relaxed in her chair and rolled her eyes. She detested Raj, and it hurt Rahul to see that disdainful look in her eyes.

"I am sorry, Miss Kher; if you think this is all disgusting why be a part of it? Didn't you come here to play this disgusting game? You can't judge the game and play it too."

"Like I said earlier I came out of curiosity." She leaned on the table, her arms folded, gazing straight at Raj.

"Curiosity or not, you came, Miss Kher, you are playing the game," he said looking straight into her eyes, "and you have to play it by the rules."

Tanya thought she saw hurt under his cool gaze.

"Now, now, this was to be an interview not a debate!" Karan Kapoor made his presence felt. "Shall we get back to the interview?"

Both Rahul and Tanya tried to recover from the outburst as they nodded, not breaking eye contact with each other.

Karan Kapoor asked questions from a sheet to which Tanya replied in a plain disinterested voice. Rahul barely heard what she said. He kept his eyes on her but his mind was racing. Had she recognised him? Was she trying to get the truth out of him? Did she know what was going on?

"Do you have any other questions? Raj?" Karan asked.

"No, I think that's it."

"In that case, thank you Tanya, and good luck."

"Thanks." Tanya got up expecting Raj to say something. When he said nothing, she left the room.

"I guess she's on the danger list then?"

"What?"

"The danger list. Don't you want her to go out? She clearly seems to hate the game." Karan knew Rahul wasn't going to throw her out, but he wanted to pry a little. Rahul looked into one of the cameras. "No, I think she's an interesting person. All the others are too sweet and unreal; it's good to have this dynamite here."

"Rahul, tell me something," said Karan looking into Rahul's eyes. "Do you like her?"

Rahul looked away from the camera and hesitated a little. "Yeah, she's different."

Karan Kapoor got up and asked Rahul to follow him. Once in the garden, Karan turned around to ensure that there were no cameras around. But before Karan could speak, Rahul asked him, "Why would you want to know if I like her?"

"Because you seem to have made your mind up about her." Karan decided to be honest with Rahul.

"I am eventually supposed to choose a girl, so what's wrong?"

"Rajsingh is supposed to keep the audience guessing. This is not Rahul's love-story. It is Rajsingh's TV show," Karan explained.

"You mean to say, you could tell I'm in love with her?" Rahul frowned nervously.

Karan Kapoor was startled. He'd expected it to be a crush but love was an entirely different ballgame.

"Rahul, between you and me, you know what you've gotten into, right?"

"I don't know Karan… I really don't." Rahul sat down on one of the benches in the garden.

"You are on this show. She doesn't even know the real you. You do know that you're probably going to get hurt here, not to mention, her feelings are at stake too!"

"You think I haven't thought about that? Of course, I know I am going down a dangerous path. It's impossible to find reason when you're in love."

Karan sat down next to Rahul. "Yes, my experience, especially in films, has taught me that. What can I say, Rahul!"

"Just don't say anything. Leave me alone to deal with it."

"I can't. I am hosting this show and I can't let you kill the show, but that is something I'm saying in the professional context. Look, young man, I like you and I can't watch you hurt yourself either," he explained. He put a hand on Rahul's shoulder.

Rahul looked straight into Kapoor's eyes. In a curious mixture of Raj and Rahul he said firmly, "Professionally, I can revive the interest in the show. I will try and act very pally with the other girls too. But on a personal level, it's too late to back out." With that, he got up and walked away.

Karan sat on the bench for a while. He said a silent prayer, asking God to give Rahul the strength to deal with the mess he had gotten himself into.

Chapter 22

After the disastrous interview with Karan and Raj, Tanya was convinced it was time to head home. Somehow, she didn't like the idea so much anymore. She wanted to stay and she wanted to play this game, Raj's game. Tanya was surprised and to an extent scared that she wanted to fight to the end. But she knew she had crossed the line and there was no way back. After hurting his ego yet again, there was no way in hell that he was going to want her on the show. After all, she had called him a 'phony'.

She knew Karan would definitely not forget to evaluate her on the disastrous interview. The 'friends' who'd been distant were suddenly hovering around her. They wanted to share beauty tips, lend their advice and be her best buddies. Tanya couldn't figure out what was happening and she really didn't care. It was Saturday and there was a party organised for the girls. Tanya was dreading the party.

"Consider it a farewell gig for those who go out tomorrow," Raj had written on the invitation note that came to each girl. Somehow, Tanya felt like the note was meant only for her.

"Thank you, Raj," Tanya thought and threw the invitation on the bedside table behind her. She grabbed her diary and her pen and started writing. She had found that she was at peace when she was writing. Her thoughts flowed effortlessly from her head onto the paper. They didn't have a chance to stop and confuse her. They didn't get a chance to trouble her. They flowed with ease, almost therapeutically.

She thought about Raj all the time, and thinking about him bothered her. Although her poetry revolved around him, it didn't trouble her. She could put her random thoughts in the book and forget all about it.

Simran suddenly burst through the door, startling Tanya. Simran was flaunting her perfectly toned body in a bikini and a sarong that was barely covering wet body. "We are so stupid! We thought we'd beat the heat but look, look what the sun's done to us!" she yelled.

Tanya didn't care if they beat the heat or the heat beat them. Tanya wanted her solitude.

Simran had asked Tanya if she'd like to go swimming with them and Tanya had declined. She had no intention of getting into a swimsuit for television. She was sure the crew was going to cover that bit of the event elaborately. Tanya had chosen to be alone in her room instead. Seeing Simran's brownish pink face, she was convinced she'd done the right thing.

"This sucks! What do I do Tanya? Say something!"

"I don't know. You're the beauty expert. I am sure you have some face mask or some concoction to fix that."

"Good idea… I'll borrow some stuff from the kitchen!" She ran out.

Tanya couldn't help but marvel at the change in Simran's attitude. Two days ago, Tanya had been a boring person and now, she rocked! There was a huge commotion outside the bedroom door. Tanya peeped out to check if everything was ok. The girls were running all over the place, some in their bathing suits, some in bathrobes and some were carrying some fancy clothes on hangers. The party wasn't until four hours later, but everyone was acting like it was the end of the world. Tanya felt insane standing in the middle of the chaos. She decided to take a walk.

The sun was blazing even though it was almost five in the evening. The air was humid. Tanya had to admit that a walk was a bad idea. She decided to sit by the pool till the chaos in the house died down. With its green cover, it would be a cool place to get her thoughts together, she figured. She sighed when she entered the pool area. It was a mess with used towels, glasses and random things lying all over the place. She felt irritated. The girls were irresponsible. How could they not clean up after themselves? She was just strolling around the pool when someone pushed her. She nearly fell into the pool, but managed to balance herself and turn around. There stood Radhika, an apologetic smile on her face. Unfortunately, Radhika's face pushed Tanya's irritation level further up.

"I am so sorry, I just came to get my stuff," she apologised as she walked past Tanya and retrieved a towel and a bottle of cream from one of the benches. She tiptoed back towards Tanya and stood a moment. "Don't be so depressed!" she said as if she was consoling Tanya and suddenly, out of the blue, she hugged Tanya. Tanya flinched and moved out of her arms.

"Why would I be depressed?" Tanya asked, flaring up.

"We all heard," Radhika said, nodding sympathetically, "how bad your interview was. PMS, was it?"

"Whatever it was, I don't really care. But how did you know?"

"The crew, they sort of mentioned it. I can't imagine anyone ever fighting with Raj. He just seems so, so sweet!" Radhika was convinced that Tanya had done something terrible to have managed to have a fight with the sweet, sweet millionaire.

"Radhika, I think you should go and get dressed. The party is in a couple of hours." Tanya looked away, in dismissal.

"I think you should go and pack your bags, rather than telling people what they should be doing!" Radhika flashed one more of her fake smiles.

That was the last straw. Tanya felt infuriated. She had to grit her teeth to keep from pushing Radhika into the pool. Everyone's business was Radhika's business and someone needed to put the bitch in her place. And then, a sudden realisation hit Tanya. The other girls were being nice to Tanya because she was not a threat anymore. She felt defeated. She didn't even notice Radhika walk away with a smirk on her face. Tanya slumped down on the bench.

"Maybe they are being nice and I am being cynical," she thought to herself, but she was convinced that was not the case.

Tanya walked back to the room, hoping to take a shower before attending her own farewell. She felt empty. As soon as she walked into the room, a strong smell coming from the bathroom stoked her anger. She checked what was going on in the bathroom, to find Simran, still in her bikini but her body covered with a whitish paste.

"Sour yoghurt, cucumber and *besan* paste. It is supposed to reverse a tan. I hope it works."

"I came back to take a shower." Tanya wasn't interested in Simran's fake show of friendliness.

"Oh! I am going to take at least an hour more. I have to get ready for the party,"

"It's 7," Tanya said, trying not to lose her temper.

"I know. It's a bit tight, but make-up takes hardly any time."

"I can't take a shower until 8 then," she said, hoping Simran would get the hint and try to hurry up.

"Kinda, but babes, I have a party to go to." She looked at Tanya and shrugged her shoulders.

"Are you forgetting that I have to go to the party too?"

"I know, but it barely takes you 15 minutes to get ready!"

"That is not the point here, Simran. I was outside taking a walk for two hours, hoping that your beauty treatment would be over by the time I got back. Be a little considerate."

Tanya walked out. She picked out the clothes she was going to wear, a simple black cocktail dress with a hint of shimmer. She lined up the shoes and jewellery and sat on her bed waiting for Simran to get done. At 7.30 she heard the shower switched on and in twenty minutes, Simran was out of the bathroom. "I'm sorry, Tanya."

Tanya just went inside the bathroom, ignoring her apology. She was glad she was going to be rejected by Raj tomorrow. The circus was getting to her. But as soon as the shower sprayed beads of cool water on her back, Tanya realised that she wanted to get all dressed up for the evening. Before her thoughts could confuse her further, she grabbed the soap and busied herself with the act of scrubbing herself clean. She was wondering why she was surprised. What had she expected of these girls? They were competing for a rich man's attention. Why was she looking for friends here? She switched off the shower and decided to stop thinking for a bit. She was fatigued by her hyperactive brain.

Simran's hair and make-up were almost done when Tanya stepped out of the bathroom. Tanya busied herself with blow drying her hair. Once she was done with her hair she dabbed on a foundation and used a bit of kohl on her eyes. She finished it up with a light glossy lipstick. As she pulled her dress on, she had a little trouble zipping up the back.

"Let me help." Simran came up from behind Tanya. Tanya didn't protest.

"I know you are mad at me about the whole outburst last week. Look, I am sorry about it, really. There is so much pressure." She zipped the dress up and locked the zip.

"It's okay. I understand," Tanya said reluctantly.

"No, you don't. I can see it. You're still mad at me."

"Seriously. I am not. I don't care." Tanya wore her earrings.

"And why is that?" Simran asked while checking her own make-up in the mirror.

"It's probably my last day on the show and I don't intend to spend it worrying about these things," Tanya said as she slipped into her shoes.

"Your last day? It could be any five of us who go home. Stop being so negative!"

"Don't pretend you don't know how disastrous my interview was," Tanya said scanning Simran's face for guilt, but Simran simply frowned.

"Yeah, Radhika did say something about it. But I should know better than to trust her. Right?" She was smiling at Tanya.

Tanya could see right through her own cynicism. She smiled too. "It's silly, this game. I am sorry too."

Tanya didn't like who she was becoming on this show. She realised that Simran looked a lot less tanned than before. "Nice tan!" Tanya said with a wide grin.

"Thanks, now let's go have fun." Simran sprayed perfume on herself and offered it to Tanya.

Tanya pulled out her own bottle from her bag and waved it at her. Both the girls took one last glance at themselves in the mirror and confidently strode out of the room.

They entered the common room. This was the same room where Tanya had first seen Raj and hated the sight of him. The periphery of the hall was lined with food-tables and in the far corner of the room was a very crowded table.

"No points for guessing where the bar is," she muttered to Simran. Pastel satins adorned all the tables and walls. Raj and Karan were nowhere to be seen. Tanya saw the crew setting up their equipment around the room. She really felt sorry for them. They deserved a chance to let their hair down too. They had been working hard through the last few weeks.

"You guys should join the party too. You deserve a break," Tanya screamed over the loud music to the two guys manning a camera in one corner.

"Thanks, but when you got to work, you got to work," one of them replied with a smile. They had been with the contestants right from the start, and yet, the girls hardly ever spoke to them.

Tanya walked over to the drinks table. Simran and Pallak had managed to get themselves drinks. The music was too loud to talk.

"We don't need music that loud. This isn't a disco and we're not teenagers." Simran sipped her drink and stormed off towards the DJ console.

"There she goes, God save the DJ!" Pallak said sipping orange juice, "So, Tanya, how are things with you. You have been awfully quiet through this week."

"Yeah, everyone has phases," she replied and smiled at Pallak.

The music suddenly turned much softer. They glanced towards the DJ. Simran was walking back towards them triumphantly. The girls casually chatted as Radhika joined them.

"Hello girls!" she screeched oblivious to the irritated look the girls exchanged amongst themselves. "Fun party, no?"

"Very," Simran replied imitating the fake excitement.

Tanya looked away at the other girls. She had no intention of talking to Radhika. Shehnaz entered the room with a bunch of girls — Khushi, Megha and Priya. She was wearing a skimpy black dress and she looked extremely glamorous. She could really carry off skimpy dresses without looking trashy. Tanya felt jealous of Shehnaz's beauty. She always felt green with envy every time Shehnaz was around.

"She makes me want to go hide under a table. How can she look so pretty, even when she's so tanned?" Pallak complained.

"She's very sweet though. She's agreed to lend me her dress for one of the dates next week," Radhika boasted and waved to the Shehnaz pack.

"Yeah, that's because she's sure you'd look like a clown in her expensive dresses," Simran smirked but Radhika didn't hear her. She had already started walking towards Shehnaz.

"She didn't hear you. What a waste!" Tanya said.

"There is always next time. Radhika can annoy Simran very easily," Pallak reassured Tanya.

"Shall we go eat something? I am starving." Tanya was eyeing the food counter. There were some nice kebabs, salads, curries and *biryani*. Tanya helped herself to all of it, while Pallak and Simran stuck to the salads.

Shehnaz came over to Tanya and looked at her plate.

"Hey, you've got an appetite! I can't imagine eating all that oily stuff without wincing about the weight I might put on," she gushed as she picked a slice of cucumber from Tanya's plate.

"Well, luckily I don't care about that." Tanya helped herself to some more *biryani*. "My friends were wondering how you manage to look so gorgeous despite the tan."

"Yeah, I heard that." She was still pecking at the cucumber. "Radhika brings all the news to us."

"God, that girl!" Tanya couldn't help but be annoyed that Radhika thought it important to report such small things. Shehnaz laughed and walked away.

Tanya quietly finished the rest of her food. She got herself a glass of water and she looked around. Raj had still not arrived. He was trying to be fashionably late.

She helped herself to another drink and eased her way through idle conversations, sipping a vodka tonic. If it was her last party in the house, she wanted to make the best of it. Before she knew it, she had downed quite a few drinks and was feeling breezy.

"I should stop," she told herself but continued to drink. Tanya was at the bar getting herself another drink when she heard a commotion behind her. She turned around and saw him enter the room. The girls crowded around him, and he smiled at them, apologising for being the last one to arrive.

Raj socialised and mingled as he made his way to the bar. He got a drink for Shehnaz. They spent quite some time chatting at the bar. Tanya felt another twinge of jealousy. However, this feeling was one she'd never had before. Tanya tipped her head to one side and watched Shehnaz being led toward the dance floor. She saw them dance and saw how perfect they looked.

Tanya kept staring at Raj, as he danced with every girl. He didn't look at Tanya even once. She felt lonely. Tanya felt sorry for herself. She never thought she'd be the girl to stand in a corner while everyone around her danced. What did she expect? She was a boring media planner, who was looking to find excitement on a reality TV show. This was where she belonged — outside the dance floor. She walked to the bar to get another drink. It was better to drown yourself in alcohol than drowning in self-pity, she told herself. She was halfway through her drink when she felt a warm hand on her arm.

"Dance with me?" It was Raj, standing right next to her looking deep into her eyes.

Tanya wanted to say no, but she found herself following him to the dance floor. She danced with him, enjoying how he held her in his arms. She loved how he pushed her away and then pulled her close. She almost felt her heart melt when he held her close and his warm breath brushed her neck. The other girls cheered and clapped as he twirled Tanya around. When the music stopped, he smiled at Tanya and walked away. She stood alone on the dance floor as he went over to Shehnaz. Tanya decided that she had to leave the party.

She waved goodbye to Pallak and Simran who were now having a blast on the dance floor and headed back to the room.

Once in the room, she tried to forget the sad, hollow feeling in her heart. Raj was smitten by Shehnaz. Tanya was nothing to him. Tanya felt another pang as she remembered the wonderful date they'd had. And then she cringed as she thought of all the horrid things she said to him during the interview with Karan. Just as she fell asleep, her last thought was that she had brought this upon herself.

Tanya opened her eyes to bright sunlight filtering through the curtain. She pulled up the sheets to cover her eyes. Her head was throbbing, her eyelids were heavy and she felt completely miserable.

She remembered all the drinks she had downed the night before and cringed. She hated hangovers. Tanya pushed herself out of the bed. She took a shower, which made her feel better, but only slightly. Simran was still fast asleep. Tanya made her way down to the kitchen. The house was eerily quiet. She felt like a ghost as she found the humungous fridge in the pantry and got herself a big bottle of chilled water and an apple. The party had gone on until late. The whole house was asleep, even the kitchen staff. The common room had a hangover too. It was messy.

The satin drapes were dangling from the walls, glasses and plates were all over the place. She wished she could help the staff clear the mess, but her throbbing head interfered with that thought. She didn't feel like eating the apple. She wanted something substantial. She went back into the pantry and found herself some leftovers from the party. Satisfied with a small helping of ice-cold biryani, Tanya decided to get some more sleep.

The day had started late. And all the residents of Jaiswal mansion were trying to rush through their schedule. The elimination process was running a couple of hours late but Rahul seemed unfazed by the delay. He waited in the study, cameras fixed on him as he evaluated each girl with Karan. He seemed animated and jovial as he went through the remaining girls. Karan then reconfirmed each one of the ten names that were placed in the danger zone.

"Let's have them come in?" Karan asked Ashutosh.

"That'll make it more dramatic. You ok with that na, Raj?" Ashutosh was the only one who knew Raj's secret among the Cee crew, but he referred to Rahul as Raj, so that he didn't accidentally call him Rahul in front of the crew.

Rahul nodded. After a few minutes, the girls started walking in. Tanya was the last one to come in. Her eyes were red and her face slightly swollen. He knew she'd had a lot to drink the day before. He wondered if he should offer her some coffee, but decided against it. Rahul forced himself to look at the other girls. They all looked nervous, and yet, managed to smile at him when they caught his eye. They didn't need to be told that they were in the danger zone, but as a formality Karan announced that they were in the danger zone. The girls gasped and faked stress for the camera. Rahul was amazed at their ability to pretend. Even though he had made up his mind about the five he'd be sending home, for the camera, he had to pretend to evaluate the ten girls and then make his decision.

Raj glanced at each of the girls, trying to remember the times they had spent together. He turned to Karan, "I'm ready."

Raj and Karan walked out of the room. The girls started talking amongst themselves. Radhika was the loudest of them all. She expressed her outrage to the camera. "I can't believe I am here. We've had such lovely dates."

Tanya had no problem believing she was there and she had already packed her bags. She had had enough of the game, Raj and the gossip. She didn't like how cynical the game had made her, she didn't like how she was longing to stay back and worst of all, she didn't like how Raj had made her feel last night. She didn't want any of it. Not anymore.

Karan came back into the room and there was a haunting silence as all the conversations stopped. The girls stared at his face nervously. Karan called out five names, including Tanya and Radhika. The girls got up. Tanya wasn't surprised, even though the other four looked crestfallen. Tanya took comfort in the fact that Radhika was getting out with her. "Radhika doesn't deserve to stay. She doesn't deserve to be Mrs Rajsingh Jaiwal," thought Tanya.

Karan Kapoor turned to the girls, looked at them and smiled.

"How does it feel girls? How does it feel to be the lucky five who are not going to be eliminated today?"

The girls looked up, completely bewildered.

"That's right." Karan turned to the five girls seated comfortably on the chairs. "Sorry girls, your quest for Mr. Right ends right here."

Tanya stared at Karan Kapoor in disbelief. He looked at her and gave her a reassuring nod. She didn't know what to make of his nod.

The five girls who were staying were sent out while the girls scheduled to leave were asked to wait for their last conversation with the camera. Rajsingh Jaiswal had once again taken Tanya by surprise.

Chapter 23

Rahul assumed that sharing his feelings for Tanya with Karan would make his heart lighter, but he discovered that his feelings weren't in the interest of the channel. Sherry and Karan had both warned him about this. Karan suggested that he put Tanya in the danger zone. "It will make sure that your real feelings aren't seen. Menon will be convinced that she's not a threat," Karan explained.

Rahul expected Tanya to be shocked about being in the danger zone, but she seemed rather unfazed. He saw surprise on her face when Karan announced she was staying. He wanted to surprise the audience and the channel. He didn't know why she was so surprised that she was staying. Rahul wanted to tell her that she was in the danger zone only because he had wanted to protect her, but that was not an option, Karan had made that clear.

Rahul forced himself to come back to the task at hand. Fifteen contestants were divided into teams of three and put in charge of the house for that day. They were to supervise, instruct and if need be, step in and make sure the house was being run smoothly. Their duties included checking kitchen supplies, finalising the meals for the day, getting the house cleaned, managing gardening, laundry and so on. Each team had to report back to Raj and Karan at the end of the day. They would discuss their activities through the day. The purpose of this exercise was to judge the girls' domestic skills. And of course there was a part that Rahul most dreaded — dates. He really didn't know how to fight the extreme boredom he felt at most of them.

Rahul looked through the notes he'd made while speaking to the team that was running the house that day. Shehnaz had no idea about managing a house, nor did she have any idea on how money was managed. Her team-mates, Pallak and Radhika complained that although she had no idea, she insisted on being the leader and meddled in everything. Lunch had not been served on time because the supplies didn't arrive. The washing machines were loaded too late and they were still whirring in the basement, which meant the laundry wasn't going to be ready in time. All in all, the Tuesday team had done a really lousy job. The Monday team had managed to finish their jobs, even though they did so with great difficulty and after a lot of fights.

He finished the meeting and geared up for his Tuesday date. He glanced at the schedule. The 8 p.m. slot for Tuesday read Khushi. He took a deep breath and set out.

Tanya was sitting with her team-mates for the week, Janaki and Priya. They were planning out how they were going to manage their chores through the day. Tanya was nervous. She had seen the toughest of the girls break down under the pressure of managing the mansion. The Tuesday team had such a hard time completing the tasks that the usually chirpy gossip queen Radhika almost cried.

"Don't you miss Aditi and Madhura? They were good at this sort of thing!" Janaki spoke as she doodled.

"I miss Madhura, she used to be my room-mate. Aditi not so much," Priya said with sly grin.

Tanya was silent. She didn't miss anyone.

"Anyway back to the task!" Tanya picked up her pen and scribbled. They divided the chores into departments and put each one in charge of a department best suited to her abilities. Priya and Janaki weren't very convinced about Tanya's divide and delegate method, but given the time constraints, it made sense to divide and delegate.

Once the departments were allotted, Janaki stretched out on the bed.

"Hey! Look, Khushi and Raj!" Priya screamed as she casually glanced out the window overlooking the garden. Janaki jumped out of the bed and dashed for the window. Tanya insisted to herself that she wasn't interested.

"I'm quite tired. I'll head to my room I think," she said.

Once she was back in her room, she scribbled into her book. "Damn you writer's block," she thought. Tanya decided to go through her plan for the next day. No matter what she did, she couldn't stop thinking about Raj and Khushi. She walked to the window and looked down at the garden. She spotted Raj and Khushi strolling through the garden. They seemed to be enjoying each other's company. Just as they came near the house, a sudden breeze blew over them, messing up Raj's hair. Khushi reached out and smoothed his hair back in place. They looked at each other, like they were about to kiss and suddenly Raj's eyes went up to the window. He saw Tanya, and their eyes met for a second. He looked at Khushi and looked back at the window again. A strange awkwardness overtook him and he ushered Khushi toward the house. Khushi glanced up. Tanya could feel the anger in Khushi's eyes. Tanya wasn't feeling apologetic for ruining the moment for Khushi. In fact, Tanya had a faint smile on her lips.

* * * * * *

Tanya didn't have time to breathe on Wednesday. She had to take care of the budget, help with the menu and supervise the setting for Raj's lunch and dinner dates for that day. She also had to make sure the pool was cleaned. She had to take an inventory of what needed to be ordered for the house. Tanya eased through these tasks one by one, without hitting the panic button. At noon, she realised she had done nothing about the lunch setting in the private dining room. There was a whole lot that needed to be done. There was no help to spare as Priya and Janaki were using all the manpower they had in the laundry and kitchen respectively. When Tanya went to them about the lunch, they promised to send someone within a couple of minutes. Tanya decided to go ahead and start prepping anyway. Tanya moved the table and chair and then climbed up on one of the chairs to pin some drapes in place. Once that was done, she rushed to the kitchen to make sure the special lunch order from Raj was under preparation, grabbed some plates, candles, cutlery, tablecloths and napkins. She had no idea how to set a table. So she laid out the tablecloth, and left the rest to the help that would come. She switched on the air conditioning before managing to acquire a vase and some flowers. Once she'd made sure the floor was clean, she sat down to breathe. Helpers arrived and she fired instructions to them.

It was only when she was supervising the setting that she realised she was getting things ready for Raj's date with another girl. She felt slightly annoyed. Tanya had stressed, rushed and troubled herself for someone else to enjoy their date with a man she herself was vying for. She looked down at her to-do list. There was no time to brood, she had a lot to do. She reluctantly filled out the shopping list for the week. She managed to order all the food items and in addition to that, disinfectants, detergents and room fresheners, in the given budget. She smiled to herself and went down to lunch.

After lunch, Tanya got busy getting the pool cleaned and she checked on her team-mates, when she could. They seemed to be well in control. By six o'clock, dinner was being cooked, laundry was done and sent out for ironing, Priya had taken over the cleaning of rooms and was almost half way through. Tanya's helpers were almost done cleaning the pool.

"We aren't doing badly at all!" Priya chuckled with surprise.

"I know! Planning in advance helped. Three cheers for you, Tanya!" Janaki started clapping and cheering.

"Come on girls, we have a lot many rooms left to be cleaned, dinner to be laid out and the pool to be finished.... So let's get back." Tanya gave each of the girls a high five and ran to the pool.

By eight that evening, everything on the checklist had been taken care of and the supplies had arrived.

The girls settled into the couch opposite Karan and Raj to discuss their day. Tanya could hardly take her eyes off Raj. There was something intriguing about his eyes. She felt like she'd known him for a long time... a past life, perhaps.

"So far, yours is the only team to have finished their tasks so well and within the given time. Also, you've managed to order everything needed within the budget. And for the first time we have team-mates giving credit to each other. So far, everyone was blaming each other and squabbling," Karan Kapoor spoke into the camera with a smile.

"It's team effort. I was lucky to be with two great managers!" Tanya smiled at the girls, who blew her a flying kiss each.

"Well, you three make a formidable team! You get the highest points so far. Unless tomorrow's group outdoes your exemplary performance, you girls will be the high scorers in this task," Raj stated matter-of-factly taking little interest in any of the girls.

Tanya searched for a flicker of a smile meant just for her but she got nothing. "Why did he choose to keep me here?" she wondered again as she walked back to her room. She was too tired to take a shower, so she just went straight to bed.

"Big date today?" Priya asked Simran and Tanya at breakfast.

"Yup. This afternoon." Tanya took a bite of her scrambled eggs on toast.

"You should be getting ready then. It's already 10 a.m.!"

"Our girl's motto is to keep it simple. She never takes more than half an hour to get ready," Simran said as she nudged Tanya. Simran took another reluctant spoon of her oatmeal porridge.

"Pull my leg all you want. I just don't have the skill or patience to paint my face. Even if I try, it always goes horribly wrong," said Tanya helping herself to another toast and buttering it, as Priya looked on in horror.

"Don't look so horrified. I am a real girl with a real appetite," Tanya said as she bit into her toast.

"Anyway, I have to get back to my tasks," Simran said. "You girls have raised the bar with the way you managed the house." She winked at Tanya and started towards the kitchen.

Tanya finished her coffee and thought about her date. She was quite excited about seeing Raj.

She drew herself a bath. Today's beauty treatment was going to be a flashback of the last time, when Simran introduced her to the concept of exfoliation, moisturisation and more. She applied the gooey face-mask imitating Simran's strokes from memory. She soaked herself in the bath for a while and then peeled off the mask. Once out of the bath, she looked at the clothes she had picked and shook her head before putting them back in the cupboard. She looked through her stuff, only to find that she had hardly any new clothes left. She found a floral skirt that Anita had put in at the last minute despite Tanya's refusal to carry it. She felt homesick, and held the skirt for a moment before putting it on.

She wore a white sleeveless shirt and blow dried her hair before pulling it back in a neat, unpretentious pony-tail. She tried out at least four different earrings before settling for a dainty silver pair. She dabbed some foundation on and powdered her face. She lined her lips and filled them in with a rich wine colored lipstick. She pouted her lips and blew herself a kiss and smiled.

She tapped all of Simran's bottles on the dressing table before finding the perfume she was looking for. She sprayed some in the air, but seemed not to like it. She turned around and hunted in her own bag. She found a jasmine body spray and sprayed it on herself. She took one last look at herself in the mirror and put her glasses on.

"Perfect," she thought. 'This is just me!'

She set out for her date and as usual she was running

15 minutes ahead of the schedule. She bumped into Simran on her way down. "Good luck!" she said as she zipped past Tanya to their room.

As soon as Simran got back to the room, she was shocked. The dressing table was a mess, Tanya's clothes were all over the place and the bathtub wasn't drained. It was very unlike Tanya to leave the room in such a mess. Simran didn't mind, she'd left the room like this several times and it was okay if Tanya did it once. But she found it odd.

Tanya was waiting in the room, expecting Raj to show up. It was well over fifteen minutes since she'd arrived. She felt slightly restless.

Rahul knew that she was waiting. "I'll be down in ten," he told Deepak who had popped in to announce Tanya's arrival. Rahul took his own sweet time to button up his shirt. He patiently smoothed his dishevelled hair down and stared into the mirror. Rahul folded his sleeves up as he thought about the date.

Tanya played with a strand of her hair and glanced at her watch. She was restless. Five minutes later, Raj walked into the dining room and smiled at Tanya. To him she looked like the old Tanya, the one he saw from behind the glass counter at the mall. As soon as their eyes met she smiled and got up.

"I am sorry to have kept you waiting. Business calls!" Raj apologised. It didn't sound like he meant it but Tanya was too excited to see him to sense that.

"I understand," Tanya replied softly. "I know how it feels to have work follow you on vacation."

"Ah of course, you used to be a workaholic." Raj poured out some orange juice from the bar. "What can I get you to drink, Tanya?"

Tanya loved the way he said her name. "Apple juice, please."

"Sure you don't want some wine? I prefer not to drink during the day but you're free to have a glass,"

"Apple juice is just fine," she said again. She realised she hadn't stopped smiling since he'd come into the private dining room.

Raj brought back the two glasses and placed hers by her plate. “I suppose you must be tired after all that hard work,” Raj asked as he sipped from his glass.

“Not really. My part of the work wasn’t physically taxing.”

“And allotting the budget was a cakewalk?”

“Of course,” she laughed, relishing the apple juice Raj got for her.

In the editing room, Karan Kapoor saw the cold vibes between them.

“*Thanda hai*, the date is not rocking enough!” one of the assistant directors said.

Karan just nodded. He was amused at the great performance Rahul was putting up for the camera. He knew the cold vibes were a sham.

“If the date doesn’t seem to be interesting, the crew just abandons it. They usually decide whether a date is hot or not within the first ten to fifteen minutes,” Karan had told Rahul. Rahul wanted a private date with Tanya and he was making sure he got just that.

“*Bilkool*, absolutely. I think we are wasting our time. Just take enough footage to describe the date,” Karan suggested with a sly smile.

Rahul loved seeing Tanya smile. He hated that he had to be curt with her, but he had to pretend for the cameras. Rahul was enjoying their simple conversation over a simple meal of *dal*-rice. He loved how excited Tanya was to eat the simple meal.

“I miss the *dal* my sister-in-law makes. This is the best comfort food ever,” Tanya exclaimed as soon as Raj apologised for the simple fare they were about to eat. Raj hadn’t mirrored her excitement. He just pushed food around on his plate. Rahul, however, wanted to know more about her sister-in-law, her family, her friends, but he couldn’t risk letting Menon in on what was happening.

Tanya looked up at Raj. She couldn’t understand why he was being so cold to her. She felt rather silly. She decided to stop talking for a bit.

"Dessert?" Raj asked her.

"No, thank you," she said rather gloomily. Raj noticed.

"Maybe we could use a walk."

She stared at her watch and looked back at Raj. "It's three in the afternoon! A walk in this blazing sun?"

He smiled at her and that smile made her concerns melt away. She smiled back and got up. Raj ushered her out of the private dining room and looked up and down the corridor. Tanya started walking towards the door that led to the garden, but suddenly Raj grabbed her hand and pulled her in the opposite direction.

"There's no one here and no cameras either. Run!" Raj said in an excited tone.

Tanya couldn't believe it. "Is this the same guy who was speaking in a monotone and responding in monosyllables less than a minute ago?" she wondered.

They sped towards a flight of stairs at the other end of the corridor. Raj pulled Tanya along as they sprinted up the stairs and before they knew it they were in another corridor leading up to his room. Tanya knew this was a restricted area but Raj was moving faster than she could think. She gave him a bewildered look as he pulled her into his room. Sure, she had made it obvious that she had a crush on him but she didn't fancy being dragged into his bedroom like this. Rahul could read the bewilderment in her eyes. He knew that if he didn't explain himself soon, Tanya was going to have one of her crazy outbursts again.

He caught his breath and said, "I am sorry, don't take this the wrong way. I only brought you here because the cameras have been making me really edgy today. I just wanted to spend some time with you away from the cameras. If you mind, we can go back downstairs..." He sounded appropriately apologetic.

As Raj looked deep in her eyes, the ever-so-bold Tanya lowered her eyes and blushed. "I thought you were still mad at me for last week," she said, uncharacteristically coy.

Rahul was still holding her close. He could sense her perfume but it puzzled him. He couldn't tell if it was a floral, fruity or a spicy fragrance that she was wearing. Her perfume was a chaos. He suddenly realised how close he held her. He let go of her and politely urged her towards the couch.

"Oh that! I should thank you. You were absolutely right. This is no way to find love." He paused a little and looked at her, "You always surprise me, Tanya."

She looked up. She was blushing.

"Would you like to watch a movie?" Rahul really just wanted to watch her all afternoon. He wanted to see her smile, blush, giggle. He just wanted to be with her.

"Sure, but don't you think the crew will come looking once they don't find us in the garden?" Tanya asked

"No they won't. I've taken care of that," he grinned at her reassuringly.

"So which movie are we watching then?" Tanya settled into the couch and winked at Raj.

After the movie Tanya sneaked out with Raj, tiptoeing down the hallway. He escorted her till the end of the corridor, where there was another set of stairs. He suddenly pulled her closer to him.

"The cameras start from here. Just go down this stairway and turn left. You'll find yourself out in the garden," he whispered softly in her ear. She could feel his warm breath on her neck and looked up at him, wondering if he was going to kiss her. Raj just tightened his grip on her hand and let go. Tanya realised that they'd been walking hand in hand. She smiled at him and walked down the staircase in spite of the fact that Raj had made her go weak in the knees. As soon as she was in the safety of the garden, she thought about her lovely afternoon with Raj. She couldn't stop smiling.

"Hey, how was it?" Simran yelled. She was fixing some stuff around the patio with a couple of helpers.

"It was okay. Nothing great!" Tanya didn't want to gloat. She didn't want any jealousy.

"Oh! I am sorry to hear that." But Simran was smiling.

"How's your task going?" Tanya asked.

"It's going okay. Did you get a bad tan or something? Your skin's looking reddish." Simran pointed at Tanya's cheeks.

Tanya turned away, and told herself that there was nothing to blush about. She walked back to the room rather quietly. Nobody seemed to take any interest in her. "The crew members must have leaked it out that I had a lousy date," she thought.

Tanya couldn't sleep that night. The butterflies in her stomach would not let her.

Karan went over each girl's progress with Rahul. They decided that seven girls had failed to perform their tasks to Rahul's satisfaction. Rahul confessed to the camera that there were a few girls on the list who were quite fake and that he loathed them.

"Keep guessing! I won't name them!" he winked into the camera. Karan scribbled down the seven names and handed it over to one of the crew members. The crew dispersed to get ready for the elimination. Karan waited for the room to be completely empty and turned to Rahul.

"So how was your date after all?"

"It was," Rahul began, then looked up and smiled goofily. "I don't know… awesome, fantastic… I don't have words Karan." He stared into the distance.

"I am glad you enjoyed it. But don't forget she's a contestant. She doesn't know who you really are," Karan said with a grave expression.

"I still don't know how to deal with that fact. Karan, I think she feels something too. Maybe she'll understand." Rahul scanned Karan's face for a response.

"Maybe she won't. Be prepared for the worst, my dear boy," Karan said, trying to reassure Rahul, while playing safe.

Within minutes, the crew was back to readjust the lights and change the camera angles to capture the girls' faces during the elimination. In a little while, the girls walked in.

Raj and Karan evaluated each girl on their performance in the task and their dates, right in front of them. Most of the girls couldn't take the criticism too well and the cameras captured the shock, the anger and the outbursts. Some girls couldn't believe how mean Raj could be. Just when the girls thought they'd heard enough, Raj got up and announced which of the two girls were to survive.

Shehnaz was surviving and so was Pallak. They both looked apologetically towards the other five, but as soon as they turned around they let out a sigh of relief. Raj and Karan didn't stay back to console the girls.

* * * * * *

Menon sat back in his chair and scanned through the names of the ten contenders who still stood the chance of becoming Mrs Rajsingh Jaiswal. Karan was doing a great job of keeping Rahul engaged in all the girls. The competition had been unpredictable so far.

Shehnaz Bharucha
Priya Gokhale
Simran Khanna
Pallak Shah
Khushi Motwane
Janaki Deo
Anuja Thakur
Neha Bose
Rehana Merchant
Tanya Kher

Something about the last name rang a bell, but he ignored it. Menon had met Tanya at many parties hosted at Blue Advertising. Quite a few people in his organisation had strived hard to please Miss Kher but to no avail. This media planner, who held the power of making key decisions about the multimillion rupee media spends, was honest to the core and was not interested in nonsense he had been told. Once she quit Blue, Tanya was discussed a bit, but easily forgotten. Her name had rung a bell among quite a few Cee employees but they didn't think it was very important to bring it to their boss's notice. Menon didn't dwell on the familiar name. He handed the list to Nina.

"Fax it over to the production department. They can co-ordinate with the sponsors," he ordered. His sales team had struck a lucrative deal with a leading fashion house to provide clothes and accessories to the finalists. Menon thought of the astronomical sum they were making over the deal and smiled triumphantly.

One of the media journals stated that the curiosity was at its peak for the first episode of the show and they predicted that the TRPs were going to be in Cee's favour by a landslide. Menon smiled yet again, satisfied.

Chapter 24

Simran sensed a change in Tanya's behaviour. These days Tanya smiled in her sleep. Her cheeks were forever a slight shade of pink and she randomly disappeared in the middle of tasks.

Tanya had been living in a bubble since her last rendezvous with Rajsingh Jaiswal. She hardly took notice of the politics of the show. She didn't care that most of the girls remaining on the show despised Shehnaz. She didn't realise that Raj made no secret of his fascination for Shehnaz. Tanya didn't notice a thing. Tanya had not noticed that her partner in the task for the coming week, Shehnaz, was closest to the man Tanya desired. What was surprising was that she didn't mind planning a formal dinner with Shehnaz. Simran found it very odd that Tanya was the only one unaffected by Shehnaz's proximity to Raj.

Tanya walked by the pool, the hectic day of planning forgotten. Even though it was a few hours past midnight, Tanya felt calm and serene. A sudden movement in the foliage behind her startled her. She stood alert as a cat, waiting to spot another movement. There was none. She turned around and started walking along the pool, remembering her first date with Raj. She stopped. She could swear she saw a shadow. She realised that it wasn't very safe to be outdoors that late into the night and decided to go back in. Just as she came closer to the little doorway, a hand shot out and blocked her way.

Tanya opened her mouth to scream but she felt a hand clamp down on her mouth. Something caught her eye and she knew she wasn't in danger. She knew who the Rolex belonged to. She yanked the hand and pulled Raj in front of her. She gave him an angry look.

"Do you realise you nearly gave me a heart attack? Are you mad?" she hissed.

"Sorry, didn't mean to scare you. I was just looking at a beautiful girl by the pool. She looks much better when she's smiling, you know?" He placed his hand on her arm.

Tanya blushed a little and then asked, "What are you doing up so late?"

Raj smiled and led her across to the other side of the pool. They both sat down on one of the benches. Raj reached out to take Tanya's hand, but he sensed the surprise on her face and stopped short. A minute later she placed her head on his shoulder and both of them sighed.

"What am I doing?" she asked softly.

"I don't know, but it feels... nice." He put his arm around her and she snuggled closer to him.

"This seems wrong, somehow." Her voice was drifting away as she sank into his arms. Raj smelt her hair.

"You know you sound like a girl straight out of a Mills & Boon drama," Raj whispered into her ears. They both laughed softly.

Rahul looked at Tanya. She was in his arms. He realised that for Tanya, these were Rajsingh Jaiswal's arms. He held Tanya tighter. They both stayed still by the pool until the sun started to paint the sky a pale orange and birds started chirping around them.

"We should go back to the house or we will be in a lot of trouble," Rahul reluctantly said, still holding Tanya tight.

"It feels like school, doesn't it?" Tanya snuggled closer.

Raj nodded in reply as they both tore away from each other

with great difficulty. When they got up, Raj pulled Tanya into his arms and kissed her forehead.

"I wish we weren't bound by all these rules," he said touching her cheek ever so lightly.

For the first time in weeks, Tanya saw desperation in Rajsingh Jaiswal's eyes. Tanya moved in closer and hugged him before walking away. She stopped at the gate and turned around to smile at him and sprinted towards the house.

A few minutes later from the same green gate, Raj emerged. Tanya tiptoed to her bed, careful not to wake Simran. She didn't want to answer any awkward questions. She pulled the sheets around her and took a deep breath and sensed Raj's scent around her. She smiled and drifted off to sleep.

In the bed by the window, Simran opened her eyes and stared at the huddled up figure on Tanya's bed.

Tanya woke up really late, almost by lunchtime. Simran had already left the room. She took a quick shower and slipped into jeans and a t-shirt before running down to Shehnaz's room.

"Sorry I'm late," she apologised.

"Don't be. But remember, you need to make sure this task works. We all know what lousy dates you've been having," Shehnaz said as she continued filing her nails.

Tanya smiled to herself at the thought of her last 'lousy' date with Raj. She shook off the thought and sat down. "I didn't hear the alarm go off," she explained with a slight blush.

"That's fine. Let's go over the arrangements, shall we?" Shehnaz took charge.

Shehnaz spent the next half hour spelling out what she wanted to do for the dinner they were hosting. Tanya was amazed that she was so confident about outdoing the other teams. "So, are we cool then?"

"Of course, anything you say Shehnaz!" Tanya was hungry and couldn't wait to go down for lunch. "How about some lunch now?"

"Sure!" Shehnaz was glad to finally be paired up with someone who agreed with her.

What Shehnaz didn't know though was that Tanya had barely heard a word of what Shehnaz said. She just grabbed a plate and loaded it with salad, fish and rice. She looked around and found Simran and Pallak chatting at the other end. She walked over to them and sat down.

"Hi!" she said with a big grin.

"Wow! You're chirpy. What's going on?" Pallak smiled at her.

"Umm, yeah, nothing really…! I finally got enough sleep," Tanya said as she took a bite.

"I'm done." Simran got up with her plate and walked off.

"What's going on?" Tanya asked as she stared after Simran.

"No idea. She definitely woke up on the wrong side of the bed today." Pallak bit into a piece of bread.

"Anyway, what do we have today? I haven't gotten the time to see the schedule," Tanya asked.

"We are getting new outfits from ShowStoppers."

Tanya stared at Pallak expecting an explanation.

"It's a fashion label. They have really nice ethnic and fusion clothing. I think they have a tie up with… what's that mall in Bandra *yaar*? *Haan*, OneStop!"

"Ah! Yes I used to stay very close to OneStop. I went there often actually." Tanya continued to eat.

"And you don't know about ShowStoppers? You're weird." Pallak made a face.

"Well, I hardly used to notice labels back then." Tanya shovelled another spoonful of rice in her mouth. "Actually, I used to hardly notice anything at all."

"You talk as if it was years ago!"

"For me, it just seems a lifetime ago." Tanya pushed the rice around on her plate. Thinking of the old days made the food look unappetising. Her life had changed so much since.

Pallak got up and said, "I have to go plan the lunch I am supposed to organise with Neha. I'll see you in the evening."

Tanya looked around her as she finished lunch. She felt like she was in a strange place, at a strange time and yet somehow it felt right. She decided to go back to her room. Right outside the dining room, she came face-to-face with Raj. She was half tempted to hug him but she didn't.

"Hi!" Tanya beamed.

"Hey! You all right?" Raj looked sleep-deprived. That would explain his dull expression, Tanya thought as she nodded. Before she could open her mouth to speak, Raj was gone.

The van carrying the girls' outfits arrived, followed by Sherry's Mercedes. She stepped out in style and glanced at the house. She made sure there was someone to supervise the unloading of the van and walked to the house. Without looking around, she made her way to the small office-cum bedroom assigned to Karan Kapoor on the ground floor and knocked.

Karan opened the door and smiled.

"I told you, you should've taken the bigger room. A superstar like you can't possibly be put up in a room simple as this!" She sat down on one of the soft chairs, crossed her legs and placed her Louis Vuitton clutch firmly in her lap before taking off her expensive sunglasses.

"It isn't that bad. I am having a ball here." Karan sat on his desk.

"If you insist! You must excuse my snobbery, I just got back from Paris," Sherry muttered in a fake French accent. They both laughed.

"Anyway, have you met our friend yet?" Karan asked.

"No. I thought I should see you first. Tell me." Sherry folded her arms and sat back as Karan began to relate the Rahul-Tanya saga. Sherry felt like Karan was narrating the storyline of one of his movies. As a young woman, Sherry had watched each and every Karan Kapoor movie possible. Nobody knew Sarita, the Bollywood fan; it clashed with the elegant social image she had worked very hard to build.

"And have you narrated this little story to your friend,

Mr. Menon?" she asked intently.

Karan was taken aback. "You mean?"

"Avinash Menon. Have you told him yet?"

"I made the mistake of confiding in him in the beginning. I am sorry, Sherry, but I trusted him. Somehow, now I get this feeling that he could go to any lengths to take Tanya away from Rahul," Karan said hesitantly.

"And our romantic hero would never let that happen," she said.

"Yes, I believe in love." He shook his head.

"What has that boy gotten himself into? She will never accept him without his money!"

"That apart, I have a feeling Mr Menon is taking a personal interest in making sure no love blooms before the finale and the audience keeps guessing. He wants the viewers to be hooked," Karan said.

"Sure he does. Everyone's so curious about the show." Sherry sighed.

Karan got up and pointed to a form on his desk.

"That's Shehnaz. Lately, Rahul has taken my advice and started ignoring Tanya; at least while he has company. People think she has been having some lousy dates with Raj and so does your husband."

Sherry leaned in and looked at the form and then at Karan.

"Raj has transferred his attention to this girl. She's pretty, she's smart, basically a good choice." He spotted the perplexed look on Sherry's face. "He just pretends to like her. This has made the show a little predictable according to your husband. Menon has arranged for her to be thrown out this time."

"But I thought Raj made the decision." Sherry was confused.

"There is a twist in the tale this time. The girls get to vote out. They can choose three contestants they dislike the most and it is quite obvious that most of the girls will vote Shehnaz out."

"Why won't they vote out Tanya?"

"She doesn't look like competition. The girl to receive the maximum number of votes gets thrown out. The others,

Raj decides."

"So Tanya is safe, as of now?"

"As of now, yes. But if anyone were to discover the secret dates..."

"You are telling me that Raj gives her no attention whatsoever outside of these private dates? And she's okay with it? She's not showing off to the other girls?" Sherry asked.

Karan shrugged and shook his head.

"Well, she's a very smart girl in that case," Sherry said raising her eyebrows.

There was a faint knock on the door and Sherry said, "I'll get this!"

Rahul was smiling on the other side of the door and as soon as Sherry opened it he hugged her.

"How have you been?" she asked, keeping concern out of her voice.

"Missing you, as always!" Rahul closed the door behind him.

"Liar! I heard that you have been spending a lot of time with a certain girl and..."

Rahul's expression changed.

"It's okay Rahul," Karan reassured him.

"I just don't like the idea of her being in this place; it's like she's out there, vulnerable. I can't protect her even if I want to."

Sherry smiled and lightly touched his arm. "If it wasn't for this show, you would never have met her," Sherry reasoned.

"That is not true," Rahul admitted

"What do you mean?" Karan was taken aback.

"Well, I know her from before the show," Rahul confessed.

Sherry and Karan stared at Rahul in shock. Although Rahul had mentioned it to Sherry earlier, she hadn't paid it any mind. At that point of time, Sherry was worried about Rahul's feelings. But now, she knew that her husband would go to any lengths to keep this game in his hand. And the fact that Tanya knew Rahul from before could create a lot of problems.

"You know it's a breach of contract from her side, right?" Karan breathed out heavily.

"No, it isn't. I know her but she doesn't know me," Rahul explained.

"Go on." Sherry sat down again, intrigued.

"Well, she was a regular customer at the mall. She never came into the perfumes section. I don't think she registered me, forget remembering me at all." He looked at Karan, hoping his story had been bought.

"And?"

"She doesn't know me. She really doesn't!" Rahul was desperate yet again.

"We know she doesn't know you, but I don't think anyone else is going to believe you." Karan looked at Sherry.

"Especially my husband." Sherry was looking stern.

"Can't we just pretend I never said that?"

Rahul received two nods.

Sherry was aware that Rahul and Karan understood the threat from her husband, but she also knew that they did not understand just how badly her husband needed this show to be in his control. Sherry attended parties alongside a gloating Menon. Even though she was dutifully fulfilling the role of a socialite, she was getting weary of acting. She heard Menon speak to his bosses about Rahul and the disdain in his voice irritated Sherry. If it wasn't for Rahul, Avinash Menon wouldn't have the show and he would have quite a few swords dangling above his head. It pained her that her husband didn't give Rahul any credit. And when she spoke about Rahul, rather fondly, she would see a hint of a fire in Menon's eyes. For the first time since she married Menon, Sherry had been scared of him.

They were expected in the library, where there was a team of stylists waiting to talk to the girls about the outfits they were receiving. Tanya waited for Simran but when she didn't show up, she made her way down to the library. She wondered why Simran spent such little time in the room these days. When she walked into the library, she saw Simran seated behind Shehnaz. She saw Tanya but she didn't smile at her. Tanya quietly sat down in a vacant chair next to Shehnaz. She tried hard to pay attention to what the fashion consultants from ShowStoppers were saying, but her mind kept wandering to Simran. She couldn't understand why Simran was being so weird.

"Each one of you is going to get one traditional outfit, two formal evening outfits and a casual outfit," the consultant said blandly.

"My colleagues here will have a one-on-one with each one of you to make sure that we provide you with outfits that compliment your personality," she continued to say. Tanya was up for the discussion within an hour. She was totally dreading it. Within minutes into the session, Tanya found that she was actually enjoying talking to the consultant about her preferences.

"I hate going over the top, and make-up is really not my scene," Tanya explained as Sherry nodded and the consultant scribbled something into her notebook.

"Fashion and style are about simplicity. I am sure we can work out simple garments that enhance your complexion, which looks fabulous. You don't need any make-up. But I do suggest some kohl to bring out the colour of your eyes."

"You know, I think she would look great in fusion wear when it comes to casuals. Don't you think?" Sherry asked the consultant.

Tanya was surprised at Sherry's attentiveness and involvement. There was something about Sherry that comforted Tanya. After much delibration, they all agreed upon a beautiful georgette *sari*, a turquoise blue gown and a black cocktail dress. Sherry insisted on the trendily cut *kurti* with jeans for Tanya's casual look. Tanya was pretty excited about her outfits which would be with her by evening. She thanked them both and as she got up to leave, Sherry surprised her with a hug.

Sherry had been watching Tanya. She couldn't understand why she wasn't showing off her relationship with Raj. Any girl in the contest would be thrilled to spill the beans and be smug about it. Was Tanya playing a game? But the fashion consulting schedule with her proved to Sherry that Tanya was smitten blind. Showing off just wasn't this girl's style.

When Tanya got back to the room, she was surprised at all the mess. She cleared around a bit before slumping into the bed. She couldn't sit still. Something was bothering her. She washed her face and retied her hair before heading to the dining room.

She got herself a cup of tea while scanning the dining room. She was hoping to see Raj, but he was nowhere to be seen. She realised just how empty the dining room felt. She sipped her tea, remembering a time when this room would be crowded with contestants. Of the ten contestants that remained, nine were always on a diet.

After tea, Tanya decided to get some books from the library. She had spotted a few books that morning during the fashion session. Tanya was browsing through books, when she heard the library door open. Tanya walked past the rows of books to see who was giving her company. She didn't see anyone, but she heard a shuffling sound. She walked in the direction of the sound and was glad to see Raj browsing through some DVDs.

"Hey there," she smiled and ran to him like a little girl.

"Hi!" Raj looked fairly surprised as he put his arm around her, "What are you doing in the library?"

"Getting a book. It's getting rather boring now that there are just ten girls on the show," she explained as they both sat down by the reading table.

"Did you find anything you like?"

Tanya shook her head, still grinning ear to ear.

"I'm glad to see you. We haven't had a chance to talk, have we?" He took her hand.

"We haven't, but I understand," Tanya said smiling as she felt her fingers entwined with his.

"Please, please forgive me for snubbing you like that when others are around. I hate doing that to you, but trust me, it's necessary."

The grin was gone from Tanya's face. She said nothing and

got up, jerking her hand out of Raj's hand.

Tanya had been in the middle of an emotional whirlpool. She had been too overwhelmed by all the things she was feeling to notice that Raj had been snubbing her. She took his aloofness as a sign of shyness. What the hell had she been thinking? How could she have missed such a thing?

Raj looked in her eyes, trying to look for an understanding glance but all he could see was pain. Just as Raj was about to say something, they heard a knock on the door. Rahul had forgotten that he had locked the door when he closed it earlier.

"Just a second," he shouted as he rushed Tanya behind a stand overloaded with books. He signalled her to stay there as he ran to open the door.

"Good you're here. We need to talk," Karan entered the library and closed the door behind him.

"I wasn't alone, actually," Rahul quickly said before Karan could say anything that could give him up.

"Huh?" Karan followed Rahul's gaze in bewilderment and he saw Tanya getting out from behind the stand. He started laughing, making the air in the library dense with discomfort. "You guys are straight out of Bollywood."

Rahul glanced at Tanya who stood looking at the ground; he could tell she was humiliated.

"We met accidentally and got talking, it's not…." Rahul tried to explain.

"Come on, it's okay. Everything's fair in love and war." He turned to Tanya, "Don't worry Tanya, I'll leave you two alone."

"I was just leaving, anyway," Tanya said in a flat, cold voice, her eyes firmly on the ground.

Rahul felt terrible for the way he had made her feel. Rahul saw her walk away in a familiar rhythm, fast and long strides. She was walking exactly the way she used to when she came into the mall. Rahul realised that she was wounded by something back then and had healed herself. He hated himself for hurting her again, but he wasn't sure what he had done.

"You embarrassed her." Rahul kept staring after her.

"So what were you two talking about?" Karan ignored Rahul's accusation.

"I was just apologising to her." Rahul sat down again.

"For what?" Karan picked up a book and flipped through it.

"For the way I've been behaving the past few days!"

"Are you out of your mind?" He continued to flip through the book.

"What do you mean?"

"For all you know she hadn't even realised that you were avoiding her all this while. She could have thought you were shy about it. Congratulations, you have now brought it to her notice." Karan kept the book down and looked at Rahul.

"I don't care. I don't ever want to lie to her about something. I had to tell her the truth."

"If you don't want to lie, why don't you go ahead and tell her who you really are? Some things are better not told, Rahul. You should've known that." Karan got up and left, leaving Rahul confused.

Hiding her feelings from the world was an art Tanya had forced herself to learn from her father. Lately, she had forgotten the importance of that art. She had let her eyes dance when they wanted to, she allowed her cheeks to blush when they felt like blushing and she always let her lips smile at every chance they got. Raj's confession made her feel vulnerable. She had made a fool of herself in front of him. She cringed every time she thought of how she had been around Raj. She was hurt and humiliated. Why hadn't she figured out what was happening? She always thought she could read people. She had let her guard down around Raj, thinking she could trust him, but she had forgotten that he, after all, was a guy.

"Enough!" she thought. She had noticed the way Raj had looked into her eyes. He wanted to know how she felt. She wasn't going to let anyone glance into her soul that easily anymore. When she came back to her room, she saw Simran search her face. Tanya looked in the mirror for a touch of sadness or a teardrop in her own reflection. Tanya saw nothing.

Why had she allowed Raj to treat her this way? Sneaking her off to his room, spending the night on the bench by the pool, ignoring her when they had company.... Why? She didn't know. But she didn't want to find out either. She didn't want to be on the show anymore. She realised that she had been the way she was for a reason. She didn't let her guard down so that people could never hurt her. She wondered how many other girls had got the privilege of those private dates with Raj. She wondered just how many other girls were okay with being ignored by Rajsingh Jaiswal in public. And she, like a fool had thought that what she had with him was special.

* * * * * *

A Match Made in Heaven was premiering. Everyone settled in front of the television as they waited for Rajsingh Jaiswal to start his hunt for the perfect bride. Some waited to be entertained, some waited to see the handsome guy and some were watching it out of sheer curiosity.

A woman sat in front of the TV, surfing, looking for something to keep her entertained until her husband returned home for dinner. She saw Raj speak in his impeccable accent, describing what he was looking for in a bride. She decided that this was interesting only because she found something familiar about him. She had met him before. Maybe she had been introduced to him at one of the numerous parties she had attended with her husband.

As soon as the next segment started, she knew who he was. She sat still, hearing her heart beat loud and clear. As the channel broadcast the making of a millionaire, Rahul Rajgopal showed up in his Tantra T-Shirt & jeans. The perfume seller's rags-toriches story was what they called it. Tears began to well up. She had always dreaded meeting him again. She never expected him to show up on the TV on an idle Monday evening.

* * * * * *

Anita and Ravi stared in shock at the drama unfolding on the television. It was incredible to see Rahul Rajgopal transform into Rajsingh Jaiswal. The girls on the show were being interviewed. They all seemed to be very decisive of winning his heart, except their Tanya.

Raj couldn't take his eyes off Tanya in their first meeting. That was the end of the episode. The sneak-peek at the next episode showed Raj and Tanya's date and Anita froze. She saw Tanya's eyes mesmerised by Rahul or was it Raj. Anita looked at her husband, her eyes full of worry.

Her first instinct was to call Gia and ask her if she had known, but as soon as she picked up her cell-phone Anita realised that Gia knew!!! She was working on the show, and the show had been going on for weeks now. Suddenly, Anita realised why Gia had been avoiding her for the last couple of weeks. She sat still, wondering what Tanya had been going through. From the looks of it, Tanya was having a good time, but then, what if she was actually falling for this guy?

Long after the television was switched off, Anita and Ravi sat silent. They both wanted to say something but they didn't know what to say. It was too late. It had been weeks since Tanya had been on the show. They couldn't do anything about it.

"I think we should go and get Tanya now," Ravi said after what seemed like an eternity.

"That was my first thought too, but it won't be easy. I am sure they have rules,"

"Anita, what are you saying? Didn't you see? This guy is a fake. My sister…."

"Tanya isn't just your sister. She means the world to me. The guy is a fake, yes, but Tanya never went on the show with the intention of winning it. So relax," Anita tried to reason.

"He couldn't take his eyes off her. I saw the way Tano looked at him. This isn't looking good. And that Gia!" Ravi was furious.

Just then Anita's phone beeped. It was a text from Gia.

"It's Gia. She is apologising. She couldn't tell us about this because she was contractually bound. She says she has been checking on Tanya through the rough cuts of the show, and Tanya is doing well." Anita read out the message.

Ravi looked at Anita angrily and stormed into the bedroom. Anita closed her eyes and prayed for Tanya.

Chapter 25

Even though she didn't want to stay on the show, Tanya wasn't going to slack on her task. Tanya just wasn't made that way. Besides, teaming up with Shehnaz worked out quite well for Tanya. Shehnaz would decide what they were doing and the execution was left to Tanya. There was no scope for fights or arguments. It was a first for Shehnaz.

By Friday afternoon, all the preparations for the dinner party were under way. Tanya was just supervising some last-minute details and finalising the seating arrangement when Simran came to the dining room. Tanya was surprised to see her. She had been extremely quiet and had been disappearing quite often. Tanya wasn't really interested in confronting Simran to figure out what was wrong. Tanya took one look at Simran and went back to work. Simran came up to Tanya.

"When are you going to talk to me about what happened?"

Tanya went on with her work. "What happened?"

"Don't act like I don't know. What's going on with you and Raj?"

Tanya shrugged. Simran was the last person she was going to confide in.

"Come on! I saw you that morning at the pool." Simran was following Tanya as she walked across the dining room.

Tanya stopped walking. She was shocked to hear about the

pool from Simran. It was her secret with Raj. After their little encounter in the library, Tanya felt terrible about these moments. The fact that her roommate knew about it, made her feel worse. Tanya took a moment to think about what she was going to say.

"You saw me, so?"

"Well, what is happening with you two?"

"First of all, I don't think it would be very wise to jump to conclusions based on one incident." Tanya had finished placing all the name cards on the table and looked Simran in the eye. "Second of all, even if there was something happening, do I owe you any explanation?"

"Yes. Yes you do. I am your friend. That's the least...."

Tanya cut in, "We are all contestants on this show. Now, if you'll excuse me. I have some work to do." Tanya left the dining room.

Tanya managed to finish all the work an hour before dinner. She went to the room to get dressed. The room was empty. Tanya suddenly felt terrible about the way she had spoken to Simran.

"What choice did I have?" she thought to herself. Tanya felt the energy was seeping out of her body. She decided to lie down for a bit. She thought about Raj and felt her chest tighten. Why had he treated her like that? Why had she let him play with her heart?

* * * * * *

Raj hadn't been able to catch Tanya after their encounter in the library. He had looked for her everywhere, but either she had been avoiding him, or she had been keeping to herself. Whenever they met, it was for one of the lunches or dinners thrown by the other girls. He could hardly talk to her while they were surrounded by people. He was hoping to pull her aside tonight. She was hosting the dinner after all and she would have no choice but to stay till late.

Raj was impressed at the sight of the dining room. At the top of the dining table sat a beautiful flower arrangement. Small cards with elegant golden writing indicated who was to sit where. Raj was seated next to Shehnaz and Karan. Deepak was seated next to Rehana Merchant who was across the table from Raj. Tanya was at the far end.

"Hey you." Shehnaz came up to him as he surveyed the dining table. She looked beautiful. She always did.

"Everything looks lovely, Shehnaz," he said as she clung on to his arm. "By the way, why isn't your co-host sitting up there with you? Team differences?" Rahul didn't want to make his disappointment with the seating arrangement obvious and so he tried to sound as casual as possible.

"Right." Shehnaz looked deep in his eyes, "Tanya wanted to sit next to her friends, there." She pointed her delicate hand towards the other end of the table.

Rahul smiled and nodded. He had hurt Tanya and now she didn't want anything to do with him. He could understand. Shehnaz excused herself and pretended to run to oversee something. She looked back and smiled at Raj. The smile made Rahul sick, but Raj smiled back.

The others came in one by one but there was no sign of Tanya. 'She must be getting ready,' he thought to himself.

Shehnaz was by the kitchen door when Karan came and seated himself.

"Nice setting; the helpers tell me Tanya has been toiling since daybreak to make sure all the arrangements were perfect," Karan said.

"That explains why she isn't here yet." Rahul gestured to Tanya's seat.

"I thought she would be seated next to us." Karan stared at Tanya's empty chair.

Rahul told Karan how Tanya herself wanted to be seated as far away from Raj as possible.

"Strange. Let me talk to her friends." Karan got up and straightened his jacket.

Karan went around the table, talking to all the girls before he came to Simran. "Good evening. How are you, girls?" he asked Simran, Anuja and Pallak who were busy chitchatting.

"I see one of your friends is missing," he said as he picked up the name card, "Ah, Tanya. She is usually early for all the events. Everything ok?"

"No idea. Last I saw her was when she went to her room to get ready," Anuja answered. She looked at Simran, but Simran said nothing.

"Well, I must go check on her then," he said.

Karan made his way across to Shehnaz before slipping out of the dining room. Normally, he would have had a production assistant go over to check. But not with Tanya. Karan himself had to find out what was going on.

He knocked on the door, no answer. He knocked again, no answer. Karan was a little worried.

"Tanya," he called, "this is Karan. We are all waiting for you to join us."

Suddenly he heard footsteps and the door opened. "I am sorry Karan. I don't think I will be able to join you. I am not feeling very well." Her eyes looked red and her face was pale.

"Shall I send for a doctor?" Karan was genuinely concerned.

"No, no, I'll be fine. I haven't slept very well. I just need to sleep it off. It's just a regular headache and fever. Don't worry about me. Enjoy the dinner." She gave him a bleak smile.

"Oh, such a shame! You went through all that trouble and you aren't attending. Can I get you something, though? Feel free to dial the emergency number." Karan left with a sympathetic pat on her shoulder. He knew that she wasn't lying. He also knew why she was unwell. He knew that, sometimes, solitude was the best medicine. He decided to leave her alone.

In the dining room, Karan announced that Tanya wouldn't be joining them because of ill-health.

"I am not surprised. She has been so disinterested in this dinner," Shehnaz muttered to Raj.

She got up to address the guests. "I'd like to welcome everybody tonight. We've picked Parsi cuisine. A change from all the Punjabi food we've been eating." She looked at the other girls. "It's a shame my partner Tanya couldn't be here. Please enjoy yourselves and have a good time."

She sat down elegantly and looked around in contentment. Shehnaz was unaffected by the fact that her partner was unwell. Rahul glanced at Tanya's empty chair once again. He looked at her friends, who continued to chitchat. Simran caught his glance and she smiled at him. He gave her a nod and focused on the food that lay in front of him.

He couldn't eat. He just wanted to go up to Tanya's room and take care of her. Karan gave him a reassuring smile, as if reading his mind and signalled him to eat.

"She will be okay. Don't worry, just enjoy the dinner," he whispered.

Tanya spent most of the next day in bed. Simran brought her cups of coffee and soup. She checked Tanya's temperature at regular intervals. She remained by Tanya's side but not a word was exchanged between the two. Other girls did knock on their door to check on Tanya, but Simran told them she needed rest. Simran knew it as well as Tanya did that most of them were doing this for the sake of formality.

Simran was on her way to get some soup for dinner from the kitchen when she met Raj on his way to their room.

"Hi, I was just thinking of visiting your room-mate."

"Oh, that is very sweet but she is sleeping. She needs rest." Simran snubbed him.

"Maybe I'll just have a look. How is she?"

"She is all right. She just needs a lot of rest, Raj."

"Should I send for a doctor?"

"She'll be fine," Simran said coldly. "I am going to get some soup for her. We are all here for her."

With that Simran left for the kitchen. Rahul stood outside Tanya's room for a long time. Simran was right. She was asleep. He walked away.

In her bed, Tanya was thinking of Raj. Why hadn't he come by to see her yet? She closed her eyes tight to stop the questions from sending her mind into another one of those trips that left her feeling sick and miserable.

Tanya finally felt hungry. She mustered up the strength to walk down to the dining room. It was just nine in the morning. The entire house was asleep. She ate alone and came back to the room to shower and dress for the day. She felt much better after she showered. She glanced over at Simran's bed. She was sound asleep. Tanya felt grateful to her for the way she had taken care of her over the last two days. Tanya scribbled down a sorry note and left it by Simran's bedside table.

She was hoping to be thrown out today; she wanted to go home to Ravi and Anita, but at the same time she wanted to stay close to Raj. Why? She couldn't quite understand why she continued to care for him after all that had happened.

Tanya had been too busy thinking to notice a pipe running through the lawn. She nearly tripped on the pipe and was about to fall when a familiar pair of hands held her, breaking her fall.

She squinted up and saw a familiar mop of hair against the sun. Raj had broken her fall.

"Thanks." She turned and began to walk away.

"Wait, Tanya." He grabbed her arm.

"Oh sorry I forgot. We are alone now, aren't we? You can talk to me now," she said glaring at him.

"What?" Raj looked at her, baffled.

"After getting to know you, I thought there was more to you than your shallow outlook towards life, marriage and other things, but I was wrong. And yeah, do me a favour. Please throw me out today. Forget getting married to you, I am not interested in even looking at you." Tanya jerked her shoulder away from his grip and stormed off.

Rahul was stunned. Tanya spoke in a calm, controlled tone. She meant every word she said. She was in complete control of herself and he could see the hatred in her eyes and he could hardly believe it. Had he really hurt her that badly? Why wasn't she giving him a chance to explain himself?

Tanya closed the door behind her before breaking into silent sobs. Simran, who was lying awake in her bed got up and rushed to Tanya.

"What happened? Why are you crying? Tanya?" She tried to console Tanya but she ran into the bathroom.

* * * * * *

"From thirty girls, it's down to just ten of you. We have come a long way," Karan said into the camera. "Over the past weeks you have come closer, gotten to know each other. Some have even become friends. You girls now know Raj and you know the other girls, your competition. So now, it's up to you to decide who fits the bill and who doesn't. Each one of you will now vote for the three girls they want to see thrown out this week. Are we clear?"

A surprised murmur rose in the room.

"Good. No discussing the votes. One by one, drop your votes and leave."

Karan pointed to the girl on the first chair. Each girl scribbled three names on the paper and dropped it in the box. They were led into another room, where they spoke to the camera crew about who they'd thought was least suitable for Rajsingh Jaiswal. Tanya wrote her own name, then Simran's and Pallak's.

"This show is cruel," she thought. "This is the least I can do for the both of them."

The crew was busy recording Shehnaz's quote, making it easy for Tanya to slip out.

Rahul sat alone in his chamber. He was trying to figure out the two names that he was supposed to hand in for the vote out.

He scribbled Tanya's name and scratched it out several times. Finally, he made his decision.

The girls gathered in the library. Shehnaz waltzed in with a bright smile on her face. She had spoken to all the girls and she was confident that none of the girls had voted her out.

As soon as Karan and Raj entered the room, the room fell silent. The girls tried to smile at Raj. He, however, seemed lost.

As soon as the three names were announced, the smile on Shehnaz's face disappeared. Tanya froze in her chair. Shehnaz, Pallak and Janaki had been voted out. Why was her name missing? She couldn't stand the idea of spending another week in the Jaiswal Mansion. She closed her eyes tight. "This has got to be some kind of a joke. Hell, no, it was a conspiracy," she told herself.

* * * * * *

The woman sat in her living room. Her 4-bedroom apartment was silent, but there was nothing new about that. She was waiting for her husband to come home after another long day at work. She always hoped he'd come home early, but not today. This time she was glad that she had the TV to herself. Her eyes sparkled with tears as Rahul's face flickered on Cee TV. She touched the screen where Rahul's face had been a minute before. The doorbell rang. And once again, Ayesha let go of Rahul to run to the man she had chosen to marry.

* * * * * *

Tanya was obviously mesmerised by the fake Mr. Right. Anita knew there was trouble brewing. Anita turned to face her husband.

"Do you see what I see?" he asked her with a sigh.

Anita nodded. She had thought that this crazy idea would have helped Tanya. She was beginning to get worried that it might actually cause damage. She couldn't bring herself to look her husband in the eye. This was one of the few times that she had been wrong. So horribly wrong!

* * * * * *

Rahul shifted uncomfortably in his bed. Tanya was forced to stay in the house against her wishes. Why hadn't he voted her out? He couldn't forgive himself, so he tiptoed down to her room. He hesitated a bit and turned around and walked down to the swimming pool.

'I hate Raj,' Tanya kept telling herself again and again, but she found it hard to believe. She had been upset when she found out that she was staying another week. But now, in her solitude, she realised that she felt glad that she hadn't been voted out. She was confused. The only thing she knew for sure was that she wanted to confront Raj about the way she felt.

Chapter 26

What was once a mansion crowded with girls, giggles and a whole lot of curiosity, had now become an empty house. The only person who wasn't bogged down by the silence was Karan. He had his hands full juggling the crew, Rahul and Menon. And he was also worried about Rahul and Tanya. He received the task for the week on email.

"It's a compatibility test. You will answer a few questions. And then the girls will have to guess your answers," Karan told Rahul. They were having tea in the garden. Rahul didn't reply. He continued to stare into space.

"Sounds interesting, doesn't it? Rahul?" Karan asked.

"Umm yeah. I don't care." He took a sip from his cup. He had grown to like chamomile tea.

"What?"

"I don't care. Tanya hates me," he said helplessly.

"Rahul! You're still thinking about it?"

"Forget it. I don't want to talk about it." Rahul walked off.

Karan sighed. He had to explain the task to the girls. As he spoke to the girls about the task that lay ahead of them, he realised that Tanya was completely disinterested. Karan decided that it was time for an intervention. Karan waited for the girls to leave. As usual, Tanya was the last to leave.

"Tanya," he said and paused to make sure that the other girls had left. "There was something I was hoping you'd help me with."

"Sure. What can I do for you?"

"Come along." He signalled her to follow him. She followed him, wondering what was so important that he had to ask for help. Karan silently walked Tanya down to his room. She couldn't understand what was going on but something told her it had to do with Raj. Tanya walked into the room rather uncomfortably. Karan sensed her discomfort.

"It was sort of private, what I had to talk to you about," he explained. "There is this friend of mine. He is very troubled you know," Karan continued.

"And?" Tanya was really not interested in Karan or his friend or his depression. She had her own battles to fight.

"There is this girl he really likes, and I am pretty sure the girl likes him too."

"Hmm…."

"A lot of people wouldn't want them to get close for some reason and these people are powerful. To protect her from these people, he has been ignoring her. He was honest with her and apologised to her for it but she never let him finish." Karan saw Tanya look up at him. She suddenly seemed interested in what Karan was saying.

"And now she's mad at him?" Tanya completed the story for Karan.

"Bingo! You're a smart girl. Now, tell me what could fix this problem? I like both of them and I hate to see them both so sad."

Tanya smiled at Karan, and blushed. "There's nothing you can do, Karan. Let the girl handle it."

She got up and walked to the door. She turned around and smiled at Karan. "Thank you," she said before walking out the door.

Karan couldn't help but think what a lovely movie Rahul and Tanya's love story would make.

* * * * * *

Tanya hadn't quite understood who the dangerous people keeping them apart were, but she finally understood why Raj had acted the way he had. She stopped in the corridor that led to Raj's room. She realised that she didn't merely like Raj. She was in love with Raj.

With that realisation, Tanya broke into a sprint towards Raj's room. She didn't care that his room was out of bounds for her. Tanya didn't bother to knock. She flung the door open and scanned the room. She spotted a figure on the terrace and smiled. She ran to him. He turned around, his face awash with confusion. She tried to catch her breath.

"What's going on?" he asked. Tanya hugged him, unable to speak.

Rahul couldn't understand what was going on. In a flash, he remembered her rash and angry words from the day before. He pulled back and pushed her away. Tanya was confused.

"I'm sorry, Raj. I never gave you the chance to explain. But I just realised, that I…"

"Leave me alone." Raj didn't let her finish her sentence.

"But I…"

"I said leave me alone," Rahul yelled again.

Tanya was startled. Just the tone of his voice struck her like a sharp branch of a tree in a thunderstorm, ripping her heart out. She turned around so that he didn't see her cry and made a dash for the door.

Rahul stood there breathing heavily, his eyes full of rage. Who did Tanya think she was? One moment she was warm to him and in the next she was as cold as ice. He was furious. He was glad he had pushed her away.

Tanya walked back to her room silently. Her head was buzzing with thoughts. "First he shows interest in me, then keeps me on the show, then he woos me, then he wants to ignore me and now he gets angry with me! What sort of a game does he think he's playing?" she asked herself as she fumbled with the room door.

Her body felt heavier than it did before and her cheeks were hot with rage, confusion and embarrassment. She dropped on the bed and started sobbing. She didn't know what she had done to be treated this way. She flinched as she remembered how Raj had yelled at her. He was supposed to be in love with her. Why couldn't he look at her the way he always did? Why couldn't he talk to her? Why couldn't he give her a chance to explain herself? After a while, a thought crept up in her head. There had to be a reason why he did what he did.

"Sleeping so early?" Tanya didn't notice Simran walk into the room.

"I'm a little tired," Tanya replied clearing her throat and wiping her moistened eyes.

"Ah, I am going to get ready for my date with Raj. Can you believe it? It's the last week?"

"I am just glad it is." Tanya wiped the tear stains on her cheeks and sat up.

"Have you been crying?"

There was no use lying, Tanya's rule was broken. Simran had seen her cry.

"Yeah. Just missing home,"

"Don't be such a baby." Simran came around and sat next to Tanya and put an arm around her. Sure, Simran felt bad for Tanya, but she had a date to go to and she sprang up and got busy with getting dressed up. Tanya laughed bitterly as she realised just how vast the dimensions of this game were.

* * * * * *

Rahul had started to act as he pleased to make the best of his last week as a millionaire. In a week, he was going to be just another perfume salesman. Rajsingh Jaiswal would be an identity dead to everyone. And Rajsingh Jaiswal would leave a ghost behind. The ghost, Rahul, could no longer be himself. He would forever be the guy who pretended to be a millionaire and cheated a bunch of girls. Most of these girls would go back to their lives, Menon would have his TRPs, Karan Kapoor's career would get a fresh shot but at the end of this drama, the only person left without anything would be Rahul Rajgopal. Who was Rahul Rajgopal? Could this person who once lived like Rajsingh Jaiswal go back to the life that Rahul once led?

Rahul stared in the mirror, trying to look for the Rahul who loved his perfumes and lived in a dingy Mumbai apartment. He tried to talk like Rahul once did, but he spoke like Rajsingh Jaiswal. And suddenly Rahul realised there was hardly any difference left between Rajsingh Jaiswal and Rahul Rajgopal. They had belonged to different worlds but they had morphed into one now.

Karan was hoping to see Rahul and Tanya together more often after his intervention, but nothing seemed to have changed between the two. Karan hadn't seen Tanya since their little talk and Rahul had been keeping busy with his duties as Rajsingh Jaiswal. Rahul had been avoiding Karan. Karan couldn't help but feel worried. He started realising that as the D-day came closer, there was very little of Rahul left in Rajsingh Jaiswal.

All Tanya wanted to do was to get through with the week and run back to Ravi and Anita. On many occasions, the other girls asked her why she was so silent. Tanya simply said she was homesick, which wasn't a complete lie. Tanya looked through her little diary. She couldn't wait to share the stuff she had written with Anita. She was the only person who would understand. She wondered if Ravi and Anita were watching the show. She wondered that they had to say about the show. Tanya sighed and got up. She locked away the notepads in her bag. She was hungry, so she decided to get something to eat.

She really wanted to cancel the date with Raj, but she wanted to confront him. She wanted to know what was going on in his head.

"Tanya!" She heard Karan's voice.

"Have you been able to sort it out with Raj?"

"Umm, no." She shifted in her chair uncomfortably and wished she had taken her snack back to her room.

"But...."

"I am sorry Karan, you were wrong. Your friend doesn't really like the girl." She got up and looked Karan in the eye.

"What?" Karan was confused.

"He told the girl that he wants to be alone." She walked towards the window and saw Raj holding hands with Khushi. "And he has had company everyday since then. He probably doesn't need to be alone; he just doesn't want to see that girl anymore."

"I don't believe that." Karan wanted to talk her into trying again. They were running out of time. Tanya had to know how Rahul felt before she found out who he really was. Tanya turned around.

"It's not for you to believe. It's for me to accept. He's a millionaire. He has his whims and fancies, and I'm a simple girl. Maybe I was just the flavour of the week. I am not interested in playing this game anymore, Karan. I tried, I really tried. But I'm tired now, Karan… I can't, I don't want to fight. "

She sounded helpless. Karan didn't know what he could possibly do to comfort her.

Tanya was to meet Raj at seven by the pool. Tanya remembered her first ever date with Raj and she felt a knot rise up in her chest. The crew had finished setting up their cameras. She did the mandatory pre-date interview with the crew. She gave some boring answers. Karan prodded her a bit but he didn't push her. He didn't feel right prodding her. Tanya looked gorgeous in her purple silk gown, minimal make up and a simple hairstyle. But something was still amiss. She didn't seem enthusiastic.

She still had a few more minutes before the date so she stepped out towards the house. She bumped into Simran who gasped as soon as she saw Tanya.

"You look gorgeous!" she said. Tanya just nodded.

"Is everything ok? Still homesick?" Simran asked.

"Yeah…," Tanya replied.

"Come on, it's just a couple of days and we're out of here!" Simran tried to cheer her up.

"Sure." Tanya looked at her watch. "I should go. Don't want to be late for the last date." Tanya really wanted to be alone but she had to drag herself back to the poolside.

The ambience was very romantic with dim lights, candles and the works, but Tanya didn't notice it. She saw Raj, already across the pool by the table and felt a smile escape her lips.

She tried to walk over the rocky path across the pool, but her heels made it difficult. The last time, Raj had walked with her, holding her. She looked up for help, but Raj was busy pouring wine into the glasses. His indifference was more cruel than the yelling, Tanya thought.

She removed her shoes and walked across. She slipped her shoes back on and greeted Raj. His calculated smile told her that he wasn't looking forward to this date either. This was not her Raj. She took a seat.

"What mood are we in today?" Raj asked as he uncovered a platter of kebabs.

"Excuse me?" Tanya tried to search his face for a hint of a smile.

"Some kebabs for you?" He ignored her reaction.

"Thank you." She was in no mood to eat, but helped herself reluctantly.

"You look nervous. Am I making you nervous?" He sipped his wine.

He was making her anxious, but somehow she didn't want him to have the pleasure of knowing that.

"No, you're not. I just don't feel very well tonight. I really wanted to cancel."

"Then what stopped you?" he asked with a smirk.

"It's the rules that we play by in this contest." She rolled her eyes.

"Or," he said with a smug smile, "you couldn't resist my charm...."

"Well, I have had to bear with your charm for so many dates now. I thought let's just get over with this one last date. One for the road!" She raised her glass, sarcasm glinting in her angry eyes. She knew he was playing with her and she wasn't going to let him win this one.

"Good food and good company are two essentials of a great date. At least we have one of those." Raj stuffed a piece of chicken angrily in his mouth.

Tanya stared at him. Where had the polite and considerate Rajsingh Jaiswal disappeared?

The crew was thrilled with the fireworks, but they didn't last. Raj and Tanya ate their meal in complete silence. The crew started to get bored. They switched off their monitors. It was a while before Tanya decided to break the silence.

"I came to apologise the other day. You never let me finish," she said in a very low voice.

Rahul glanced at the cameras from the corner of his eye. He might have hated her arrogance, but he still wanted to protect her. If the crew found out she had stepped into his room, she could get into trouble.

"Don't worry about it. These things happen," he said between bites of barbecued *paneer*.

"No, they don't. I really thought we had this connection. I felt like I could tell you what was on my mind. These past few days have changed that. I don't think you are Rajsingh Jaiswal."

Rahul stopped eating and stared at her. What did she know?

"What do you mean?" he asked, in an arrogant tone. Who was she to question his performance?

"Raj would never treat me this way." Her eyes were slightly moist, but she wasn't going to cry in front of him.

"In what way?" Raj asked impatiently.

"First, you woo me, then you ignore me when we are around people, then you come and tell me that you've been ignoring me. What am I supposed to do? Take it lying down that a guy who's been sneaking off to see me alone ignores me when we have company?" she looked at him angrily. "But as soon as I realised why you were doing what you were doing, I came to apologise. And then you yell at me. Look at you, right here, you're clearly telling me you hate me. Who treats a girl the way you've been treating me?"

"Tanya, in the past you have ended up saying some nasty things to me. I want our last date to be cordial. I want to part on good terms, so let's not discuss this right now." He nodded towards the camera. Tanya didn't catch the nod.

"It's all about what you want. This show is all about what you want. But in the past few days you made me realise that you were all that I wanted and now you want things to be cordial," she said and getting up, she began to walk away. She hopped across the pathway through the pool but she was barely halfway across when the combination of too much wine and heels got her. Tanya tripped and toppled into the pool. Rahul who was standing by the table watching her, immediately dived into the pool to rescue her from drowning in the shallow pool. Rahul swam across with an urgency, as if she had fallen into the ocean and was about to drown. By the time he got near her, Tanya had steadied herself. He offered to help but she pushed him away. Even though her face was wet, Rahul could tell she was crying.

"Are you ok?" he asked with concern, trying to look in her eyes.

"No!" she screamed. "I am not okay. I am on a stupid television reality show, I am fighting with the guy I am supposed to have wooed, I have fallen into the swimming pool and I have ruined a very expensive silk gown. You think I...."

Before she could say anything else, Rahul bent down, pulled her close and kissed her on her lips. Tanya had no choice but to shut up. She was startled but she didn't want to fight it; she closed her eyes and kissed him back, surrendering to the warmth that engulfed her. She didn't care that her face was stained by mascara, she didn't care that they were in the water, all she cared about was how much she had longed to be held the way Raj was holding her right now. Rahul broke their kiss to look at her. Suddenly she looked up at him. A warning bell went off in Tanya's head.

"I think I should go," she said, pulling herself away. She dragged herself out of the water and ran across to the house.

Rahul stood there, in the middle of the pool. He was shaking. His lips still tingled from the short but passionate kiss he had just shared with the woman he loved. And from the way she had dissolved into his arms, he knew that she loved him. He smiled. And with a euphoric wave of his hand, he plashed the water around in the pool.

"How was your date with Tanya?" Karan asked Rahul as they worked on shortlisting the top three girls. The finale was slated for Sunday. Rahul didn't care about any other girls. He just wanted to give one name and walk away with Tanya. He had known she was the one, right from the start. Rahul wanted Tanya but Rajsingh was yet to decide.

"It was ok," Rahul replied reluctantly.

"It was rather quiet," Karan probed.

"Yeah, very quiet." Rahul scanned Karan's face for sarcasm, but he was relieved to find none.

"We stopped filming when you guys started eating in silence. The crew felt there wasn't going to be anything else worth filming." He paused and looked up at Rahul. "Rahul, I know enough about romance and I know something happened. The silence was the calm before a storm."

"How do you know?"

"It is written across your face. It is written across her face," Karan explained as if it was the simplest thing to read.

"Well, she does love me. But...."

"But?"

"Rahul Rajgopal is in love with her, but what about Rajsingh Jaiswal?" Rahul asked.

"At the end of the day aren't Rajsingh and Rahul the same person?"

"No, they aren't! She is in love with Rajsingh Jaiswal. She

doesn't even know someone called Rahul Rajgopal exists." Rahul was exasperated.

"You said you were yourself around her. So, she loves you; what's in a name?" Karan tried to reason with Rahul.

"She thinks I am a multimillionaire from the UK. She has no idea who or what I really am!"

There was an awkward silence.

"That's what this show is all about. We'll see tomorrow."

The two of them went into the study to discuss Rahul's experiences as Rajsingh Jaiswal for the final episode. Rahul spoke about his friendship with Sherry, Asif, Pervez, Shruti, Sudha and Karan. Rahul got nostalgic about the Karjat days.

Rahul narrated his special moments on the show. Karan could see that Rahul had forgotten the entire Raj vs Rahul debate that they'd had earlier. He was now at his job. Rahul was a natural in front of the camera and he was one heck of an actor. Karan smiled. He had an idea, but it could wait until the end of the show.

Tanya couldn't stop thinking about what had happened the earlier night. Even though she blushed as she thought of how Raj had kissed her, she also felt confused. The kiss was one of the most special things she was going to take back with her, but she knew it was going to be painful going away from all the madness that she had hated all this while. Just before the kiss, she had looked at Raj and it felt like the water had washed away a mask from Raj's face and the Raj she loved had re-emerged. Tanya couldn't figure him out, but she knew she loved him.

"So, all packed?" Simran came into the room

"Yeah! Almost!"

"Great, I am sort of nervous about tomorrow,"

"Why?"

"I know I am not winning it. I probably don't even want to, but still! For the sake of my self-esteem, I'd like to be in the top three." Simran started dumping some of the bedside things into her bag.

"Going by the dates I have been having, I won't be surprised if I am the lowest. I wonder why I have come as far as I have." Tanya sighed.

"Hah! Very funny! I know you like him. I know he likes you. All this talk you're giving me is a result of some misunderstanding, but I don't want to know." She smiled at Tanya.

Simran was more than just a roommate or a co-contestant. She had come to understand Tanya. She was a friend. Tanya was going to miss Simran

Saturday morning brought an air of nostalgia with it. The contestants were gushing about their wonderful time together, among themselves and to the camera. The domestic staff was busy winding things up. Packed suitcases were being wheeled around. The afternoon arrived and it was time for Rahul to pick the top three.

"I have zeroed down on," he said moving a chit to Karan, "one of these three."

"Fantastic. Ladies and gentlemen, we have the three girls who stand a chance to marry our Prince Charming. We will announce the names right after the commercial break,"

After a moment's pause Karan started again. "I promised to give you the three names after the break and here they are — Khushi Motwane, Simran Khanna and," he looked anxiously at the camera, "Tanya Kher!"

He paused another moment and turned to Rahul. "Why Simran, Khushi, Tanya?"

"Khushi has lived abroad, she knows how to manage a social life. I guess managing the home is secondary, she can always hire help. She projects an image of perfection despite her flaws."

"And why Simran?"

"Because, we all know, she is hot!" Both of them laughed before Rahul continued. "She is extremely passionate and speaks her mind. The thing I liked the most about her was her ability to be a loyal friend to her co-contestants on the show."

"We all know how much you enjoyed both Khushi and

Simran's company, but why Tanya? I know you guys started off great but your dates with her were dull, sometimes boring and at times volatile? I am surprised you chose her to be in the top three."

"I can't explain why. There is something very intriguing about her. We started off great and yeah, we had our bad times, but she was great at her tasks, she's had a successful career. So, she has beauty and brains. I wouldn't say she's the ideal wife but she is an interesting match."

"But you wanted an ideal wife..."

"Well, there is something very endearing about her, and I think maybe if we gave this another chance, away from the cameras it would be different." Rahul shrugged.

"You are aware, Rahul, that the girl you choose has to accept you as who you really are for you to get the big prize and you are also aware that they do not know about this little condition. Do you think any of these girls will choose love over money?"

"Karan, I can't speak for the girls, but I hope my charm works."

"I guess we can only wait and watch then," he smiled into the camera. "As the audience, you've been a part of this journey with Rahul. Who do you think Rahul will choose? If your guess is right, you could win a special 'Royal Tour' with Globetrotters! SMS your answer to 5758 followed by the name of the contestant to participate. Tomorrow is the day. See you, same time, same place for the final episode of *A Match Made in Heaven*!"

"Cut. That was perfect, Karan," Ashutosh yelled.

Rahul went back to his room and made sure everything was in order. He fished out his backpack from under the bed. It contained his clothes — Rahul's clothes. He zipped up the backpack and kept it ready. He didn't want to take anything that didn't belong to him, but he didn't want to leave behind what was rightfully his. Those things may have cost only a few hundred rupees but they were precious to him.

He gave his backpack a satisfied look. There was something

that was in this house that he wished belonged to him. But he wasn't sure yet if she belonged to him or to Raj.

As the sun rose on the final day of the reality TV show that had gripped the nation, Jaiswal Mansion was once again filled with a bustle. The girls were all packed and settled in the library when Karan Kapoor walked in.

"We have the names of the three girls who are most likely to get the chance to be Mrs Jaiswal, in this envelope. I am afraid, the remaining four will have lost their chance to be a millionaire's wife, but they will not be sent away empty handed. Our sponsors, Globetrotters, The Travel People, are giving away an all-expenses-paid 10-day trip to Singapore on a luxury cruise-liner," he announced.

The girls clapped and cheered. The tension was obvious on their faces.

"Neha Bose." Karan's voice brought the cheering to a halt. "Rehana Merchant, Priya Gokhale, Anuja Thakur."

The girls looked at Karan's face smiling ear to ear, not realising that he had announced four names. "Neha, Rehana, Priya and Anuja will be heading to Singapore!"

The four girls almost screamed with joy before they realised that they were not one of the top three.

"I give you our finalists, Simran, Khushi and Tanya!"

Khushi beamed at the cameras and acted like she had just been crowned Miss World. Simran looked at Tanya and smiled. Tanya smiled, but not because she was in the top three. She smiled because Simran had got her wish.

In the adjacent room, Rahul wrote a name down and sealed it in an envelope. The assistant took the envelope and muttered something on his headset.

"Don't worry girls. You won't miss the finale. We've arranged for you to watch the rest of the show from a special location. And cheer up, you'll meet your old friends there. Khushi, Simran and

Tanya, get ready. In an hour, we will know who gets to marry Rajsingh Jaiswal," Karan said.

There was a lot of crying as the girls parted. Simran and Tanya came back to their room to gather their things.

"That was all so fake, we were happy they lost! They were not happy that we were in the top three. Why so much drama?" Simran stuffed all the bottles on the dressing table into her bags and zipped them up.

"Aren't you happy? You got your wish. Maybe he is going to ask you to marry him!"

"I don't care! I just wanted to be in the top three. But yeah, I'd happily lose to you, but I'd love to win against Khushi."

"You always know what you want! I envy you," Tanya admitted.

Simran shrugged. Their stuff was packed and sent down. Both of them stood in the room, took a last look at it and walked out.

Karan toyed with the envelope. He knew very well who the winner was. There was no question about it. Rahul was up in his room, winding up his things. Sherry was on her way to see the final episode live in action. She too had guessed who the girl was. She glanced at her husband and wondered if he knew. She wondered if she knew him at all anymore.

All the other twenty-seven girls had gathered in a house not far away from Jaiswal Mansion. The channel didn't want people to know who had been voted out. The channel also didn't want to let the girls know that they had been ousted by an ordinary salesman. It was a treat reserved for the finale. The twenty-seven girls settled in front of the large screen that was to telecast the final episode live to them. They couldn't wait to see which one of the three girls was going to live her dream.

The screen flickered on. Tanya, Khushi and Simran were dressed elegantly, ready for a proposal in the study. Rajsingh Jaiswal walked in with a huge smile. There was a different glow to his face, but the girls didn't notice that. They noticed the television in the study.

"Today is the day, we find out who amongst the three lovely ladies, is going to get the proposal they have been dreaming about." Karan smiled at the three.

Tanya remained calm and composed, Simran indifferent and Khushi was simpering as if she was in a beauty pageant that she knew she was going to win.

"There were many others who kept us company through the past few weeks. And today as we wind up the hunt for the perfect wife for Raj, we have invited them all to share this moment with us in another part of the house."

Shehnaz, Pallak, Radhika and all the others smiled and waved at the camera.

Ravi and Anita were watching the show from a hotel room close to the Jaiswal Mansion. They had been watching the show, and they weren't sure what was going on with their Tanya. They were both very glad that they were going to meet her in a couple of hours and that this drama was going to be over.

Families across the country were tuned into the live episode that would conclude their favourite reality drama on television. Everyone wanted to know how the girls would react when they found out the truth. They were curious to find the girls' reaction to Rajsingh Jaiswal's real identity. They felt like Rahul's confidantes, knowing all along, who he really was, while the girls assumed he was a millionaire.

Rahul was now talking to them. "When I came on this show, I was a simple man, a perfume seller with simple dreams. One feels lucky to be surrounded by so many beautiful people. When the show started, I didn't think much about what would happen when it all ended. Now, I am at the end of the show. These girls want to marry a millionaire and the truth is — I am not one. It's highly unlikely that they will still want me when they learn that I am just a salesman. But if the one I have chosen does, I do get to keep a lot of the good things I enjoyed here, so keeping my fingers crossed." He smiled into the camera and the final episode of the most watched show in India went on air.

* * * * * *

"Papa I am sure it is Tanya!" said a young girl watching the show in her living room in Delhi.

"He will choose Khushi. He said it clearly yesterday! Khushi is perfect wife material," said a housewife to her husband in their bedroom in Mumbai.

Everyone was predicting Rahul's choice but they were equally curious about which of the three would accept Rahul for who he was.

"He is such a darling! I would want him, even if he didn't have the money. Oh, I love Rahul!" a teenager gushed on the phone as she watched the final moments of her favourite show.

"Man! I wish I was in his place. What fun *yaar*! Pick any girl you want," a 23-year-old told his flatmate in their Bangalore apartment.

* * * * * *

"We have a little something for you," Karan said to the three finalists, pointing towards the television. "It's a snapshot of Rajsingh Jaiswal's world outside the four walls of Jaiswal Mansion."

The television flickered on in the study where the three finalists were seated. The large screen in the dining room came on with a picture of the OneStop Mall. The camera went into the perfume section and somebody who looked like Raj was now talking. What followed had the girls gaping at the screen — some in shock, some in anger and some in contentment. They stared as the video unveiled the real story behind Raj. The three finalists tried to maintain their composure but couldn't hide the shock on their faces.

"I must say he did a good job. I mean, he's a salesman, but look at his performance! I feel so bad for the girls up there, I mean, they are finalists, sure. But to marry a salesman?" Radhika was speaking into one of the cameras.

"I guess the transformation is phenomenal and not once did I think that he wasn't Raj. He's a brilliant actor." Madhura was smiling her 'Madhuri Dixit' smile into the camera.

As Tanya stared at the television, she remembered her friendly neighbourhood mall. She suddenly remembered buying a perfume from Raj or was it Rahul. She felt angry. She felt betrayed. The drama unfolded as Rahul Rajgopal transformed into Rajsingh Jaiswal. Rahul saw the video in his room. He was as shocked as the girls. He felt cheated. He had no idea he had been filmed right through that stage.

Finally, when the video ended, an assistant summoned him into the study. He walked in to see Khushi looking at him with disgust, Simran in anger and Tanya in recognition.

"Ladies, I give you Rahul Rajgopal, popularly known as Rajsingh Jaiswal." Karan was clapping with the crew. The three girls stared at Rahul in disbelief. He felt naked in front of them, stripped of the identity he had been living with for the past few weeks.

"I feel lucky to have spent all this wonderful time with all you girls. It's good to finally get rid of that mask. It was getting heavier and heavier." He smiled at the girls and turned to Karan. "Being Rajsingh Jaiswal was very, very special because I got to meet you all and for that I have to thank Mr Avinash Menon. I couldn't have transformed myself into Raj if it wasn't for Sherry and her team. You just saw them on the screen. Give it up for them!" He started clapping. Everyone clapped, reluctantly.

Tanya was amused by the ease with which he was speaking. She realised that this was the salesman who had sprayed perfume in her face. She smiled at him. She was the only one of the top three smiling. The girl in Delhi let out a scream!

"She's smiling! She's going to accept him for who he is!" she yelled.

"The time has come to announce the future Mrs. Jaiswal."

Karan handed the envelope to Rahul, who tore it open. He decided to keep the girls guessing. He looked at them and asked, "Who do you think it is?" then he looked into the camera and said, "Who are you crossing your fingers for?"

Everyone waited for him to read out the name. He smiled. It was a crooked, condescending smile that he threw at the camera before he spoke.

"In my opinion, the perfect choice for Mr Rajsingh Jaiswal, would be Khushi Motwane." There was no emotion in Rahul's voice as he glanced at Khushi and then at Tanya.

There was a Miss World moment for Khushi, as Tanya tried to hide her disbelief and Simran her anger. But one look at Rahul and Khushi stopped and looked at Karan.

"Khushi, do you accept this proposal?" Karan asked her.

She looked puzzled as she realised that Mr. Jaiswal was a fantasy figure. It was Mr. Rajgopal, a salesman who had chosen her. The winning smile disappeared from her face.

Khushi gave him one last look of contempt, "No!"

"I am not surprised at all." Before anyone else could speak, Rahul cut in. "Khushi is perfect for Rajsingh Jaiswal. What makes Raj ideal for her is the fact that he can give her a lavish life and she will never have to work hard for it." He looked at Khushi with contempt as the confusion levels rose around the crew.

"That works for Raj. He doesn't care what the girl wants from him. He only cares about what the girl has to offer him. Raj is not real. What is real is Rahul Rajgopal. And Rahul Rajgopal doesn't want anything but true love. And I do not believe in finding it like this on a TV show. Love happens when it has to. You can't force people to live in the same house and find love through tasks that measure the girl's ability and compatibility."

He looked at Tanya. "I did however find a woman who kept searching for the man beneath the layers of Raj's fake personality. And I am sorry I had to lie to her about who I really was. I chose her to be one of the top three because I believed that if we got another chance, she may be the one for me — Rahul Rajgopal."

Rahul turned to a camera and he froze right there. The recording stopped and Karan ushered the girls to another room for their bytes.

Khushi and Simran spoke to one camera team and Karan spoke to the other to record the closing segment.

Khushi said angrily into the camera, “You can’t cheat girls like this. You’re playing with their emotions. This is a ridiculous game show. And I am disgusted with Raj, sorry Rahul or whoever he is,” and she stormed off.

Simran went ahead to record her own byte.

Rahul and Tanya were the only ones in the study. Rahul couldn’t bear to look at Tanya. He was scared he would see the same anger, contempt and pity that he had seen in Khushi and Simran’s eyes and that would have broken him.

Tanya, however, was smiling. It all seemed like a joke to her. She looked at Rahul, unsure of what to do. Suddenly, she knew what she wanted. She got up and walked over to him.

“Hey, I am Tanya Kher, do I know you from somewhere? You look very familiar,” she said, the big grin not fading from her face.

He turned to face her. Although he was bewildered, he smiled because he loved her smile. Hell, he loved her!

“Rahul, Rahul Rajgopal. I see you at the mall every day. How about a cup of coffee?”